THE CENTRAL SPHERE

By

Nigel S. Griffen

Published by

Merad Tylaire Ltd.

Published in the UK in 2004 by
Merad Tylaire Ltd.

ISBN 0 9547903 0 8

Printed by Latimer Trend & Company Ltd, Estover Road, Estover, Plymouth, Devon, PL6 7PY

Published by:
Merad Tylaire Ltd.
PO Box 68, Kingsbridge, TQ7 1ZN

For James

With grateful acknowledgment to
Diane Griffen, Valerie Griffen and Laura Griffen

My thanks also, to the management and staff at Milklink, Plymouth for their continuous interest and support.

Cheers Digory.

THE

CENTRAL

SPHERE

First Edition

CHAPTER ONE

The world was once again on fire. Slobber, half dressed, leant out of his bedroom window, and stared into the glowing red of the rising sun as it poured over the top of the valley wall. The remnants of saliva from his drool pouches, trickled from the sides of his large mouth, down onto the ungrateful flowers below. He drew a deep sigh as he pulled the palm of his large, blue hand down over his face. “What was I thinking about?” he asked of no one in particular. The large Tanglepine tree outside his window said nothing, not because the question was largely rhetorical, or indeed because it was incapable of verbal communication. No, it offered no reply because Tanglepines in general, choose not to converse with their neighbours – unless they happen to be another Tanglepine, that is. This rule goes doubly so in the small town of Kettles Reach, where the favoured pastime of the inhabitants is to while away the evening in one of its 237 alehouses. Subsequently, early morning questions such as: ‘What was I thinking?’, ‘What on earth was I drinking last night?’, or ‘Who are you?’ are common and really not worth an intelligent tree’s time!

The large, blue man inhaled deeply of the morning air before offering a single nod of decision. He had agreed to do it and, even though it was 5 o'clock in the morning, and even though he was nursing an uncommonly oppressive hangover, Slobber was a man of his word. He removed his head and shoulders from the open window and drew himself up to his full height – his bold stripe of orange hair just brushing the relatively low ceiling of his room. "Let's do it!" he said, before setting off for the bathroom to continue his morning regimen.

Down the narrow corridor he shuffled, moving sideways to avoid his large, rounded shoulders knocking the gallery of family portraits which occupied the wall. Paintings and photographs of Slobbers past and occasionally present – the gallery of blue faces all smiled at him, their dark blue eyes following his large frame as it shuffled by: Uncle Slobber, and his wife Slobber – who used to run an alehouse – his parents, Slobber and Slobber – before retiring to Flagrantstool, they had run a local greengrocers shop; his favourite ex-girlfriend, Slobber – she still worked as a chemist in town; and then, there at the end of the passage, an image of an ancient monarch, whom all Slobber tend to claim as a relation, the last King – Bob…Bob Kanstandandkipwhilewaitingforabus, or to give him his full title: King Bobbingforapplesintherainwaiting-foratrainpeeingdownthedrain Kanstandandkipwhilewaiting-forabus. This bizarrely long, and some might suggest daft name is what prompted his Highness, at the end of a full week of celebratory drinking with his subjects – following his invention of probably the best pint of beer anywhere in the universe – to make a proclamation: "Henceforth," he slurred to his scribe, whose name was Trav, or to use his full name, Travelroundtheworldwithyourbuttocksstapledtoatreeandsee-howfaryouget Canyoustandonthegroundinatheatreinthe-round,whileholdingapickledonion, "all subjects in my land are ordered to change their name to…to", he faltered, apparently – so the tale goes – looking around the room for inspiration.

A drunk king, of course – or indeed a drunk anyone – will often lack true inspiration. This fact is clearly displayed by the name Bob finally chose.
It took very little imagination on his part – bearing in mind he was sitting in a large room filled with large, blue people, all of whom had one unfortunate evolutionary trait…they drooled! They didn't just drool a bit, oh no. They drooled a lot – so much so, that over time, pouches in the cheeks had developed to catch the vast quantities of gob-juice that just one native could accumulate in a matter of minutes. Back then of course, before devices had been invented to remove the mouth-water, people had to make frequent visits to Slobber Vats – placing their chins on the cushioned rests and delivering their reservoirs into its gaping mouth. This activity was referred to as 'having a Slobber'. Seeing his subjects 'on the Slobber', and eager to make a decision before refilling his tankard, King Bob continued: "SLOBBER!" he shouted, piercing the gentle silence of insobriety that had speedily reoccupied the room. All eyes looked in his general direction as he rose to his unsteady feet. Swaying gently, as if a reed caught in a breeze, the King, having the general impression that the attention of all was now firmly fixed upon him, looked out across the room. After taking what seemed like an age to adjust, and re-adjust his crown, he spoke again. "I, King Bobbingforapplesintherainwaitingforatrainpeeingdownthedrain the Third, of Trippleippleippletroopwooplewoop, on this day do announce that I am changing my name." He paused for a moment to allow his announcement to sink in to the inebriated minds of his company. "Henceforth, I shall be known as King Slobber." There he stopped, awaiting the gasps of amazement from his audience.
"What will that be short for Highness?" whispered Trav, hoping to break the awkward silence that now filled the room.
"What!?" replied the King with impatience. "Short for!? It's not short for anything!" he said, attempting to fix his servant with a firm stare, his eyes overshooting with each exaggerated movement of his thickening head.

It took its time of course, but eventually the silent sounds of bafflement coming from his audience, at the absurdity of his announcement, began to filter down his ears and into his brain. Quite obviously he wasn't properly conveying his message – as is often the case with the drunk, since they all too often think they've said something when they've only thought it, and say something when they've only wished to think it.
Bob slumped back down into his throne and beckoned the congregation to draw near. Once done, and with his large goblet now full again, King Slobber attempted to explain himself properly.

The basic theory behind his radical decision was this: Trippleippleippletroopwooplewoopians are, even when sober, a warm, friendly and generally polite bunch. Having such peculiar names made it difficult for outsiders – and, it had to be said, even insiders – to remember who it was they had been talking to. Far worse, members of the same family would often have to go to written reminders, just to send a birthday card. In the past, memory hadn't been a problem since all Trippleippleippletroopwooplewoopians were gifted with extremely good ones. However, since the recent preoccupation with consumption had occurred, memories had begun to suffer and the chances were this trend would not reverse itself.

The King explained that he was fed up with constantly having to repeat his name whenever he gave it. Moreover, since his signature took over five minutes to sign he was sick of writing it…with the amount of time a King spends, signing this order or that proclamation, the collective time spent on autographs alone ran into hours. And it wasn't just him. Filling in a census form, for example, could take a large family several weeks! "Let's make all our lives simpler", he suggested. "We all know who we are. Let's go by one name and let that name

be Slobber. A name that defines our wonderful individualism as a race."
Perhaps it was the beer or the fact that he was King, that prevented anyone from arguing the point. Indeed, many in the room on that day saw an amount of logic in the plan.
The King, finding new inspiration in the lack of criticism, continued: "Wherever a Slobber goes, they will not be a stranger, for everyone will know his name. Parents will no longer waste precious time arguing over what to call the baby. Never again will your name be forgotten." He felt a true sense of purpose rising in him, as he rose to his feet: "If a fellow hits his head and is taken to hospital with amnesia, the doctors and nurses won't have to worry about what to call him – his identity would be confirmed immediately."
The King stepped from his small stage and moved slowly among his subjects, his voice and articulation of upper limbs adding greater weight to his speech. "No longer will two-thirds of a company's expenditure go on ink. No more will class-room registers dominate the entire school day…teachers will actually be able to teach! Postal workers' bags will shrink, and recipients of post will no longer spend the morning hunting through the interior of four-foot-long envelopes, looking for the piece of correspondence. Personalised vehicle number plates will no longer be a danger to pedestrians…" His message began to catch the imagination of his companions. Like a bush fire, ideas suddenly caught hold and began to sweep through the area, as others began to add their own ideas to the ever-growing list: "Marriage ceremonies will be shorter," shouted one holy man, "and gravestones won't need to be the giant monoliths we have today."
"Cheque books will be shorter," said a banker, "and credit cards will actually fit in your back pocket".
The King's eyes flashed with excitement, as the room filled with further suggestions. He was thrilled. Other than the recently brewed pint of excellent beer, he rarely had truly brilliant ideas. This one, it seemed, was proving to be not only

brilliant, but popular as well…perhaps even brilliant, and popular enough to become the stuff of history!
With this notion beginning to make a home in the King's mind, he permitted himself a smile of self-satisfaction: *Other Kings may come and go,* he thought. *What contribution did King Doolyoolyoolyoolyoolyoolyoolyhowmanyoolysarethereinhisname make, or Queen Nicedress-doyoulikethedress-whatsyouraddress-ismyhairamess? None! I bet I am the only one here to even remember their names!* King Slobber was indeed right, he had secured his place in history. Even the following civil war – which broke out roughly two weeks later – had little, eventual effect on his standing. In fact, the war itself may have even elevated his standing still further. This was perhaps because, interestingly enough, the entire war – which only lasted a month – was fought and won without any violence or bloodshed whatsoever…gallons of spit, but no bloodshed. Not only that, but the eventual outcome of the war had little or no effect on history: The war had been fought by two factions…the monarchists – or Pro Slobber league, and The Other Lot – the title given to the Rebels by historians. The Other Lot had, of course, been fighting for the right to not change their names, and it was they, in fact, who actually left the 'battlefield' victorious. The heads of both armies met at the Palace, to sign and witness the surrender. Whilst there, the King suggested they seal their treaty with a pint or two of his rather splendid creation. It was during this knees-up that The Other Lot had a complete change of heart about the whole idea, and decided they liked the name Slobber after all!

Now, everyone born of Slobber – the logical new name for Trippleippleippletroopwooplewoop – is Slobber, as well as being a Slobber.

Slobber stared at his reflection in the bathroom mirror, as the light shroud of mist closed in. In no time at all the clear image of his large, blue face dulled. Now, the steam from the hot

water tap at the sink below, permitted Slobber's reflection to appear as nothing more than a vague, though still blue, image. Turning off the tap, he reached up to a box on the shelf and gently raised its carved, wooden lid. "A little early today lads. Get prepped", he gently commanded.
"Sir!" came the disciplined, unseen response.
Having washed and shaved, Slobber sat himself down on the toilet. He reached across and unhooked the suction cup, attaching it to his mouth before switching on the vacuum.

With both his bowels, and saliva pouches emptied, he returned to the sink – staring thoughtfully at the de-misted mirror, into his own dark blue eyes, as he washed his hands.
"Ready, lads?" he asked, his gaze unshifting.
"Ready when you are, sir!" came the clear reply, as five, small, wetsuit-clad figures jumped out of the box and stood in a line on the shelf. Slobber opened his mouth as the five tiny Toothwranglers, under the command of Sergeant Enamuelle, took aim and fired. With consummate precision, the tiny suction cups found their mark in Slobber's mouth. Stability checked and the ropes tied tight, the Toothwranglers – with the skill of a commando brigade – hooked up their harnesses and slid down into the gaping cavern below. Upon safe landing, they quickly released themselves from their entry ropes and secured their safety harnesses – thrusting the tiny pins into the gaps between Slobber's rounded teeth. These harnesses were without doubt, the most important part of a Toothwrangler's equipment. If not securely fastened a Wrangler could easily slip in the waterlogged mouth of a healthy Slobber – as Gobswane, the youngest of Slobber's crew once discovered to his terrifying cost two years earlier.

He was cocky, as the young often are, and eager to please his new friends. His pins improperly fastened, he slipped as he scrubbed a particularly grimy molar. His desperate attempts to find a footing on Slobber's tongue were to no avail, and his team-mates watched helplessly as he slid down the gaping

throat. His commander was frantic – he had never lost a man in action. Slobber too, was beside himself with worry – he tried to make himself sick but only a tiny tooth-scrubbing brush appeared.
Gobswane survived however, surfacing some 24-hours later…found clinging to the side of the toilet bowl. His physical injuries were nothing compared to the terrible emotional trauma caused by his journey through Slobber's digestive system. Toothwranglers are a tough breed – adventurers in dental hygiene – but his journey proved to be nearly too much for the little guy. Nearly, but not quite. The excellent medical insurance Slobber had offered as part of their employment package, provided a first-rate counsellor, and three months after his disgusting ordeal Gobswane was back to work – a little older and a lot wiser.

Their meticulous scrubbing complete, the team gathered at the bottom, front row of teeth. "Detach ropes!" ordered Enamuelle.
The suction cups quickly freed, the group sounded off – one to five. Satisfied that all were present and correct, the Sarge shouted to his commander – "Ready for elevation, sir!"
Slobber, in accordance with this statement, searched for the small stool with his foot. Quickly finding it, he pulled it into position and carefully raised himself up onto it. When the Sarge was satisfied that safe height had been achieved he gave the order to jump, and in quick succession his team did just that. Their parachutes opened immediately and the team glided effortlessly back to their shelf base – landing in turn with total accuracy, on their x-marked spot. Slobber ran the tip of his tongue over his now polished gnashers, "Thank you, gentlemen. Excellent work."
"Our pleasure sir", came the unified reply, accompanied by a salute so sharp you could slice cheese with it. "Tonight, sir?"
"Not tonight Sarge", replied Slobber, hoping to disguise his unease with an authoritative tone. "Gentlemen, I am going away for a couple of days and while there's no one I'd rather

have with me on this expedition, I need to pack light…" He shuffled his feet a little and tried not to look at the ground… "For that reason, and that reason alone…I…I…I will be taking a brush."
"A brush, sir!?"
"I'm sorry Sarge," said Slobber, quickly turning to the door, "that's the way it's gotta be. You boys take a little R & R. I'll leave food and beer on the landing." Slobber quickly shuffled back down the corridor and into his room.
He didn't like leaving the guys behind, but what could he do? Besides, they deserved a vacation. He would see if his ex-girlfriend could pop round with her all-girl crew – a gesture, he felt sure, all would appreciate.
His conscience a little clearer, Slobber busied himself with getting ready. He quickly clad himself in his favourite 'adventuring' outfit…actually, Slobber had never really been on an adventure – unless you count going to the fish and chip shop of a Friday night – so they were just his normal weekend clothes: Waterproof woollen sweater; waterproof trousers; and waterproof walking boots. It wasn't that he was expecting rain you understand, it was simply that with an individual Slobber capable of producing around 50 gallons of mouth-water per day, pretty much everything a Slobber would wear, carpet their floors with, or anything really, is waterproof.
Clad in his finery, Slobber threw a few things into his weekend bag and bounded down the stairs.

CHAPTER TWO

The ground shook, as it had been in the habit of doing of late. The residents of Flintlewood held their collective breath and waited for the tremors to pass.
Potfondle, the eldest son of a gardener, lay in his bed, his hands clasped behind his head, and stared at his ceiling light as it swayed to the motion.
Its hypnotic effect was only broken when a small piece of plaster fell from above and hit him on the forehead. "Great globs of steaming goo!" he exclaimed. He threw off the bedclothes and leapt to his feet like a gazelle.
He then, very quickly fell backwards, back onto his bed – having not taken into account that his floor was still shaking.
"Great globs…" he began, before becoming a little more resigned. "Ah well", he said philosophically.
After a few minutes, the shaking subsided and the still dressed Potfondle rose to his feet once again. "What a night!" he sighed to no one in particular.
"You're not wrong", agreed his Bonsai Tanglepine tree, its voice slightly muffled due to it still being in Potfondle's 'going out' bag. "Any chance of some daylight?" the tree said, a hint of irritation in its voice.

"Smack my Rodney! I'm sorry!" said Pot – as he was generally known.
He pulled the tree from the bag, and put him in his pot of soil on the windowsill.
"About time!" said the tree, angrily. "36 hours! I can survive without soil for 36 hours! Three – Six! How many times!?"
Pot looked at his shoes, guiltily trying to draw a circle with his heel, whilst his toe remained fixed to the same point on the floor. "Sorry!" he said. "Won't happen again."
The pair stood, if a tree in a pot can be described as standing, in silence for a while before Pot – anxious to change the subject, foolishly asked, "What was I drinking last night?"
The tree was silent for a while, looking at Pot's face, which seemed to cry out for forgiveness. Not being the sort of tree to hold a grudge, he replied: "It's stupid questions like that which prevent my species from having very much to do with your two-legged sort!"
"So?" said Pot, too slow to pick up on the tree's sardonic wit.
"Far more than any sane creature would ever consider!" the tree replied, sighing regretfully to itself that it had ever decided to converse with Pot in the first place.
"Great night though", said Pot. "That guy we were drinking with…"
"*You* were drinking with", interrupted the tree.
"OK. That great guy I was drinking with…whatsisname?"
"Slobber!?" replied the tree, stunned that Pot couldn't remember.
"Yeah! Slobber. What a great guy. Anyway, what are you complaining about? You must have been given enough water to last a month!"
"You didn't have to leave me on the floor. Took care of yourself though, didn't ya!? Sitting on a chair...on the bar!"
"Of course", said Pot. "I can't swim!"
"Never fear", said the tree, the sun's rays starting to have an effect on its mood. "As well as extremely efficient drainage, all public buildings in Slobber are required, by law, to provide adequate numbers of life rafts", he joked.

Pot gave a courtesy laugh and walked over to the dressing table to empty his pockets. "Smack my Rodney", he shrieked in disbelief, as he surveyed the lack of cash. "I spent a fortune last night!" He went quiet for a moment, his face displaying a vacant expression as the cogs of his mind slowly turned – doing the maths. Looking to the ceiling, presumably for inspiration, he began mumbling audible evidence of his calculations: "40 or so for drinks; 10 for the obligatory takeway; and...bloody hell!" He frowned, quickly recalculating, hoping he had made an error. "55 for a cab!?"
"Would have been cheaper to stay in Kettles", suggested Tree, his quiet observation somewhat unhelpful after the event. "I did actually suggest it at the time", he added smugly, his reminder met with disdain from Pot, who treated Tree's 'I told you so' comments as though they were a bad smell someone had just let into his room. "Anyway", said Tree, following an agonising moment of uncomfortable silence, "55's not too bad. After all, it was past midnight...international travel."
Pot thought for a while, eventually deciding that firstly, he hadn't been ripped off and secondly, complaining about it now was pointless. With the delivery of a deep, and philosophical shrug of his shoulders, he simply dismissed his expenditure during the previous evening – "Ah well!" he said with a sigh, "I think I'll have some breakfast. See you in a bit, Tree", and with that, he bounded out of his room and down the small, wooden staircase.

Tree, whose actual name is Butsmell but who, for obvious reasons, tells everyone his name is Tree, had been with Potfondle for nearly 20 years. A present from Pot's father, he was a splendid looking little fellow – his shimmering silver bark complimented beautifully by his gold and red foliage. Being a Bonsai of course, he was somewhat smaller than most Tanglepines one is likely to meet, and his size may well have been the root cause of his sometimes entertaining, cynical take on life. It was in fact, Tree's size that had forced him to communicate with Pot in the first place.

Potfondle was nearly eight when they first met. A little Pillick then – full of hope and the promise of opportunity. Now, as he approaches his thirties, and standing nearly three feet tall in his stockinged feet, Pot is regarded by many as a great Pillick.

At the age of 12, Pot decided that keeping a tree in captivity was cruel and unnecessary, so with purpose in his heart, he took the little plant out into the wilderness, eventually selecting a small piece of ground in the midst of a Tanglepine wood, in which to re-home this small growth.

He carefully dug a small hole and placed Twig – as he had named him – in the ground, giving him plenty of water to help his roots settle. With a tear in his eye, he bade the little chap farewell and turned, slowly plodding back in the direction whence he came.

"Oi!" came an indignant shout, stopping the little Pillick in his tracks.

"Oi! Furball..!" said the small voice, drawing Pot's amazed attention towards the small plant. As he moved closer, his eyes growing wide as he considered the possibility that he had found a Tanglepine that was actually willing to communicate with him, he spoke: "Twig?" he said softly, "Is that you?"

"So. You were just gonna leave me here were you!?" said Twig, his obvious ingratitude throwing Pot a little.

"Well…" stumbled Pot.

"No, no. That's alright", said Twig, playing the wounded party. "Don't you worry about little me. You leave me here among these giants."

Pot was confused by Twig's reaction. He thought he had done the right thing, placing him here, among his own kind.

"Don't you want to live here?" he asked with surprise.

"Of course I don't want to live here!" replied Twig. "I'm a domesticated tree, Pillock!"

"Pill-ick!" corrected Potfondle.

"Really!?" replied Twig sarcastically, aware that his comment had gone way over the child's head.

"Do you like living with me then?" asked Pot with cheerful surprise.
Twig neither liked nor disliked living with a family of Pillicks. He frankly considered it the lesser of two evils since, as a Bonsai, he would have the mick taken something rotten, if he permitted himself to remain among his much larger cousins.
"Well are you taking me back or what?" he said, deftly avoiding the question. "You can't leave me here, out in the elements, surrounded by giant trees and dangerous animals…I could freeze to death, or a big tree could fall on me. Worse still, dogs could urinate on me, drowning me in a sea of pee."
Pot curled his nose at the thought of the latter. Certainly he wanted no harm to come to his little friend…especially since he was now talking to him.
"I tell you this, my furry friend…" continued Twig, hoping to drive the final blow of his argument, "leaving me out here would be tantamount to murder."
Pot reeled, "Murder!?"
"Yep! Homicide, my boy…well treeslaughter at the very least."
Pot, not wanting to harm his little friend, carefully dug Twig out and listened carefully to the rules of communication…
"OK," said Tree, as he advised Pot of his 'real' name, "you have a Tanglepine that talks to you. This is not altogether unprecedented, although it is unusual, so don't think that because I talk to you, I'm gonna go around talking to everyone...my cousin did that and he ended up as a circus attraction. Not the life for me, baby! Understand?"
"The circus!?" Pot parroted excitedly.
"Concentrate!" demanded Tree. "You and me. We can be mates, but try getting me to talk to anyone I don't want to, and you'll end up being the biggest Pillick that ever lived."
"Great!" said Pot.
"That's not what I mean, furball!"

The adult Pot, having broken his fast with the now cold takeaway he had apparently bought the night before, went back upstairs to see how Tree was getting on. "You asleep?" he asked.
"Yes. Go away", said Tree.
"Today's the day", said Pot excitedly, as he quickly rubbed his hands together.
"The day?" quizzed Tree.
"That big, blue fella…said he'd come over and help us track down the cause of all these groundshakes."
"Ah!" sighed Tree. "That day. Hope you've got an umbrella."
"He said he'd be sure to pack his outdoor Vacuhat, whatever that is."
"It's a big hat, which sucks away the saliva from his mouth and then blows it, at high pressure, up into the sky. If the weather's hot enough the water evaporates before it hits the ground. If not…"
"What?" said Pot, his imagination already starting to create comic images.
"Depends on how cold it is", said Tree. "Just right and it turns to snow.
Too cold and you get pierced by a spear of your own spit!"
"What if it's neither hot nor cold?" enquired Pot.
"Rains a lot in Slobber, don't it?" said Tree, wishing he had eyebrows he could dance up and down to highlight his comedic point.
"I need a shower", announced Pot quietly.
Pot stood under the cascade of clean, warm water. To see him naked, for those unfamiliar with Pillick physiology is, to all appearances, to see him dressed. Pillicks, you see, are covered in a light, downy fur that grows all over their body – apart from, curiously enough, their face and neck, their wrists and hands, and their ankles and feet. Those Pillicks who wear shorts and 'T' shirts a lot also tend to shave their arms and legs. The life of a professional swimmer therefore, tends to revolve around the barber's shop!

There was, of course, a time when Pillicks didn't wear clothes at all, and some would argue that they really don't need to wear them now, since a naked Pillick looks like a dressed Pillick...albeit in a rather boring boiler suit.

The Pillick rag-trade appeared at the beginning of their industrial revolution – chiefly for the design of protective clothing. As the number of wealthy Pillicks grew, new demands were made of the emergent fashion industry. People wanted to show off their wealth – look good. Suits, cocktail dresses, smart shoes...the works. In time of course, the range of leisure clothes (or play clothes, as the general workforce called them) increased and the prices came down. It is now highly unusual to see a naked Pillick wandering the streets!

The showering done, Pot dried his brown 'boiler suit', and strolled into his bedroom. "Where's my rubber gear?" he asked rhetorically as he began to turf through his wardrobe.
"Didn't your ex-girlfriend keep it?" said Tree.
"The recreational stuff? Yeah, she did. Wouldn't be any good anyway...too many holes." Pausing for thought Pot added, "I did look pretty sexy in it though, didn't I?"
"Seeing you naked is bad enough. I chose to be asleep when you were in here with Gwendolyn", replied Tree.
"Ah! Here it is. My Wetaway 2000, with specially adapted tree pocket and brolly", said Pot trying to impersonate the voice on the commercial – "Whether you like walking in the rain or are planning a trip to Slobber for business or pleasure, you'll find that nothing keeps you drier than the Wetaway 2000. Its triple-lined rubberised exterior carries a lifetime guarantee, and its specially ventilated, realistic fur lining will let you stroll through showers, or conduct that all-important business meeting in total comfort."
Picking up on the particular reference to the specially adapted tree pocket, Tree piped up. "I don't have to come! Why do I

have to come? I like the shaking. It aids my defoliation process."
"I'm not leaving you here to rifle through my stuff", said Pot.
"I'm a tree, butwart! How can I rifle through anything? I don't have hands", said Tree defensively.
"You've got limbs though, ain't ya?" chuckled Pot, punctuating his 'comic' remark with a gentle jabbing of his fingers, against the small plant's container.

CHAPTER THREE

"Dressed, weekend bag in my hand, nibbles and drinks for the lads on the landing. OK. Ready to rock", said Slobber confidently as he stood at the foot of his stairs. At his front door he paused, and read the badly written note he'd left for himself the previous night:

Pot can't swim!
Check weather reports and take appropriate Vacuhat.

"Nearly forgot. Well done me. Nice note", he punctuated as though on some new kind of word diet. He went to the under-stairs cupboard and, after pondering for a while, selected the 'Vacuhat Excelsior', with high-powered fine-spray attachment. He placed the stylish, red hat on his head and carefully inserted the mouth tubes in his drool pouches. With powerpack belt in hand, he went out into his front garden before securing it around his waist. He then relaxed his large, round belly bulge, and allowed its 'flop-back' action to activate the power cells. In moments a jet of water fired out of the exhaust nozzle, protruding from the top of his headgear.

Slobber raised his eyes, being careful not to affect the angle of his head – there being a visiting group of brollyless schoolchildren passing his house. "Hmm", he said as he adjusted the fine spray control.
"Hey whale boy!" shouted one of the children.
Slobber switched off his Vacuhat and allowed a decent quantity of liquid to accumulate in his sacks. Then he returned the control to 'straight jet', took careful aim and hit the 'on' switch. "There she blows!" he shouted, as the child in question was caught in a deluge of well-aimed spittle. He then re-adjusted the spray control to the 'mist' setting and, safe in the knowledge that the heat of the day would evaporate most of it, strolled down his short path and out onto the street – chuckling loudly to himself as he passed by the schoolboy, now being given CPR by one of his teachers.

As Slobber strolled through the town, he passed EGGIES pub… Then NAREDOOWELLS; TODDHOPPERS EMPORIUM OF INSOBRIETY; 10 SLOBBERS'; and 51 BOB KANSTANDANDKIPWHILETWAITINGFORAPINT'S. He strolled straight passed GOTYOCASH'S, where he'd spent the previous evening, and headed straight for The Jetty.
This was no ordinary jetty, however. No ordinary, run-of-the-mill, wooden protrusion. No simplistic construction, for the purposes of landing small boats, or for fishing off the end… This was the Sentinel Jetty, which, at some 42 miles in length, is probably the most impressive piece of ocean-invasive architecture ever created by man or beast. Its existence is due, wholly and entirely, to the curious geography that exists in Kettles Reach specifically, and the general law of life and land. Kettles, as it is simply known by the locals, sits in a very deep valley, surrounded on three sides by a vast and ancient Tanglepine forest. In itself this wouldn't be much of an issue, other than the fact that Tanglepines are, even though terribly rude and ignorant, sentient beings – feeling and self-aware – and as such, protected by the general law of Life Respect. Since space in the valley is therefore limited – rather foolishly

dominated as it is by so many 'Cathedrals to booze' – the only option for the local town planners was to expand into the sea.

Slobber hailed a cab, and instructed the driver to deliver him to Slobber's Ferry & Taxi Services, International Rank – a destination some three miles down the pier.
"Hello Slobber," said the driver, as Slobber settled himself into the back seat of the conveyance, "how ya doin?"
"Slobber?" said Slobber, quickly identifying the driver, as he carefully pointed his Vacuhat exhaust out through the small hole in the roof, "Gods man, I haven't seen you in ages...didn't you emigrate to Driesville...to help with their drought problem?"
"Certainly did", said Slobber, "Didn't like it much. Money was good but there's something undesirable about eating produce that has been propagated with the assistance of your own spit."
"Why would that put you off?" asked Slobber, removing a mouldy cheese sandwich from the crack in the seat.
"Everything begins to taste the same. Even the beer."
"I could see why that would be a problem", said Slobber, slowly realising why he hadn't been terribly upset when his second cousin – Slobber – had left for Driesville.

The journey to the International Rank was short, but not too short for Slobber to bore his cousin rigid with tails of woe from the land of Driesville: "And I'll tell you something else about spit propagation," said Slobber, "not only does the food start to taste like saliva, but your saliva starts to taste like food."
"Really?" said Slobber as he tried to decide whether or not a person could actually commit murder with an old cheese sandwich.
"Spit – food. Food – spit", continued the driver. "I'm serious. You can't tell the difference."
It was at around this time that Slobber's brain – well past the point of simple tedium – was taking serious consideration to the possibility of creating its own haemorrhage. Finally, it

decided that suicide was something of an over reaction and instead plumped for astral projection.
Slobber's face slowly dropped. Bit by bit the signs of occupancy left his features as his consciousness slowly left the cab and went for a quick pint.
"No charge", repeated the driver.
"What?" said Slobber, his mind slowly returning to the here and now.
"No charge for family", said his cousin. "It's been great talking to you again. Do you still live round here? I'll have to come and visit."
"No", said Slobber. "Just visiting one or two old haunts. I now live..." his attempt to think quickly of the name of some faraway land was hampered by his now tipsy, travelling mind. Suddenly, a moment of inspiration: "I've moved to Driesville", he said, "I rather enjoy the taste of my own spit."
"Shame", said the driver. "Well. Enjoy your trip back. See ya round, then."

Slobber strolled up to the booking desk. The well-dressed agent smiled politely though insincerely as he approached.
"Can I help you sir?" he said, as though it was the millionth time he'd asked that question today.
"Single to Flintlewood please. No luggage."
"Flintle - wood", parroted the clerk slowly, a slight furrow appearing on his brow.
"It's on the banks of the river Twit, in the land of Gweep", said Slobber, seeing the clerk – whose badge proudly gave his name in bold silver letters, ***Slobber*** – was in some small state of uncertainty.
"Of course", said the clerk, clearly relieved by the assistance. "Sorry about this. It's only my second day. To add to my problems, my hat broke down this morning and nearly drowned some poor old lady."
Slobber smiled at the notion and listened politely as the clerk continued, obviously glad to find an appreciative audience for his amusing anecdote. "She was apparently here visiting

family, to discuss her will or something...they were all here, down to meet her…actually," said the clerk, as he thought about the scenario, "they seemed quite disappointed when she choked off her drenching and laughed: 'Only in Slobber can a lady get such a welcome from a handsome young man', she said..."
"How much?" asked Slobber, anxious to bring this conversation to a conclusion without causing offence.
"15", said the clerk, handing over a boarding pass.
Slobber handed over the cash, offered the clerk the cheese sandwich he was still carrying, and made his way to the jetty.

"Matchwood", said Slobber to himself as he read the name on the bow of the boat.
"That's me!" said the taxi enthusiastically.
Slobber couldn't believe it, a talking boat! And an eaves-dropping, talking boat at that.

Talking boats are, of course, not beyond the realms of possibility. There are, it must be observed, such things as talking lifts, talking cars, talking watches, even talking kettles. This particular talking boat however, didn't rely on computer chips or other forms of mechanical gismo. This boat was made from Kia Willow wood…Kia Willow wood, from a Kia Willow tree.
Wow! thought Slobber, as he pondered the wonder of it…
Kia Willows are a relative of the Tanglepine, only they are not so choosy to whom they speak. In their natural state they can grow to about 80 feet in height. The bark on their thick trunks is coated in fluorescent silver algae, which complements perfectly the pale gold leaves, that cover their thin limbs, which, in fine Willow style, cascade elegantly from the tip of the trunk to form a beautiful fountain effect.
What made them so precious to the boat building trade was their extremely flexible, yet durable wood. So much so, that in years gone by Kia Willows were brutally felled in response to demands from that particular industry. Their even greater

usefulness lay in the fact that the wood, and therefore their intelligence, doesn't diminish once they are separated from the roots. A healthy Kia Willow can, in fact, continue to 'live' for several hundred years after felling. Another curious fact about this particular tree is that its molecules are wholly independent of one another. Provided you have enough gathered together in one place, their individual personality and faculties, remain.

Another reason, if more reasons where required, that Kia Willow was so attractive to the boat building industry was that a Kia Willow boat was capable of not only self-navigation, but also acting as tour guide, administrator, and provider of general conversation on long, lonely voyages. Their consummate honesty – or at least the perception of it – combined with attention to detail, also dissuaded dishonest sailors from petty pilfering.

The decline in the use of this wonderful material can be accredited to several factors, the most significant of which is the fact that in order to build a large ship, hundreds of trees are needed. Owing to the Kia's unique qualities, the resulting vessel could become argumentative and, effectively, fall out with itself. This would inevitably result in poor navigation, lousy tours, and unreliable cargo manifestos. Not only that, but a crew…often just a small housekeeping unit, could be driven insane by planks from different trees, destroying any peace and quiet by bickering and arguing all night long!

It was not unheard of for ships to run aground, or even allow the majority of their cargo to be stolen, simply because none of the emergent personalities could agree on who had overall responsibility.

The problem was further compounded by the frequent occurrences of trees being separated during construction. More often than not, pieces of the same tree would end up in several different ships. When vessels met in mid ocean, days could often be wasted, sitting motionless, while ships chatted and effectively caught up with themselves. On one particular occasion, the felled Kias decided to hold a grand reunion party. Hundreds of ships, as well as poorly conceived furniture, houses, and modes of land-based transportation, converged on one port and clogged it for over a month. It was decided, when all was said and done, that there were far more cons than pros to using Kia Willow for anything other than self-opening doors. These were great at parties, since they not only announce the guests, but provide instruction on where to leave your coat and so on. Most other items constructed from Kia Willow have long since been disassembled, properly collated and either released into the wild (stacked neatly in a field somewhere) or turned into doors. There was a fleeting industry in the construction of road signs but, since travellers had to stop in order to ask which town or village the sign was pointing to, this idea quickly died off – much to the delight of the Amalgamated Sign Writers' Union.

"My name…" said the boat, drawing Slobber out of his stunned silence. "Matchwood is my name."
"I'm sorry", said Slobber after a lengthy pause, "It's just that you surprised me. Are you Kia Willow?" he asked, hoping to bring a little of the conversational control back in his direction.
"You bet I am!" replied Matchwood, "Kia Willow, and fiercely proud of it!"
"Really!? That's amazing!" said Slobber. "I didn't think they made guys like you anymore. My Grandad told me…"
"Yes. Yes, I know", interrupted Matchwood. "Some of us asked to be turned into small boats after the great port clog of ten-o-nine. Me and some of the other lads couldn't face forced retirement after a life of travel". Matchwood went on to describe how he feared that retirement would promote the onset of rot and that this had led him to work as a small taxi, ferrying people between Kettles Reach and Flintlewood.
"Don't you get bored?" asked Slobber.
"I have to admit that the last 70 years have been a little tedious. Still, I can't complain. I'm not as young as I was. I

doubt I could manage anything more strenuous", replied Match. "Still..." he added, his voice drifting off into a thoughtful silence.
Slobber smiled to himself and nodded in silent agreement with the boat's unfinished sentence, filled, as he assumed it was, with reminiscences of the past and inferred regrets over the present.
"I guess I'm too old for all that now", said the boat unconvincingly.
Slobber left a polite pause before his curiosity got the better of him – "How old are you?"
"Two-hundred-and-seventy-eight", replied the boat. "You?"
"A mere 33", said Slobber with a vaguely embarrassed smile, almost feeling the urge to apologise for his youth.
"I was felled at 33", said Matchwood, pausing thoughtfully for a moment before continuing. "I became part of the port bow section of a warship. First to see it coming," he said heroically, "first to get hit. I don't talk about it much...too painful", he concluded enigmatically. "You going to Flintlewood?" he asked, changing the subject.
"Certainly am!" replied Slobber.
"Well climb aboard son and make yourself comfy. I'll be damned if I'm gonna hang around here all day", said Matchwood with adventurous impatience.
"What about the other passengers?" said Slobber as he turned his head to see a small group of people starting down the corridor that linked the departure lounge to the jetty.
"Too bad for them. They'll have to catch a boring old metal job. Move it fountain features! You coming or not?

CHAPTER FOUR

Being that he was now in the middle of a wide expanse of calm sea, and being that there was no one else around, other than his mode of transport, Slobber set his Vacuhat to jet, and threw his head back over the stern. The frequent squirts arched out from the rear of the boat, gliding through mid-air before hitting the water. Glistening in the sunlight as they flew their arch, Slobber's saliva shots looked like silver eels jumping for fun.

Other than humming to itself Slobber's travelling companion had been uncommunicative. The gentle sounds of Matchwood's humming suddenly developed some lyrics:

I was a Kia Willow, but now I'm a boat.
I've been part of a great, big ship that sunk.
But I'm still afloat.

From sittin' in a wood, to sailing the ocean wide.
I've been bumped and bombed and nearly drowned.
But I'm still alive.

I sat in a dry dock, tryin' to decide.
What to do with the rest of my life.
What I'd like to try.

Now I'm a sailing a boring 'A' to 'Zee'
All things considered.
I wish I'd stayed a tree.

The song began to tail off…

Dum-dum, di dum-dum.
Dum di-dum-dum-dum.
Diddle I dum, diddle I dum.
Dum-diddly-um dum-dum.

…and ended with a half-hearted rebel-yell, *Yeeeehaaw!*

"So my blue, fountain-headed friend…" said Matchwood suddenly, realising that his little song could be overheard.
"The name's Slobber", said Slobber lazily, making a gentle point.
"Why do all you folk stick to the same name? Doesn't it get confusing?" continued Matchwood, seemingly unconcerned that any offence may have been caused.
"Course not!" replied Slobber, vaguely irritated by what he felt was quite a rude question. Adding in a quietly, sulky voice "Personally, I like my name… Anyway," his voice now slightly raised, "what about you lot!?"
"What do you mean us lot!?"
"Well…" began Slobber, already realising that what he was about to suggest could be viewed as having racist undertones. "Well…once felled, beings formerly known as Kia Willow trees are simply a collection of planks… Intelligent planks, I grant you, but planks all the same. How do you know that plank 'A' is called…say…Trevor, and plank 'B' is called Dorothy?"
"Stupid names!" said Matchwood.

"Well?" Slobber felt confident he had his new found friend on the ropes, and wasn't going to let him get away with avoiding the question.
"It's obvious innit!…We…"
"Yes?"
"Well…" apparently struggling, "Well…it's…" Matchwood paused yet again before being suddenly struck by a moment of genius... "Sound of voice of course. Obvious!" Oh yes. He had it alright. No argument to that.
The pair sat, observing an uncomfortable silence before Match, concerned at last that his original remark had caused offence to his large, blue companion, decided to clarify his point. "I wasn't suggesting all Slobbers look alike, you understand... Let me put it this way. What's your mum's name?"
"Mother!" replied Slobber without hesitation, a childish smile of self-satisfaction on his face.
"No. Her actual name", insisted Matchwood with a sigh.
"Slobber."
"And your dad…and don't say Father…" He'd let the 'Mother' thing go without comment but was disinclined to be so charitable again, "we are still some distance from land you know!" he remarked, offering a veiled threat that Slobber might find himself with a long swim if his pitiful attempts at humour persisted.
"Slobber!" said Slobber, the sharp end of the boat's point beginning to stab at his ego.
"Your girlfriend?"
"Ex-girlfriend!" said Slobber. "Slobber."
"And the names of the kids in your class?"
Slobber huffed the sigh of irritated defeat. "Slobber, Slobber, Slobber, Slobber…"
"Describe Slobber to me", interrupted Matchwood, very matter-of-factly.
Without hesitation, Slobber immediately delivered a detailed description of his best friend. Chuckling at points as the verbal map of his pal suddenly found itself triggering a golden

memory of fun and general tomfoolery.
For the first time Matchwood began to feel the glory of victory slipping from his grasp. "No", he said, desperate to stall for time. The pause created by his insurgence into his companion's reminiscences hadn't even begun to make its presence felt before Matchwood saw the light of a brilliant question… "Not Slobber. Slobber."
Slobber thought for a moment before, with a look of general puzzlement, asking the question Match had been hoping for: "Which one?"
"SEE!" shouted the boat. "Oh yes. Destroyed by superior logic!" Matchwood started to rock from side-to-side by way of a victory dance. In time to the motion he taunted his defeated opponent with another little ditty, this one utterly intended to be heard by his passenger...

I am a boat.
You are a biped.
You'd drown in a moat.
Once your legs got ty-red.

"You really should consider writing musicals", sneered Slobber sarcastically.
"Do you really think so?" replied Matchwood.
"No", came the dismissive reply.
Matchwood, again concerned that offence had been taken, quickly offered an apology which Slobber, after a deal of silent sulking, accepted.

The discomfort of a pregnant pause sat over the duet. Slobber, feeling suffocated by the deafening nothing, piped up – cheerfully offering to change his name…just for the duration of the trip, of course.
"Don't be silly", replied Matchwood, "It's who you are. Change your name if *you* wish to, not because a foolish old vessel makes a joke at your expense."

The journey was beginning to get a little dull for Slobber. Matchwood had been whiling away the time by quietly humming his little tune to himself. Slobber wanted to ask whether, whilst working as part of a warship, he had been bombed, or whether he had just manipulated events to fit the rhyme, but decided it would be a little impolite.
"What takes you to Flintlewood?" enquired Matchwood cheerfully, finally choosing to make idle conversation.
"Just visiting a friend", said Slobber.
"Girlfriend, boyfriend, old friend, new friend?" sang the boat.
"New friend actually. Little furry chap I met in the pub last night. You'd probably like him since he is in the habit of communing with nature."
"Eh!?"
"Talking to wood", said Slobber, referring to his drinking companion's pet Tanglepine.
"Ah, you must mean the Pillick, Potfondle", said Match, much to Slobber's surprise. Matchwood went on to explain that he'd taken Pot home the night before, and although Pot himself had passed out roughly ten minutes into the trip, Match had enjoyed a lengthy conversation with Tree. He'd heard all about their night on the tiles, their failed attempts to pick up two rather attractive waitresses, and their plans for high adventure that had begun to formulate after they had both passed the eight pint mark.

Matchwood had already heard of the groundshakes being experienced by that region of Gweep, and that the scientific community – apart from a representative from the Seismology Department of the National University of Gweep (she being on holiday at the time) – having conducted literally a month of solid research into the matter, had returned a casual verdict of: 'NON CONCLUSIVE…SORRY!'
The fact that the scientific community of Gweep (who don't get out much, and had blown the whole research budget on a luxury break for 50 in the paradise of Shallowpool – '***The only place to beeee on your holideeee***', as the extremely

repetitive advertising campaign never tired of announcing, in an overly happy and irritatingly chirpy voice) managed to get away with presenting a three-word, totally worthless report, left many observers with a sense of forehead-smacking frustration. 'We really need to start taking an interest in local politics', is now a phrase in regular use around Gweep. What made the whole thing all the more irritating was that, had the Seismologist been vacationing at Shallowpool, their wasteful use of public money might not have been so evident. As it was though, she knew nothing about their presence at the resort – truly exasperating, since she was just a few miles down the coast, on a snorkelling break in Lesser Shallowpool…their ad campaign simply states: ***'When you can't afford the other place, come see us!'*** Curiously enough this seemingly laid-back, 'we don't actually need your business' approach has proved terribly effective. So much so, that their next campaign, which is expected to suggest: ***'Come to Lesser Shallowpool if you want. Actually, we don't really need your business'***, is expected to be so successful that five new hotels are already under construction in order to meet the anticipated increase in visitor numbers. Thankfully, the following slogan to this – ***'Bog off you sick-faced tourist! Come to Lesser Shallowpool and we'll break both your legs!!'*** – which was written by the same 'Ad-man' – was dismissed as being a little too insulting for general use.

The little boat had heard how, whilst sipping their way through the twelfth pint, Slobber and Potfondle, now totally carried away with their new sense of eternal friendship, had decided that the weekend would provide ample time to trace the source of the problem *and* plot a solution. Two pints later, Potfondle had stood in the pub and, whilst swaying gently from side-to-side, announced, in words so slurred as to be unrecognisable as any form of language, "I go now to Flintlewood, for tomorrow our quest begins in earnest!" At that point, his unfocused eyes glazed over and his legs decided it was time to kiss the floor.

That morning Slobber had considered, as he walked from his house to the jetty, that Pot had most likely forgotten the whole conversation. In his mind, he had constructed an image of an ashen-faced Potfondle answering the small door of his house and, upon seeing the smiling face of a positively charged Slobber, saying something along the lines of "Who the hell are you!?" This, he thought – having had some experience with hangovers – would likely be followed, after a brief period of reflective silence, with a thoroughly downbeat exhalation of "Oh no!"

"So…" said Matchwood. "Think he'll remember the ambitious plans you made last night?"
Slobber had to admit, as his destination grew closer, that there was a distinct possibility of Pot having no recollection of their 'quest' whatsoever.
More likely, he thought, that having been reminded of the previous evening's conversation by Tree, Potfondle may have decided to leave town for a while.
Match suggested that the most realistic possibility was that Pot had remembered some of it, Tree had filled in the blanks and they had both come to the conclusion that Slobber, if *he* remembered at all, would not bother making the trip – deciding instead to put the whole idea down to 'the beer talking'. "After all," said Matchwood, "if you weren't actually making this trip, what are the chances that the three of you would ever meet up again?"
"Pretty remote", nodded Slobber in agreement. After all, he and Pot hadn't originally met by appointment. Pot had simply come to Kettles Reach for the same reason anybody goes there…to enjoy the hospitality of its many alehouses and get well and truly hammered. Slobber – who himself had just popped out for 'a couple' – had tried to discover if there was any particular reason Pot wished to get drunk, but the little

Pillick had simply replied: "Oh. You know..."
As far as Slobber was concerned, this simple answer was a perfectly acceptable reason for a person to destroy a large quantity of his or her brain cells, whilst spending their hard-earned money on an evening that few remember. Not wishing to press the matter, Slobber had just nodded and said – as people often do in response to such a statement – "Yeah. I know what you mean", not actually knowing what he had meant at all!
"Can you swim?" asked Matchwood.
"What do you think?" said Slobber, gesturing with his hands and raising his eyes – alluding to his hat, still pumping away. "50 gallons on average," he added. "Fifty! Why do you think Slobber buildings all have such terrific drainage systems? You don't actually think this is regular sea water we're sailing on?" concluded Slobber, leaning back in his seat, a wry smile creeping across his face.
Matchwood was pondering the revolting prospect of a life spent on an ocean of spit when suddenly, and without warning, he jolted to a stop, violently throwing his passenger forward. He then shuddered slowly forward, accompanied by an unfriendly scraping sound coming from the bottom of his hull – vibrating through his sides. The boat stopped again, and was suddenly pulled down – not all the way but far enough for some water to slosh over the sides. Here the pair sat for a moment, confusion and panic preventing any comment, before the unseen grip released its hold and the little boat shot back up again. Thrown by his own buoyancy, Match almost left the surface altogether, before splashing back down, sending enough spray out to rival the amount produced by his fountain-like friend.
"WHAT IN THE NAME OF BETTY'S ARMPITS WAS THAT!?" cried Slobber, now lying in a heap.
"Ssshhh!" hissed Matchwood, still rocking from side-to-side, the only visible ripples on the water being those created by him. "Can't see anything. Can't hear anything. Can't smell anything."

"What good is a self-guiding boat..." Slobber began calmly, as he picked himself up off the floor "THAT CAN'T AVOID ROCKS!!!" he shouted angrily.
"WASN'T ROCKS, FOUNTAIN HEAD!" replied Matchwood with equal irritation. "If you knew anything about nautical navigation you would know that this particular stretch of water is too deep for rocks!" he continued, angry that this 'land-dweller' had the audacity to question his seafaring skills. "And can you please point that thing over the side. There's enough water in here as it is. What are you trying to do, capsize us!?"
"Right!" said Slobber, feeling a little out of his depth – in more ways than one. He reached up and adjusted his Vacuhat exhaust nozzle, bent by the force of his fall.
"Right...OK...Sorry!" said Slobber, realising the harsh reality that all there was between him and an abyss was Matchwood. "Not rocks...OK. A whale?" he suggested, his anxiety clearly displayed in his now shaky voice.
"A whale would have tipped us for sure", said the boat quietly, as though thinking aloud. "You'd now be swimming and I'd be juxtaposed."
"You'd be a what!?" asked Slobber, his still present frown of concern now joined by one of ignorance.
"Match-wood!" said Matchwood, "I would *be* match wood...by nature as well as by name."
"Oh", replied Slobber after a pause for thought, "Sounds painful."

The silent pair sat motionless – other than their now gentle rocking from side-to-side. Surrounded by water and hearing only the sound of it gently lapping at Matchwood's hull, along with the occasional splash of yet another saliva jet diving into the sea, Slobber could contain his fear no longer. "CAN WE PLEEEASE GET OUT OF HERE!?" he cried.
The boat took a deep breath and then exhaled loudly. After a further silent pause, he started to move forward once more.

CHAPTER FIVE

Potfondle stood heroically, admiring himself in the mirror.
"Whether you like walking in the rain or are planning a dangerous adventure, the Wetaway 2000..." he said quietly, in his best 'hero' voice, attempting to parrot yet another commercial he'd heard.
"Oh Gods!" sighed Tree, interrupting Pot's ramblings. "So this is it then, is it? You, me and the rain gear?"
"Wetaway 2000", said Pot proudly, placing his hands on his hips and striking another pose.
"Not taking food, a tent, some sort of compass?"
"You don't need any of that stuff. *You* are a tree", said Pot now standing with his legs apart and pointing into an imaginary distance.
"Yes", said Tree patronisingly, as though speaking to a young child. "I get my nutrients from the soil. Plant me anywhere and I'll be OK, but *you*, and presumably the big, blue, drool factory, need fooooood."
"Good point", agreed Pot, taking a break from his posing but retaining his heroic voice. He turned on his heels, pointed skywards and cried "TO THE ATTIC SPACE!"

Pot ascended the ladder, carefully cradling Tree under his left arm. He placed the small plant on a box and stood, scratching his head in thought as he looked around his attic for inspiration. "Hmmm", he pondered as he stood, surrounded by stacked boxes and dust, "A bag might be a good place to start..." *No,* he thought, *not a bag. A rucksack, perhaps two.* With this simple expression, fresh in his motivated mind, Pot sprang into action, busying himself by locating the items on his quickly improvised list:

Sleeping bag	x 1
6 sleeping bags zipped together to form one big one	x 1
Torch	x 2
Matches	1 box (large)
Compass	x 2 (just in case one gets lost)
Map	x 1
Camera	x 1 (for the taking of official photographs)
Saucepan	x 2
Frying pan	x 1

"That'll do", he announced, once his treasure hunt was complete. "We don't want all the comforts of home. This is, after all, supposed to be a weekend of 'derring-do'. We will procure our groceries from the fine trades-people in the village."
"Any chance you'll be dropping that stupid hero voice any time

soon?" sighed Tree.
"No, my sarcastic Tangletwig", Pot announced, as he wrestled with the rather large rucksack he had hastily packed. "Smack my Rodney", he puffed in his normal voice, after fighting a losing battle, "This thing's gonna end up wearing me." He decided that the most sensible course of action was to trundle the bundle down to the river and let Slobber carry it. "I packed it," he said with a pronounced nod of satisfaction, "he can carry it!" delivering, this time, a pronounced nod of decision. He slid the bulging bag to the hatchway; carefully positioned it at the top of the ladder and then let it go. It didn't budge an inch. Pot tentatively pushed on it - still no response. He pushed again, this time with both hands and a little more force.
"Too fat?" suggested Tree.
Determined not to be beaten by an inanimate object, Pot pushed again, and again, and again.
"Listen", he said to the bag. "You're going down boy, and there's not a damn thing you can do about it!" He then, out of sheer desperation, jumped on it.
"ARE YOU ALRIGHT?" shouted a concerned Tree to his friend, who was now lying in a heap at the bottom of the ladder.
Pot lay on his back, looking up into the gloom above, before slowly moving his head – looking about him. He gently patted himself down as he checked for obvious injuries and breakages. "No obvious damage", he announced in due course. Feeling nothing more than a little foolish, he decided to get to his feet but found the task curiously difficult. It was then that he noticed it was not in fact the floor that had broken his fall. Nor was it that upon which he now rested. Somehow, as both he and the giant rucksack had dropped, the straps of his large bag had managed to secure themselves over his shoulders. Pot lay there for a moment, on top of his luggage, and considered his options. He nodded to himself. He had a plan.
He began by frantically kicking his legs about, in a desperate

attempt to make contact with the floor. Then, mustering all his strength, he began to struggle – twisting his body from side-to-side, hoping to create a rocking motion that might eventually roll him, and his luggage over. As his efforts continued and his speed of motion gained, he managed to rock with sufficient force to place him on his stomach.

Now he had a new problem…the weight of his ‘passenger’ now pinned him firmly to the ground. For a moment he lay, gathering his strength before pushing up with his arms until he could lock his elbows straight. With his face reddening and sweat pouring – a clear display of the sheer effort he had been forced to exert – he slowly drew in his legs, eventually resting on all-fours.

“Is there a problem down there?” quizzed Tree from the heights of the loft.

“No…” puffed Pot, anxious for his voice to sound as normal as possible, “No problem here”, he lied.

With the weight of the rucksack preventing him from raising his head, Pot was forced to scour his limited field of vision for some method of getting to his feet. Eventually, his eyes fixed on the foot of the ladder, just visible to his left. Slowly, and with his full measure of strength and concentration, Pot managed to shuffle over and grab at the bottom rung, gripping with his single hand for all he was worth, and transferring his weight to it – steadying himself and the ladder, while he brought over his other hand.

Keeping his body close to the ladder for stability, he slowly clambered up it, pulling with his arms and pushing with his legs until eventually he was upright.

On his feet, with his legs taking the strain, Pot felt confident enough to leave the pack where it was, as he waddled over to the top of the stairs. Gripping the handrail with such strength that his knuckles turned white, he slowly turned and, like a mountaineer making his descent, he very cautiously moved one foot back and down – finding a sure footing on the step below.

His descent took nearly two hours but he managed it. Upon reaching the bottom, Pot turned again and leant forward as he struggled to the front door and opened it. There he stood for a moment, looking out into the world with a sense of true achievement, stroking his chin thoughtfully, and paying close attention to the width of the opening. It didn't take a genius to realise that, with pack on back, he was now wider than the door, but rather than do the sensible thing and attempt to remove this burden, Pot permitted a curious thought to run through his mind. He edged back a couple of feet and carefully turned his back to the exit. Carefully, he checked his position in relation to the aperture, before suddenly springing with his legs and launching himself like a bullet at the opening.
"Smack my Rodney!" said Pot, quietly to himself as he dangled there, stuck fast, six inches from the ground – his legs swaying freely.
There he hung for a moment, looking at the ground for inspiration, which did eventually come. All of a sudden, Pot began to twist himself violently, and kick frantically, as his level of desperation reached its climax. Tree, not being deaf, shouted down – "Everything OK down there?" as the sound of Pot's grunting drifted up to the roof space.
"Fine", grunted Pot. "Won't...be...a...sec. Hang...on." He continued his efforts with greater determination, as he felt the pack begin to give.
"YES!" shouted Pot triumphantly, now lying on his back once again, but this time on the path – outside, looking towards the heavens, the pack still attached like some demoniacal limpet. Once again Pot began his struggling tortoise routine – rocking once more from side-to-side, gathering momentum and eventually rolling on to his front again. Squashed by his 'shell', he lay there for a while, his face cooling on the stone of his path while he caught his breath. Continuing the reconstruction of his earlier success, he raised himself to all-fours again. Now looking more like a small donkey than a tortoise, Pot looked around for the ladder. "Globs!" he said, out of breath – a hint of defeat starting to creep into his voice.

"No ladder!" He looked around the ground of his small front garden, hoping that he'd left a spade or hoe lying around. "Right! So that's the way it's going to be, is it?" he said, as no available assistance presented itself. He stood for a moment, his face contorting, as the effort of forced inspirational thought stuttered through his mind. "Of course!" he finally exclaimed, wanting to smack his forehead in disbelief at how stupid he'd been, but terrified that a shift of weight would have him flat on his face again. He gently moved forward, realising that the doorframe would provide him with ample support. This it did admirably. His task of getting to his feet completed for a second time, Pot rested against the white-painted woodwork, before finally acknowledging the error of his ways. Carefully he worked, freeing his frame from the evil passenger that had, so ruthlessly robbed him of his energy and his dignity. His cruel limpet, however, was not yet finished…it had still one more blow to deliver to its unsuspecting victim. As the heavy sack crashed to the ground, Pot was suddenly greeted by a round of enthusiastic applause from the large crowd that had steadily gathered to watch the entertaining spectacle he had been making of himself. "Globs!" he said to himself through a smile of gritted teeth – trying to hide his obvious embarrassment as he gave a triumphant wave. "Thank you. Thank you all very much", he said with a low bow. "My name is Potfondle the Tortoise..." he continued, as he made his way casually round the side of his house – heading for the peace and safety of the back garden. "I'm here Tuesdays and Fridays. Always available for Weddings, Birthdays and Bar Mitzvahs."

"What was all that cheering?" quizzed Tree, as the now packless Pot clambered through the hatch and back into the attic.
"No idea!" said Pot with a half convincing shrug of his still aching shoulders – "Must be a party down the road or something", he added, quickly grabbing his potted friend and returning sharply to the ground floor.
"Wallet!?" said Tree as they speeded towards the back door.

“Pocket”, said Pot, quickly exiting his domicile and locking the door behind him.
“There we go”, said Pot, gesturing towards an empty wheelbarrow.
“Where’s the bag?” asked Tree.
Pot gave no reply. Instead he placed Tree on the ground and, with the stealth of a great hunter, slinked his way back around the house, out to the front. Hugging the wall as though coveting it as a second skin, the little Pillick gently peered around the corner. He slowly looked left and then right, checking to ensure that his previous audience had now fully disbanded. All was clear. Quickly, he returned to the barrow.
“What are you doing!?” quizzed Tree.
Pot chose an offering of silence in response to the perfectly logical question. Ignoring his foliaged friend completely, Pot simply picked up the wheelbarrow and quickly trundled it around to the front of his house. It was with surprising ease that the small, furry chap managed to load his vehicle.
“All aboard”, he cried as he pulled back to the rear.
Tree decided to say nothing, now of the sincere belief that his mammalian pal was steadily losing the plot.
With a profound lack of ceremony, Pot grabbed Tree’s bucket and threw him on top of the loaded carrier. As he rounded the house once more, he made another, quick reconnoitre – ensuring once more, that his audience had gone. That fact now certain, Potfondle tightened his grip on the barrow handles and prepared to make his exit: “We go now,” he said, choosing to return to his ‘hero’ voice, “into that great unknown.”
“If you mean the village, you need to turn left at the garden gate”, sighed Tree, finding solace in sarcasm as a way of dealing with his disappointment at having to join this seemingly pointless endeavour. Pot chose to ignore his friend’s negative attitude and, unzipping the front of his coat for greater ventilation, the pair commenced their journey.

CHAPTER SIX

Pot and Tree sat on the bank, looking out over the moorings at the wide expanse that is the river Twit, awaiting the arrival of the third member of their expedition. Pot lay back on the grass with his hands clasped behind his head, as the gentle breeze cooled his exposed torso. Tree sat, still in his pot, on top of the rucksack barrow – blowing raspberries at any approaching dog. "Take your urine and go", he said to one small canine, as it sniffed around the vehicle's sole wheel. "In case you didn't get it", he added, "that's a polite way of saying pi…"

"You know," interrupted Pot, still gazing into the vast expanse of blue hanging overhead, "I haven't felt this level of nervous anticipation since…" he tailed off, struggling to think of a comparable moment in his life.

Tree didn't see why such great excitement was being attached to this weekend. After all, just what did *they* expect to find in two days that the scientists couldn't discover in a month – ignorant of their holiday in Shallowpool, which was never made public. *The most exciting thing likely to happen to us this weekend,* he decided, *will most likely be getting slightly lost in the woods. As for 'deeds of derring-do'*, as Potfondle had put it, *we'll be lucky if we have to run away from a wasp nest. Basically,* he concluded, *this is just another camping trip. We'll end up with aching feet...well, the bipeds will, sore limbs, bad backs...well, the vertebrates will, and food poisoning. We'll smell bad, particularly those dressed in fur-lined rubber, and we'll get home vowing never to do that again...just like the last camping trip!*

Tree continued his train of thought, really starting to enjoy his negativity. *The blue guy isn't even going to show up...I wouldn't if it was me. No. We're just going to sit here for an hour or so, before going back home via the nearest KANSTANDANDKIPWHILE-WAITINGFORAPINT'S. Pot will end up trying to cook whilst drunk, and burn the house down. I, being made of wood, will blister and blacken before...*

"Ahoy!" came a voice from the water, interrupting this bleak train of thought. "Ahoy on the bank!" shouted Slobber.

Pot sat up and looked over at Tree, both giving the same unspoken signs of surprise that he'd actually turned up.

"I suppose we could go for a quick pint before we set off proper", said Pot, more to himself than anyone else.

"You're not telepathic, are you?" quizzed Tree, concerned that his private thoughts had been invaded. "If you get hungry later, though…just one word. Takeaway! I do not look good in blisters."

Pot frowned away his utter confusion and waved to the new arrival. He then said one of the most obvious things that anyone can say in such a situation – "You made it then."

Tree, already pumped up by his earlier negativity, upon hearing this question, began muttering his favourite 'soap box' conversation to himself: "No, he's not here. That is an optical illusion. Next, why don't you look up at the sun and ask if he thinks it's a nice day?"

Pot, familiar with this common diatribe hissed, "Shut up stick insect. Don't tell me you weren't thinking the exact same thing!"

Slobber's small boat drew up to the little pier. Slobber, unused to boats and still a little shaky after their earlier fright, stood unsteadily – anxiously awaiting the time when it would be safe for him to make his nervous jump to dry land. "Nice day isn't it?" he said, pointing into the sky with one hand while trying to steady his balance with the other.

"Give me a break!" sighed Tree.

"Be nice!" said Pot in a quietly threatening tone.

Just then, Tree noticed the name on the boat. "Hey Matchwood. Fancy seeing you again so soon."

"Hey yourself!" said Matchwood enthusiastically and, forgetting his standing passenger, he delivered a vigorous wave of greeting.

The trouble with a boat wave is, that because a boat generally has no arms, any 'physical' gestures one makes are transmitted through its body, resulting in a rocking motion. The more vigorous the wave, the greater the rocking. Unfortunately for Slobber, Matchwood was unexpectedly pleased to see Tree, and his wave had been particularly generous. Slobber jerked this way and that, in an attempt to steady himself. Matchwood, realising the unintentional result of his gesture of greeting, tried to calm his motion. Pot and Tree watched helplessly for what seemed like ages as the offshore action headed towards its foregone conclusion. Slobber danced his feet and threw the top half of his body this way and that, as his arms flailed wildly – as though conducting some chaotic orchestra. Then came the moment of disaster... Slobber, for just a split second, lost concentration. His uncoordinated, though to this point effective efforts, began to have the opposite to their desired effect, and the big, blue man began to fall backwards over the side. The next couple of seconds seemed to occur in slow motion... Pot rose to his feet, as his hands came up to clutch the sides of his head. His face lengthened, his eyes widened, and his now gaping mouth cried out, "NNOOOO!!!"

Matchwood, still desperately trying to steady his swaying, suddenly realised that all was lost and a quiet resignation filled

his soul.
Slobber, still falling backwards like a freshly felled tree, had begun to rotate his arms wildly, whilst repeatedly shouting the word "WOAH!" The apparent attempt to turn himself into a helicopter had little effect and, after what seemed like an age, he tipped over the edge of the boat and landed with a loud splash in the river.
Tree said nothing.
Pot rushed to the water's edge and instinctively thrust out an open hand, attached to his very short arm. Slobber rose to the surface and began to wave his arms. "Help!" he shouted, in automatic panic.
"Grab my hand!" yelled Pot.
"Stand up", offered the calm voice of Tree.
"Put your feet on the river bed and straighten your legs", expanded Matchwood.
Slobber did as he was instructed. His feet touched the accumulated, soft mud of the river bed; his legs straightened and the top three feet of his body slowly rose up out of the water.

An embarrassed Slobber stood silently, waist high in water, avoiding eye contact with Pot. "Ah", he eventually said. He retrieved his Vacuhat and placed it carefully back on his wet head. Slowly, he waded to the shoreline and climbed out. Pot climbed into the boat and heaved out Slobber's comparatively giant bag.

Slobber flopped heavily to the ground next to the wheel-barrow. His head hung in shame, he sat with his forearms resting on his bent knees. A jet of water, which also contained two small and very frightened fish, shot from the top of his hat, narrowly missing the approaching Potfondle, before conveniently splashing back into the water.
"Did you fall in the water?" enquired Tree, his voice laced with irony.
Slobber, still staring at the ground, saw the joke and smiled.

"No", he said, "My Vacuhat's malfunctioning."
Pot dragged Slobber's bag to where he was sitting and collapsed in a heap, next to a very damp Slobber.
"Heavy bag?" asked Tree, who had now decided to see how many stupidly obvious questions he could ask in the course of one day.
Pot, choosing to ignore 'the forest of one', turned to his large companion: "I suppose you're a naturally quick-drying man?" he offered in consolation.
"Slobber skin has a degree of natural protection from water", he replied, turning his head slightly to look at his companion. "The clothes are waterproof, but they aren't designed for diving."
Slobber removed the Vacuhat tubes from his mouth, pushing one up his jumper and the other down his trousers. "That should take care of the trapped stuff," he said through a slightly dribbling smile.
As the chuckles died down, Tree requested that Pot take him down to the water's edge. He wished to speak with Matchwood and didn't fancy shouting. A compliant Pot slowly rose to his feet, collected his friend and sat him down on the pier, by the side of the little boat.
"Thank you, servant", joked Tree, "You may go."
Pot delivered a deep bow of false respect and walked back to his patch of flattened grass.
Match and Tree sat silently until Pot was out of range. "So?" whispered Tree.
"It happened again", replied the boat, matching Tree's volume, "Not in exactly the same place mind, but close."
"Did you get a get a better look at it in the daylight?"
"It was big. Bigger than any swimming thing I've ever seen before, and I've seen pretty much everything in my time!"
"Did your passenger see it?" asked Tree.
"Don't think so", replied the boat.
"Lucky he was the only one on board."
"It wasn't luck", said Match, "I left before the other passengers could board."

Tree sat quietly for a moment, unsure why Matchwood had allowed anyone to board him at all.
After the same thing had happened the night before, they both decided that Match would return the following day and, with the assistance of better light, try and discover what exactly had held them up. “Why did you let him board you?” hissed Tree, a little irritation beginning to show in his voice. “We agreed. No witnesses. If anyone should discover…”
“I know what you think it is”, interrupted the boat. “I don’t agree. The last of *them* died off long ago. This is something different. Something never seen before.”
“Even more reason not to tell anyone until we are sure!” Tree’s whisper grew in volume, as the frustration at his co-conspirator’s apparent lack of co-operation increased. “We are talking big money here, remember!”
“Don’t panic”, urged Match, “I’ve convinced him to keep shtum! Anyway…” His attention grabbed by the approaching figures, forcing him to attempt a little verbal misdirection. “Yeah..!” he said with a laugh, raising his voice so as not to arouse suspicion, “I know...I’ve never heard snoring so loud either… Hi Slobber”, he said interrupting himself, in an attempt to alert Tree to the presence of the big, blue man.
Slobber wasn’t fooled by this obvious charade, but decided to say nothing. “We are just going to pop into the village for a few odds and sods”, he said, directing his comments to Tree, before thanking Matchwood for conducting his safe passage, and wishing him a safe return trip.
“If you want to save a little time,” cried out Matchwood, to a retreating Slobber, “you should go up river – it runs right through the forest. Besides, those bags look a little heavy. I’d be more than happy to offer my services…at no charge, of course – just for a bit of fun. I’ve been promising myself a day off for ages.”
“Really!?” said Slobber, enthusiastically. “That’d be really great. Thanks.” He ran back to where Pot was still lying and gave him the good news. He then effortlessly picked up the wheelbarrow, tucked it under his arm and threw his own bag

over his shoulder. "Right! Me and Pot are just popping into the village to get a few provisions", he said, once Match had been loaded up. "Back soon. Don't go away."
As Slobber and Pot strolled out of sight, Matchwood continued his previously interrupted sentence… "Anyway", he said, "This is not just a matter of money. We are way beyond circus's now! This thing IS HUGE, it could've pulled me under the water without thinking twice!"
"Not easy to catch, I'll warrant", mused Tree to himself, his mind filled with the sounds of ringing tills and jangling coins.
Matchwood sat silently, realising that he was fighting a losing battle. His tiny partner was consumed with the idea of catching this thing and flogging it off to the highest bidder. At least Match *hoped* Tree wanted to sell it, whatever *it* was. He barely allowed himself to speculate about the possibility that Tree had desires of donning a Ring Master's suit, standing in front of a giant goldfish bowl and yelling 'Roll up. Roll up!'
"You're not listening to me, are you? Let me spell it out for you. This thing is very, very big", said Matchwood, swaying from side-to-side in an attempt to emphasise his point. "Big! Understand? Large, enormous in fact. Big body, huge fins, and its teeth…"
"Teeth!?" shrieked Tree, butting in. "You saw it clearly enough to see teeth!?"
"Teeth that size are difficult to miss", said Match, concerned that Tree might realise he was drifting into the realms of exaggeration. "I tell you this my sticky friend…a dentist could retire after only one visit from this thing!"
Although loath to admit it to himself, Matchwood's confidence had been severely dented by his most recent encounter with the creature. His first, which had happened the night before, was nowhere near as frightening. On that occasion, he had just felt a rough edge brushing along his keel – more than a tickle, but not enough to hurt. He had rocked a bit and had almost been caught in a small whirlpool, caused by the wash from the creature's tail. Being a moonless night, neither he nor Tree had seen very much, but Matchwood's obvious

surprise and alarm had given rise to Tree's imaginings of mythical creatures of the deep. For the fun of it Match, rather foolishly as it turned out, fuelled these tales with myths of sea giants sinking much greater vessels than he. The rest of their trip back to Flintlewood had been filled with Matchwood's fanciful nonsense about bits of friends washing up on beaches, screaming hysterically about 'the rhythms of the deep' before dying and being used on barbecues.

What Matchwood was keeping to himself is that this time, it being daylight, he had managed to get quite a good look at the cause of his anxiety. Slobber, having been thrown in a heap on the floor, hadn't seen anything. Match had actually managed to get more of a glimpse than he would have wished on this fine and clear morning. He had sat silently on the water, trying to make sense of what he knew could not be true.

Matchwood's early days of seafaring had been spent in military service, and he had seen many a strange thing on, and under the sea. As a young set of planks he had heard tall tales – not only from older parts of the boat but aging and experienced sailors too. Several of these taller tales told of a species of sea beast – 'the giant of the deep', is what many had named it. This 'giant' was said to be over a hundred feet in length, with enough power to sink a battleship with one flick of its mighty tail. Its teeth, it was said, were kept razor sharp by the constant gnawing of the bones of sailors. This creature, referred to by one very old and well-travelled Captain as Nassian – which in the ancient tongue means 'destroyer' – was thought to have been extinct for many an age, and Match, quite sensibly viewed these tales as being nothing more than sea-dog folklore.

That morning though, he found himself thinking back to the stories he'd once heard. Sitting there, the sound of Slobber's pleas to get to shore had been drowned out by the voice of a former Skipper…the Captain of a fishing vessel Match had

become part of after 'retiring' from military service. "Nassian", he had often been heard muttering, "Destroyer."
"Well!" whined Slobber, pulling Matchwood from his thoughtful trance. "What the Hell are we waiting for!?"
Match was forced to concur…departure from this place was a sensible notion.

As their journey continued, Matchwood found himself drifting back to the words of that old Captain. His tales and descriptions of the beast he called Nassian:

'As children, we are told by our mothers that all the monsters are long gone. That the giant lizards all shrank and now scurry under rocks at the sound of our approach. That dragons and trolls were wiped out by men of courage and honour. The serpents of the deep oceans are nothing more than ripples on the surface, transformed by bored imaginations. The monsters that sink ships are merely rocks and icebergs, and sailors who become lunch are just gobbled by sharks and eels.

I, like all children, believed my mother. Mothers don't lie, after all. My mother believed what she told me to be true. There was no reason to think that monsters really exist, since she had never seen one and despite the tall tales of many sailors, she had never met a one of 'em who – in all honesty – could claim to have actually seen an unnatural creature.
Aye, my fine ship. I stand here to tell you… I have seen such a thing. 'Twas as a young deck hand on a fishing vessel that I saw Nassian. The Destroyer – the last of its race.
Aeons ago the Gods of the sea decided that they should be the only beings to live forever. They commanded Nassian's race to give up its immortality, which they themselves had given them. These creatures, being loyal to their creators, agreed and slowly they became extinct. Nassian was the last to be born. It had spent most of its life alone; watched as its family and friends died off; its anger at the Gods growing with

each passing century. No longer immortal it eludes death's eyes by hiding – asleep for centuries at a time. It was after one such period of hibernation that we met. Our first encounter, thank the Gods, was also our last.

Centuries had passed and Nassian had become nothing more than a legend to be told on long voyages. I was on such a trip – out at sea for months, looking for fish. We had had a good haul, and were preparing to return home, our holds full and our nets bulging. As we sailed for shore, our ship slowed and then shuddered to a halt. I looked out and saw the giant creature devouring the contents of our nets. Its long, snake-like tail rose out of the water thirty feet into the air, before smashing back down – the waves it created in its feeding frenzy near wiped us out, several men fell overboard as the chaos tossed our ship like it were a child's plaything.
Our nets empty but its hunger unsatisfied, the creature writhed about, wrapping the netting around its long body, reeling us in as we would reel in the fish. Our ship moved backwards at such a speed that I near thought we would capsize. Water crashed over the stern, flooding our holds and cabins. Masts and spare rigging toppled overboard and I knew my short life was already at its end. Once the creature had brought us close enough it flexed the razor sharp fin, which ran the length of its shiny, black back, and cut through the nets with great ease. All fell silent, and seeing other ships in our fleet charging to our aid, those left aboard praised the Gods for our salvation. It has been frightened away, we thought – how wrong could we have been! This was, it seemed, to have been the literal calm before the storm – and what a storm it was.
We pulled our half-drowned shipmates back on board and waited for our saviours to arrive. It was then that we heard it. The 'Rhythm', my Captain called it. The 'Rhythm of the Deep' – a sound so strange…at first I thought it were the engines of our sister vessels, as they steamed towards us. It was only the face of my captain that made me think different. Normally

a red-faced man, all the colour had washed away and he now stood white as a ghost – even his bushy, black beard had turned icy white. "We're done for lads", he sobbed, before putting the barrel of his own musket to his head and pulling the trigger.

The sound grew louder, a bumping, crashing, thrashing sound. A giant, grating heartbeat coming from the depths. Then a roaring, like a frightening wind from nowhere. The ten of us who remained then wished we too, had owned muskets. The creature had never left us. It had been watching silently from the murky depths. Like a mountain, it raised itself out of the gloom. Towering above us, it looked at each man in turn, its lifeless eyes sucking the very souls from our bodies. Terrified, I shut my eyes tight – 'tis, I believe the only reason I am alive today. I fell to my knees, sobbing like a child, my hands clasped tightly together in prayer, I called upon the Gods to save me.

I heard the screams of my mates and the crashing of wood all around me. The water rose up around me as the ship began to sink. My eyes still shut, my prayer still being muttered, I became separated from the deck. I scrambled my way to the surface, and breathed what I thought would surely be my last. The creature seemed to be all around, its 'rhythm' still loud in my ears. "I shall not see you", I screamed. "There are no monsters!" Then, suddenly all fell silent. I felt something hit my head – my eyes still shut, I believed it was the creature's teeth and I prepared to meet my death. It bumped me again and, half opening one eye, I turned to see the bottom of a rope ladder – t'other end secured to another ship. I scrambled up its length to safety.

I awoke from my fever days later. We had reached shore, and I was in my own bed – my sweetheart sitting by my side, like an angel in the candlelight. I tried to speak but she placed her dainty fingers over my lips. From the darkness of a corner, the owner of the fleet appeared. He told me that I was to

speak of what I saw with no one…ever! " The ship," he said, "hit rocks." This is what the men on the other ships had said. "There are dozens of them," he said, his eyes boring in to me like a drill, "and only one of you. Tell stories of monsters and the townsfolk will think you mad. They will lock you up or drive you away. You have a lovely girl here, and a fine career ahead of you if you stick with me." My sweetheart nodded to me, with a smile that seemed to plead with my heart.
I agreed that rocks had caused this terrible tragedy. All my shipmates were dead, and it seems the men on the other ships had seen nothing of a monster. The fleet owner made good his promise and I made Captain quicker than any before me.

Now the fleet owner is long dead, and the ship I captain today is my own. I tell this story from time-to-time, to remind myself of what really happened on that day, and to honour the men who died. Only they and I remember.'

After retelling this story to himself, Match decided to follow the example of the fleet owner. He had managed to convince Slobber that it was 'just one of those things'. He had beaten him into submission with examples of his greater knowledge of the sea and all that is in it. Now, floating at the river's bank, he wondered if he shouldn't tell the story of Nassian to his small friend. After all, when he had heard the story it had terrified him. Over time he had forgotten about it, but the events earlier that day had brought vivid memories flooding back.
Matchwood wrestled with his conscience. *If it truly is Nassian, do I not have a duty to alert people? People would think me mad,* he concluded. *That fleet owner was right then. He'd be doubly right today!*

CHAPTER SEVEN

Matchwood caught sight of Potfondle and Slobber, waving as they approached from the town. He was very pleased to see them, since he had had little success in convincing Tree that the creature, whatever it was, should be left alone. Rather than tell him the story of Nassian, Match had managed to shut his friend up with a convincing lie. "Alright," he had said, "if you're determined to seek this thing out, I will talk to some friends of mine in the fishing fleet. If they can't catch it, no one can."

Tree had no choice but to agree, since there was no way Matchwood was going to be big enough for the job.

Slobber – who, being the biggest, carried the most – strolled down to the boat and started loading the provisions:

- ✓ 152 bottles of *Hapsnaggers Finest Ale* – a particularly fine brew, produced by the KANSTANDANDKIPWHILE-WAITINGFORAPINT brewing company.
- ✓ 30 Kittersloth brand sausages – according to their advertising slogan *'The finest banger this side of the frying pan'*.

- ✓ 2 large bags of Wippleweed – the bags have to be large, since each Wippleweed leaf is 14 inches in diameter. This widely available salad product is bright purple in colour and despite its foul smell – a little like old socks – it is surprisingly tasty and great with sausages.
- ✓ 12 packets of ready salted crisps.
- ✓ 8 large potatoes.
- ✓ Some tea bags.

Potfondle freed himself of his heavy load – 1 small bag of apples – and the pair climbed aboard with Slobber taking particular care so as not to repeat his earlier soaking.
Pot, now seated, stretched out his short arm and collected Tree. "If everyone's ready," announced Match, "let's be away", and with that he gently moved out from the bank, into the middle of the great river Twit – a surprisingly short name for such a mighty waterway – and started up river.
"Are we off, then?" enquired Tree, thinking with quiet smugness – *that's three!*

As they began this early stage of their journey, Matchwood – being something of a waterways historian, began his 'tour guide' lecture of the history of this most mighty of rivers:
"The Great Twit is Gweep's mightiest river", he said, "It begins in a set of small springs, in the high mountains of the far north, and meanders 732 miles before emptying into the sea, 12 miles south of Flintlewood. At its mouth, it is nearly a mile wide and at its deepest point – a 57-mile stretch, starting just north of The Great Chasms of Strooth but ending 42 miles short of the sea, it can easily accommodate the largest ships. Years ago, the Port Establishment Agency nicknamed this noble river the Useless Twit, since the river bed for the 42 miles from sea to deep water, is Zintal rock – the hardest substance in the natural world. Since, according to modern science, the only thing hard enough to cut through Zintal rock is another piece of Zintal rock, no one has yet been able to cut a piece off for use as a drill bit! Villages like Flintlewood,

which occur within that 42-mile stretch, have thus been prevented from becoming major ports."

Like a disinterested Museum curator, Match continued: "From its humble beginnings in the mountains, it meets its first tributary 73.5 feet from its spring of origin. Its second adds its water to the Twit's flow after a further 91 feet, the third 8 feet after that…"
"Oh smack every Rodney on the planet!!" exclaimed Pot with a huff. "My apologies to you Match, but this part of the story could take an age… For those who don't know – and I being a native of Gweep am not one of you…the spring from which the Twit technically begins is one of over three thousand in that region. The area is known, unimaginatively, as Springs and covers an area of three square miles..." Pot was really getting into his stride now. He stood up and was holding his hand over his heart, as though clutching an imaginary robe. "Nearly all of those springs," his voice resounding with great authority, "feed the growing stream which, by the time it reaches the base of the north mountain range is in fact The Great Twit." Satisfied that his point had been made, he bowed deeply to his captive audience before sitting back down.
"Proud of yourself, Pillick!?" asked Tree. "I for one, was actually listening to Matchwood here – springs are a hobby of mine."
"Really?" said Matchwood, rather surprised, and quite grateful, that at least one life form had sprung to his defence.
"Are you stupid!?" replied Tree. "I know as much about the origins of the Great Twit as this Pillick here. I'd have added a couple of rings to my trunk by the time you'd managed to get anywhere near an even vaguely interesting fact."
Match went very quiet. If he had any form of facial expression...or any kind of face at all, for that matter, he would have looked for all the world like a lost puppy.

It was Slobber who eventually, and rather unwittingly, broke the ice. He first caught the attention of Pot who suddenly noticed, through this uncomfortable curtain of silence, the slowly changing expression on Slobber's face. First his eyes narrowed, then his tiny nostril began to flare. His large mouth opened, as though about to issue a half-hearted yawn, and his eyebrows lifted high into his forehead. Pot, as it slowly dawned on him what this contortion meant, had slowly created a frown of sheer concern across his brow. It was only when Slobber began making a curious sound, that the others found their attention centred on that part of the boat.

All listened to the repetitive sounds of vocal inhalation, and all watched, as with each utterance of "Uhh", that Slobber made, his head moved further back.

"No he isn't!" said Tree, hoping that his denial would somehow halt what was about to come.

"This is not going to be pretty", sighed Match, his voice laced with the quiet resignation that comes with experience.

Pot, for his part, said nothing. At least if he did, nobody heard, hiding – as he now was – under the wheelbarrow.

The last few pants of breath inflated Slobber's chest – "Aahhh...aaahhh... aaaahhhhchoooooooooooo!!!" The Vacuhat tubes flew from his mouth – closely followed by roughly eight pints of drool, which shot out of his now trumpeted lips like some kind of demonic fountain. This flying testament to over-active saliva glands, left Slobber's body with the force of a cannon ball. Thankfully his sneeze, as sneezes often do, occurred just as his head was beginning its journey down towards the floor. The long spit-bullet flew through the air like a javelin, narrowly missing his companions. Like a glistening, wet missile it sailed out over the water, shooting through the air, mere feet above the surface, until finally, and with the impact and precision of a slicing blade, it connected with the muddy bank. The force of its impact drilled a hole a couple of inches wide and nearly three feet deep – invading the privacy of a Twit Rat's burrow. The Twit Rat unsurprisingly, since the water had disturbed him and his mate in bed, was furious. He raced his small body to the burrow's entrance and stood, angrily waving his paw and swearing, or rather squeaking noisily, at the obvious source of this offensive intrusion into his love life.

Raising his hand in an apologetic salute to the rat, Slobber yelled out: "I am extremely sorry, rat. Please forgive me", completely unaware of exactly how untimely the appearance of his 'water sword' had been.

The rest of the party looked at each other, then at Slobber, and finally in the direction of the frantic squeaking. Match, Tree, and Pot slowly began to understand the circumstances behind the rat's anger, quickly filling any missing bits of the puzzle with imagination. Then, suddenly, the three of them burst out laughing. This, of course, only served to anger the rat even further. It was this increased level of anger, accompanied by even more frantic squeaking, combined with Slobber's pointless attempts to calm the situation, that served to fuel his companions' fit of the giggles all the more. Slobber too, though valiantly fighting against it, found he had little choice but to give in, and succumb to the infectious laughter being generated by the other three. Though he fought against it, his mirth dam eventually burst, offering a flood of titters that had been steadily building behind its barrier, since he first saw the rat. It was funny, no two ways about it. The three of them – not counting Slobber, since he was behind the sneeze and not likely to receive a drenching – had been within feet of it! Poor old Matchwood was in contact with the cause of it, with seemingly no possibility of escape whatsoever! Yet, with all that in mind, the only creature to be affected by this 'jet of death', as Tree had termed it in between giggles, was a Twit Rat living over 40 feet away.

Pot managed to calm himself long enough to ask Slobber about his Vacuhat, "I thought that thing was supposed to take care of your spit reservoir?"

"It is", replied a still chuckling Slobber. "It..." struggling to catch his breath "It..." already starting a fresh round of giggles – knowing that what he was about to say was likely to get everyone else going again too, "It must be broken…It hasn't been sucking properly since I put the tubes down my trousers!"

That pretty much did it for all of them. The giggles gave way to waves upon waves of relentless laughter. Match had been swaying so much that you could have been fooled into thinking he was in a waving competition. Being continuously thrown about in his shell, far from angering his passengers, had made them laugh even more. Pot had rolled himself into a ball, hugging his now aching stomach; Tree had been tipped out of his bucket, and Slobber was now on his belly – the top third of his body hanging over Match's edge, his arms and the top of his head trailing in the water.

The rat, who was moving further into the distance, was still energetically waving his clenched paw, and shrieking.

As the four travellers began to calm down, Pot glanced behind them, "That rat's still pretty peeved", he commented. The others followed Pots line of sight to the hysterical rodent, at the precise moment when the bit of muddy bank, on which he was stamping his little feet, suddenly gave way. The rat slid at great speed down the bank and into the water, still squeaking angrily.

…It has been suggested that it *is* possible to die laughing. None of the four adventurers actually died from this final nail in the comedy coffin, but they came pretty close. The site of the angry mammal suddenly not being where they were looking was bad enough, but the fact that he continued his anger towards them as he headed for his bath, really set the seal. Matchwood exploded with loud, energetic laughter as his swaying turned into violent rocking, causing his passengers to be tossed about like corn popping in a pan. The wheelbarrow jumped up and fell overboard, and it was only Pot's quick thinking – as he reached out and grabbed Tree – that prevented the little plant from doing the same. Slobber scrambled to gather their bags – his greater weight providing him with more stability. "Here we go!" yelled Matchwood, knowing he could do nothing to prevent the inevitable, "All ashore who are going ashore!" Unable to stop his laughter, he knew that his ever more violent rocking motion could lead to only one eventual outcome…he flipped over.

Pot and Slobber, ready for the disaster, leapt overboard. Still clutching his little friend, Pot somehow managed to scramble to the shore.

In the water, Slobber allowed the bags he was still shepherding to float free, as he grabbed for Matchwood's bow. Swimming strongly with his legs and one free arm, he managed to guide the upturned boat on to a small beach before quickly turning on his heels and heading out again for their luggage.

Pot and Tree watched from the shore as Slobber swam out to the bags and successfully gathered them around his neck. He then decided to go for the wheelbarrow, which had now floated close to the Twit Rat's home, where the offended creature now stood – back at his burrow entrance – bent double with laughter as he now took his turn to enjoy the spectacle of others receiving a drenching.

Slobber, with the rat's laughter ringing in his ears, approached the wheelbarrow. Remarkably, it had managed to splash down the right way up and had been gently floating – not a single drop of water in it. Noticing this, Slobber began to very carefully load the bags into this makeshift boat.

Amazingly it remained buoyant, as Slobber began to swim for shore, holding the barrow ahead of him – pushing it through the water.

Pot, Tree and a still upside down Match, cheered as Slobber neared the beach. As he drew nearer, only about eight feet from the shore, all of a sudden, without any warning, he sank straight down like a stone. The cheering from the bank stopped abruptly and Pot's mouth – as he was actually the only one with a mouth – dropped open, his eyes widened in shock, and he sprung to his feet. He stood for a moment, scanning the surface of the now still water. He could see no evidence of his big, blue friend, the bags or indeed, the wheelbarrow. His feet started to nervously run on the spot, whilst his surprised mind decided what action to take next. His legs took the initiative and he found himself running to the water's edge and entering the river. It was when he was neck-deep that his brain took over – *Can't bloody swim!* remembered Pot, angrily. It was all he could do to hold his ground and continue scanning the water.

If Pot was frustrated by his own lack of ability, Matchwood – lying upside down on the bank – was approaching a level of severe anger. Immediately realising the invaluable role he could play in averting this potential disaster, were he the right way up, he had been 'waving' furiously. The anger and frustration he felt was clear, his energetic action causing him to rock violently from side to side. He knew his efforts were pointless, but his feeling of total inadequacy left him with no choice but to at least make the attempt. Tree for his part had quickly realised that, being something of an inanimate object, he was never going to be of much assistance. Safe in this knowledge, he had successfully relieved himself of any feelings of guilt and uselessness, and contented himself with merely watching the events around him with a profound sense of fear at what might be the eventual, unhappy result. In his mind's eye, he had already witnessed Slobber's large, blue body surface, floating face down – his arms floating out at his sides.

Slobber, while all this frantic activity was going on above him, was now standing on the hard river bed – the wheelbarrow, still fully loaded, secured by the grasp of his strong arms. He felt no panic, he knew he was close to shore and he remembered – from Matchwood's interrupted lecture – that not only was this part of the river fairly shallow, but that its bed was Zintal rock, so the chances of him finding a small pocket of quicksand, or something equally disagreeable, were remote.

He rose to his feet and, quite naturally, changed his hold on his cargo to allow him to grip the handles in the usual manner. This done, he took a very casual look at his new surroundings before continuing on his way to the bank.

"Look! Bubbles!" shouted Pot, pointing hopefully. These bubbles were closely followed by the sight of Slobber's Vacuhat and for a dreadful moment Pot's hopes were reduced by the belief that this was simply the first of the floating debris they could expect. It was therefore, with utter joy that the sight of Slobber's smiling face was greeted. Pot shouted "YES!!" as he jumped, punching the air in relieved triumph.

"Hello lads", said Slobber as continued to march forward, all the while his smile growing with each relieved cheer that sounded from his friends. He strolled up to, and past, Pot.

"Alright there Pot… Taking a bath?" he said with the off-handed chirpiness of a man just out for an afternoon stroll.

"Thank the Gods!" sighed an extremely grateful Pot, jumping as high as he could – managing to successfully deliver a suitably masculine slap to Slobber's shoulder.

"Lads", said Slobber casually, to his two remaining comrades, as he released his grip on the barrow and sank to the sandy ground, the last of his energy used up on trying to appear cool to his friends. He rolled onto his back and lay, out of breath, the joyful sound of his cheering friends still surrounding his body and filtering into his ears, his large mouth still grinning from ear to ear. "Wow!" he eventually said, "That was kind of interesting."

"What happened?" asked Tree.

"Just caught my breath I guess", replied an honest Slobber. He had briefly considered suggesting that he had been pulled under by forces unseen – a monster, perhaps – but the fear of their encounter at sea, still fresh in his mind, he decided against it….no need to spread the seeds of fear in his companions.

The excitement and relief slowly dying down, the two bipeds – Pot and Slobber – began to straighten things out. Pot

checked the luggage, draping anything wet over the branches of nearby trees and bushes. Slobber was standing at Matchwood's rear, preparing to right him. As he placed his hands on either side of his stern he suddenly noticed two seemingly hollow tubes running the full length of the boat's underside – narrow at the back, with a sort of trumpet end at the front. "What are these for?" he asked with a frown of genuine curiosity.
"Propulsion of course", answered Match, a tone in his voice which inferred to Slobber that he'd just asked a stupid question.
"Your engines, you mean?"
"Of course", said Match, "What'd you think!? I had two, big, paddling feet down there!?"
"How does it work?" asked Pot, whose aroused curiosity had compelled him to join them.
"Work!?" Match couldn't believe that neither of them had ever come across Filer Tubes before. "Well, they're quite simple really", he said. "Water goes in through the front and comes out the back." The stunned silence with which he was greeted forced him to elaborate: "Inside each tube there are thousands of tiny paddles, which hinge back and forth really fast. Their movement causes a rippling effect down the length of the barrel so, by the time the water is ejected out of the back, it's moving pretty fast…"
"It's a jet!" interrupted Slobber, proudly. "I get it. It's just like a jet!"
"Of course", piped up Pot, not wanting to seem stupid. "That's why you start really slowly and steadily speed up."
"Exactly!" confirmed Match. "The faster I move, the faster I can go. The Filer paddles are made from my wood, so I control the rate at which they hinge. The faster they move, the faster the water comes in and the faster I move forward."
"Cool!" exclaimed Slobber, truly impressed by the elegant simplicity of it all. "How fast can you go, then?" he added, after a thoughtful pause.
"A damned sight faster than you leg-boy", said a proud

Matchwood. "But I only get up to full speed in open sea... Takes a while to stop, you see."
"Well I think it's pretty amazing", said Slobber, slowly heaving Match the right way up.
"Me too", nodded Pot in agreement, as he helped by steadying the bow.
"Don't have leaves though, do ya?" added a quietly jealous Tree. Still, he had to admit, Filer Tubes were pretty clever.

Matchwood successfully righted, Slobber set about gathering fire wood. He was happy to discover that the trees in that area were just regular trees – neither Tanglepine, nor Kia Willow. He could therefore set fire to the gathered wood, safe in the knowledge that he wasn't committing some terrible crime against tree-kind. Taking a box of matches from Pot's pack – which miraculously had not received a drenching in the river, due to Pot having packed them in the middle of the sleeping bags – he lit the fire, holding the flame of his ignitor against the bundle of dry grass he had placed in the middle of the pyramid of twigs. Having nursed the small flame into a glorious camp fire, he took a larger, 'y' shaped branch and buried one end deep into the ground – leaving the end 'v' suspended high over the flames. Next he grabbed one of Pot's saucepans and filled it with water from the river, hanging it by its semicircular metal handle on the stick. "Anyone for tea?" he asked to the group in general.
"Tea!?" exclaimed Potfondle, taking another swig from his recently opened bottle of beer. "Tea is for breakfast. This lovely fire," he said, kicking a pointing foot at the crackling, orange, provider of heat, in front of which he was now standing, "will provide heat to dry our bodies and bedding. Beer," he said, holding up a freshly opened bottle, "will help me to overcome the shock of believing you drowned!"
"Drowned!?" said Slobber. "You thought I was drowned!? Not a chance. You don't spend your entire life with saliva glands like mine, and then go and let yourself get drowned... I'd be a laughing stock back home!"

Slobber removed the boiling water and the stick, as Pot handed him a bottle of ale – nicely cooled by its dip in the river – and the pair lay on their sides watching the ballet of dancing flames. Tree, at his own request, had been taken out of his bucket and placed in the earth at the head of the small beach.
"At least that damned rat has finally stopped laughing", remarked Pot.
"He had the right", suggested Slobber philosophically.

CHAPTER EIGHT

The group of four sat quietly for a bit before Match – suddenly remembering his unfinished lecture – shouted out "Great Twit!" breaking the harmony of the gathering.
"Where?" said Tree, before realising he'd left himself wide open to comment from the others. Quickly he covered himself, "What about it?"
"The Great Twit", repeated Matchwood. "Now, where was I before I was so rudely interrupted?" rocking himself gently, gesturing in Potfondle's direction, "As my learned friend," again rocking in a gesture to Potfondle, "had so concisely informed us all..."
"Hello", interrupted an unfamiliar voice.
"Oh for the love of..." said a frustrated Matchwood, in response to yet another interruption. Pot and Slobber quickly turned their heads in surprise to see who was responsible for the unexpected greeting.
"Hello", said Frutely again.
"Hi!" said Slobber in reply, offering a polite salute with his beer-clutching hand, "Where'd you come from?"
Frutely – a two-and-three-quarter-feet tall Pillick, stood high on the bank, just behind the tree line of the woods – "My name's

Frutely", she said. "Frutely Gaiberond. I heard a lot of laughing…"
"That was us", cut in Tree, eager to make his presence felt since he was in her direct path, should she decide to venture further into the camp.
"*Doctor* Frutely Gaiberond?" asked Matchwood, "Gweep's one and only expert on seismic events?"
"Yip!" replied Frutely enthusiastically. "That's me. The quake girl."
"Great!" said Tree. "You can save my weekend! What's the story with all these groundshakes, then?"
"Don't know", replied Frutely, striding confidently into the improvised camp.
Pot lay on his side, motionless. His eyes wide and his mouth open, his bottle of beer tilted in his hand, its contents slowly pouring onto the sand. He was mesmerised – transfixed. All he could see was this beautiful woman, dressed in tan shorts and a light blue 'T' shirt. The dark blonde, downy fur carefully shaved from her legs and arms, her ankles clad in pure white socks and on her feet, she was wearing light brown walking boots. The fur on her face was very fine, and the fur on her head had been allowed to grow to collar length. The dappled light, shining through the canopy of leaves above, made it seem to Potfondle that this vision before him was standing in a hollow of stars. Everything else around her began to dissolve, in his eyes. To him, she seemed to move in slow motion, each gentle turn of her head causing her hair to flick gently about her shoulders. Time seemed to slow to a gentle crawl, and Potfondle immersed himself in the blissful vision that had suddenly appeared before him.
"Is he OK?" asked a concerned Frutely, who by now had not only walked into the camp but was sitting cross-legged, near the fire.
"Fine", said Slobber, handing her a freshly opened bottle of beer. "POT!" he shouted, hoping to bring his lost friend back into their midst.
A startled Potfondle awoke from his daydream. Slightly

embarrassed, he blinked himself back to consciousness. With a degree of surprise, he quickly looked about him in an attempt to regain his bearings. Realising what had just happened, a furtive Pot set himself the task of trying to reclaim at least some of his composure. He righted his bottle of beer so fast that it sent some of its remaining contents spilling out of the neck, over his hand and onto his bare chest.
Slobber, forced to witness this bizarre display, decided to rescue his love-clumsy friend: “Pot. I’d like to introduce you to the eminent Dr Frutely Gaiberond.”
Pot wiped his beer drenched hand on his chest fur and nervously stretched out his arm. “Enchanted”, he sighed dreamily, grinning like an idiot.
“Oh please!” offered a cynical Tree – more for his own benefit than anyone else’s.
“Call me Frutely”, offered Frutely, along with her hand.
“My pleasure”, said Pot, gently taking the offering and giving a single shake of welcome.
Tree gave a cynical sigh, once more for his own benefit. He considered asking for a bucket to be sick in but dismissed the idea, firstly on the grounds that his bucket was the only one available and secondly, on the grounds that plants don’t actually vomit.

Matchwood, keen to continue where Tree had left off, pressed Frutely on the question of groundshakes. Frutely explained that she had returned home to discover that her fellow scientists – none of whom knew anything about quakes – had frittered away a sizeable amount of money on nothing more than a holiday. Her anger had however, been contained by the government’s offer – very keen for the public to remain ignorant of the previous waste of funds – to give her another grant to see if *she* could come up with a better answer than: ‘NON CONCLUSIVE…SORRY!’
Dr Gaiberond, rather than follow the example of her fellow scientists, had decided to actually research the question. For weeks, she had been trudging around, setting up sensors,

investigating damage, and shining her torch into deep caves. After studying the data, collected during a period of significant activity, Frutely was still no closer to solving the mystery. Very recently however, and at long last, her equipment finally produced the data she had been searching for…the location of the quakal epicentre – the central starting point of the quakes themselves. Upon receipt of this vital piece of information, she had been about to give a shout of triumph, when her attention had been caught by a great deal of laughter coming from the river.

"So, where is the epicentre?" pressed Matchwood.

"North", replied Frutely, "about 70 miles north." A strange silence settled over the group and then, as if some telepathic agreement had been reached by the four travellers, Slobber took Frutely into their confidence. He explained what it was that the five of them had in common. He detailed the events of the previous night, and the decision for exploration that arose. It seemed perfectly appropriate that they, who after all were heading in that direction, invite the good doctor to join them. After all, the four of them, with their virtually non-existent knowledge of seismology – the science of quakes and such – were unlikely to do anything else with their weekend other than drink beer, and risk food poisoning. Much to their combined surprise, Frutely agreed. Pot, it must be said, was not only surprised, but elated that she was going to join their company, since he could think of no other occasion where he could spend so much time in her presence. It is safe to say at this point, that Pot was smitten – the whole 'love at first sight' deal.

Those with legs, spent the remainder of the day moving Frutely's gear from her camp in the woods to theirs on the beach, and with daylight fading fast, the group decided to turn their temporary camp into a permanent one. Slobber rebuilt the spit, while Pot loaded the ends of several sticks with sausages – stabbing the splinters of wood into the ground and allowing their sausage laden points to hang directly above the heat of the fire.

CHAPTER NINE

The light from the rising sun danced across the gently flowing river, causing sparkles of light to dance in a shimmering ballet. The camp was still, with everyone snoozing peacefully. The smoke from the terminally ill fire rose straight up from the embers, disturbed only by the occasional light breeze, as it twisted and swirled towards the sky. The three bipeds had arranged themselves in a triangle around the fire. Slobber, lying on his side, his drool glands now fully active again after their nightly dry time, permitted the eight-pint reservoir within his pouches to escape – the water carving a gently curving stream down towards the river. Potfondle, presumably imagining situations of fairytale romance with Frutely, was lying on his back, his arms crossed, with each hand gently stroking its opposite shoulder, his face dominated by a smile of absolute joy and contentment. Frutely, for her part, had found that her peace had been disturbed. Initially, she enjoyed dreams of glory – awards won and speeches given on her successful research, but later her mind had become tormented with subconscious concerns – unknown fears at what her research might uncover; the possibility of ramifications too terrifying to contemplate. It was those fears, which she had barely allowed herself to consider, that now allowed the scarring of a frown to curse her brow.

The still beached Matchwood could be seen to occasionally shudder in his full-body dozing – the only outward sign that he was dreaming at all. His mind was consumed with imaginary constructs of Nassian. It created horrific images of a giant demon: a slick, shining creature – its skin a terrifying but beautiful black, shining like a mirror – a mirror that reflects only death and destruction. Its body long and sleek as it swims through the Idyllic sea, this powerful, terrifying vision could not be kept from Matchwood's imagination. "Destroyer," Matchwood muttered in fear, quietly in his sleep – not for the first time that night. Matchwood's mind decided to focus on the creature's head, as if to study it, allowing him to recognise it should their paths ever again cross. Its head was large but, like everything about this nightmare, beautifully shaped for a life under water – "No wonder the Gods gave your race immortality", he muttered to an unaware crowd. "What grace…perfection!" Its head seemed at first glance as though it did not fit. It should not be there.

To describe this vision as though it were a worm would be criminally disrespectful. Matchwood's mind was alive, like it hadn't been in many-a-year. The construction of this creature's head, given it by Match's imagination, was like nothing he'd ever been aware of seeing before: Its head, as heads often do, starting at the top of its neck, then like a skilfully cut diamond, this almost triangular torpedo begins to exert itself. Like a door wedge, its seemingly abrupt beginnings angled down towards a blunt nose with, oddly enough, nostrils; its elongated mouth filled with shark-like, triangular, razor-sharp teeth; its nostrils, located slightly above the top of its upper jaw, flaring as it strikes; its large, almond shaped eyes, wide – glowing deep red with anger – as

its brow furrows hard to the front, permitting any victim to be fully aware of its wrath.
Tree who – even with the inclusion of Dr Gaiberond to their group, still considered this weekend to be little more than a complete and utter waste of time – simply slept. No apparent dreams, no obvious concerns. Although of course, Tree being a tree – albeit a relatively talkative one – has a tendency not to move a lot anyway, even when engaged in strong debate. It is, therefore, difficult to say for sure what was going on in his mind.

Matchwood was the first to wake, startled into consciousness by a particularly disturbing image. His emergence from sleep was so violent that his front end lifted a clear six inches from the sand. The sound of his tussle with gravity caused the others to begin stirring. Slowly, the eyes of the rest of the group began to open. Tree, who was closest to the boat, gently shook his branches as he stretched and yawned.
"Wow!" he said, "What a night! I haven't slept that well in a while."
Slobber, stretching out his arms towards the sky, yawned in agreement – "Mmmmm!" he hummed, his face lighting up with a broad smile of relaxed contentment.
Pot, his face still occupied by a grin, rolled onto his side and, looking in the direction of Frutely, offered a cheerful, "Good morning."
This was disguised as being a greeting to the camp in general, but it was pretty obvious to any onlooker that Pot's beaming smile was directed, primarily, in Frutely's direction. Frutely replied in turn, her eyes fixed on the chimney of smoke from the fire. Match, after taking a while to compose himself, simply enquired if everyone was OK.
Bit by bit the group stirred themselves into action. Slobber excused himself and strolled off into the woods...
"Where are you off to?" enquired Match, still somewhat concerned for their general welfare, following his nightmare.
"Where do ya think!?" replied Slobber's back, as he held up a

hand – displaying a large bunch of leaves.
Pot, eager to impress, set about refuelling the fire in preparation for breakfast.

When Slobber returned from 'reading his newspaper', tea and sausages were well on their way. Strolling through the wonderful smells of breakfast, Slobber guided himself to the shore where he quickly squatted to wash his hands in the cool waters of the Great Twit.
"Right…" he said, rising quickly to his feet, punctuating his word with a decisive clap of his wet hands, turning his attention towards Matchwood, "Let's get you back in the water, my buoyant friend." Much to Slobbers surprise, Matchwood's reply seemed completely devoid of the enthusiasm he expected: "Yeah. I suppose so", he said. With merely a lightly snorted laugh, signalling his relative dismay at Matchwood's lack of enthusiasm, Slobber moved to his stern and took a firm grasp. "Could probably do with a small hand or two," he said, looking at neither Pot or Frutely specifically – choosing instead to allow a willing volunteer to step forward. Since Pot was on chef duty, Frutely quickly moved to assist: "Where do you want me?" she enquired, with a flirtatious smile. Slobber directed her to Matchwood's bow, and instructed her on how she could best be of assistance to the brute force he intended to exert. With a growl of supreme effort, Slobber guided his companion back into the water – his single-minded efforts firmly aided by the small hands of Frutely, who pushed with all her might from the front, while he pulled from the back.
With Match's stern now floating in the shallows, Slobber waded back to the bank and moved to the bow, relieving an exhausted Frutely, her face red as the sweat poured from her brow – a visual display of the amount of effort she had delivered.
"You alright there?" asked Slobber, showing a measure of gentlemanly concern.
"Oh yeah…" panted the Pillick, "fine thanks...You?"

"Mmm", replied a smiling Slobber. "Good morning exercise this is!" he added, thrusting his shoulder hard against Matchwood's front and pushing the rest of him into the water.

Slobber stood waist deep in Twit water, surveying the now fully floating Matchwood. With a true sense of satisfaction in a job well done, Slobber leapt up, punching the air with one hand, growling "Yyyyess! Who," he said upon landing, and turning to face his companions, "is the daddy?" He found it unnecessary to wait for any kind of reply, as their smiling faces turned to see what all the fuss was about – "ME!", he shouted, "I – AM – THE DADDY!"

"You're the man!" came a jubilant voice from the water, as Matchwood, re-immersed and filled once more with the joys of being water-bound, began to flex his nautical 'muscles'. He had been a boat for many years – either in part or entire – being on land had made him feel queasy, not to mention stagnant. Now back in the water, he was fully mobile again. He flexed his Filer Paddles, causing them to hinge back and forth furiously. Water filed into his tubes at an ever increasing rate, and from slow beginnings Match began to accelerate. The four land-dwellers watched in amazement as their comrade expressed his joy at being back in the wet – racing up and down the river, suddenly braking with one propulsion tube, and allowing himself to 'donut' – spinning round and round on the spot. At one point, Match surprised even himself with his own energy when, from a standing start, he caused water to shoot through his tubes at such a rate that he actually 'wheelied'. His front end lifted out of the water by a clear foot, and he maintained this position for over a minute, as he raced up the river. "It's me!" he shouted with energetic excitement. "Me! I am the daddy!" as he raced passed his land-based friends, watching in amazement from the bank, as this water-bound rocket shot past, heading up river and out of sight.

"Oh yeah!" came the triumphant sound as Match sped back into their view, slicing through the water, rocking from side-to-side.

Match, full of energy, headed towards the bank – "Incoming!" he shouted, as his rate of knots showed no immediate signs of dissipating. Slobber's face suddenly began to show signs of concern: "Look out!" he shouted, as his friend headed for a small submerged rock. Match heard the warning, and quickly realised to what it referred. He slammed on his brakes – causing all his Filers to stop, blocking his tubes. He then threw the Paddles of one tube into reverse, causing an immediate and violent swerve. He tipped high on one side – the heads of his companions (those who had heads) retracted into their shoulders, and their hands rose to clutch the top of their scalps – each of them drawing air quickly over their teeth as their genuine concern peaked. Matchwood turned sharply, the side nearest the rock was so low that he took on a little water.

The faces of his friends screwed up as the sound of rock against wood pierced their eardrums. "Ow!!" exclaimed Tree with genuine sympathy, as the unpleasant sound of splintering wood struck a nerve with him.

To Match, the sound, let alone the feeling of this encounter, seemed to last forever. When he eventually did come to a stand-still, it was with the assistance of Slobber, who had jumped into the water with the intention of acting as a buffer. Although he had been too late to do anything about the initial contact with the rock, he had managed to successfully push Match out of its way a little – minimising the damage a bit.

Slobber guided a shaken Matchwood back to shore, and the expedition stood surveying the damage. As had been stated by Match, it wasn't actually that bad – more superficial than permanent, just a little scarring. The main area of damage was at the top of his port side, where a strip of wood – about 30 centimetres in length – had been virtually torn from the rest of Match's body. "That's alright", said Match, attempting to console his concerned friends, "Doesn't hurt. I can make a temporary repair, which will hold for the time-being".

All watched in respectful silence as the end of the

disconnected Match splinter slowly reconnected itself, adjusting slightly as some of the wood molecules began to knit themselves back together. It was still quite loose but, advised Match, as long as he acted his age for the rest of the trip, it would be fine. “I’ll get repaired properly after I’ve dropped you lot off”, he assured them.

CHAPTER TEN

The four travellers sat silently, as Matchwood once more set off up the Great Twit. They had eaten a hearty breakfast and drunk some relatively good tea; they had properly doused the fire and done all the other things responsible campers are supposed to do before departure. Their belongings and themselves safely loaded into their nautical companion, all they could do now was sit, open mouthed – still in some awe at Matchwood's biological magic.

Matchwood himself couldn't see what all the fuss was about. "Really," he said, "it's nothing terribly clever… My physiology, unlike yours, has a certain amount of cellular independence, that's all!" He thought for a moment, realising that his attempt at an overly simple, and basically dismissive explanation was not going to do the trick. "OK", he said after a brief period of thought, "Lets say, for the sake of example, that Potfondle here lost a small part of his body…" This non-specific reference, it very quickly became clear, was a mistake as both Pot and Slobber began to omit childish sniggers. Their emerging immaturity, which catches everyone at one time or another, had taken a split second to quickly list the small extremities that exist on a person's body – a male person's

body, to be specific. This schoolroom giggling soon infected Frutely, but it was when Tree piped up with the comment: "Aha! Seen the little puff-ball naked then?" that Matchwood felt a very real need to remind everyone of their age.
"Alright. Fair enough, bad example", he said. "It is, perhaps, unlikely that anything that small would be able to hold a significant proportion of intelligence."
"Hey!" frowned an ego-bruised Potfondle.
"Sorry, Pot. Cheap shot, couldn't resist", offered Matchwood in apology. "Anyway", he continued, choosing an alternative analogy with more care, deciding to liken what had happened to Slobber, Pot or Frutely losing a finger. "Instead of rushing around, allowing blood to spurt all over the place – damaging your home furnishings and what-not, what if you could simply instruct your body to stem the flow of blood while you, having located your misplaced digit, placed it up against your hand – soggy end to soggy end – and let it re-attach itself?" His audience was gripped, although Potfondle was clearly attempting to disguise a touch of squeamishness.
"This temporary repair," Match continued, "would be more than adequate to allow you to do a little shopping, perhaps stop off for a pint or two at your local pub... Ten-pin bowling would probably be a little risky but you would have more than enough time to take a leisurely stroll down to your local shipwrights, or hospital, and get it repaired properly." Proud of his lecture, Matchwood concluded his talk with: "And ladies and gentlemen, there you have it", as his bow bobbed, suggesting a single nod of final punctuation.
Matchwood managed to hide his slight disappointment, that no one saw fit to offer applause. The reason for this was simple. His companions, although finding his attempts at reducing their ignorance very interesting, also viewed his lecture as totally unnecessary. They all understood the basic concept of molecular individualism, it was just that none of them had ever seen a practical demonstration before. It was only through politeness that no one had interrupted Matchwood to tell him,

seeming as he was to be enjoying himself.
Two hours flowed gently past, as if carried off in Matchwood's wake. Slobber quietly tinkered with his Vacuhat – attempting to return it to working order; Potfondle had slipped back into his love-filled daydream, involving Dr. Gaiberond and lots of slow-motion imagery. Frutely herself continued to be totally oblivious to the fact that she had become the object of such romantic visions, immersed as she was in her scientific data that had been collected by her equipment further down river. Occasionally she would look up from her notes, causing Pot to avert his eyes, and stare into space for a while, frowning as she wrestled with a clearly curious question rattling around in her head. From time-to-time she would shake her head and mutter, "That can't be right!" Tree was sitting silently in his bucket, planning and scheming, trying to conceive of a way to capture the sea creature that he was now partially aware of. Matchwood silently steered their course ever further up river, not entirely sure how far his passengers wished to go, but generally happy to be engaged in something a lot less boring than sailing between Kettles Reach and Flintlewood twice a day (once on Sundays.)
"Match", said Frutely "Do you think you could pull up to shore? I'd like to take fresh readings."
Matchwood quite happily agreed and headed for a small beach just a little further ahead. Pot and Slobber offered no argument, since it was approaching 11 o'clock and the idea of a stretch of legs, and a quick beer or two was not unwelcome.

The boat steadied himself as his passengers alighted. Frutely grabbed her large pack and walked quickly off into the woods that had been their constant riverside companion. Slobber retrieved half-a-dozen bottles of beer from a bag that had been allowed to hang over Matchwood's side. Tree declined Potfondle's offer of a quick planting, and chose to remain on board, anxious to continue his conversation with Matchwood, which had been interrupted the previous day.

Slobber and Pot followed Frutely's course into the woods, eventually meeting up with her in a small, sunlit clearing. She had produced from her pack a small, cylindrical object, and was busy planting it just beneath the surface of the ground. Once done she retrieved a small 'Lectron Brain' and connected its interface lead to a socket in the exposed lid of the cylinder.

"Beer?" offered Slobber, his hand offering a green glass bottle.

"Thanks", replied Frutely with a smile, accepting the offering, "This should only take about 20 minutes."

"Don't these things need a quake to happen before producing any information?" enquired a surprisingly informed Potfondle, talking more to himself than anyone else.

"That's right…" replied a vaguely surprised Frutely, "Well normally. This one's a bit special though."

The three sat on the grass and listened to Dr Gaiberond's enthusiastic description of this excellent piece of technology… Frutely had for years been tinkering around with a device that could measure the size of a quake without actually needing to experience it. She had become frustrated with having to bury lots of seismographs all over the place, and periodically go around checking them all. *Why not*, she had thought, *invent something that can tell you all you want to know after a quake had happened?* The idea was a good one, although seemingly impossible to realise…impossible, that is, until Frutely experienced, about five years ago, a moment of blinding inspiration. *The ground shakes the earth, trees, buildings, rocks...everything. Everything moves, just like a footprint in the mud,* she concluded. This simple thought had led her to the invention of the 'Comparometer'.

"This device," she proclaimed to her small, beer-swigging audience, "doesn't need to be in the ground when the quake actually occurs. It just needs to have been planted at some point before it, and then again, within a 24-hour window, after the quake has happened."

Her amazed companions listened intently as Frutely explained that the drum, now in a hole, sends out millions of electric signals – using everything they come in contact with as a natural conductor, and causing a gentle knock-on effect. "Since everything in or on the ground is in constant contact with something else – even air – the connection between the drum, and the end of its signal is never broken..." Seeing that she was beginning to lose the understanding of Pot and Slobber, she decided to explain by simple example. She picked a long blade of grass and stretched her arm out in Pot's direction. "Now," she said, holding one end of the grass between her thumb and forefinger, with the other placed in Pot's bottle of beer, "you and I are touching. I'm holding the grass, the grass is touching your beer, your beer is touching the bottle, and the bottle is in your hand."

"Oh I see," said Pot, his eyebrows raised and, surprising himself with his apparent understanding of this complex subject, suggested, "and if I move, even just a little..."

"That's right", Frutely cut him off as she excitedly wanted to get to the point, proud as she was of her achievement and more than a little impressed that Pot understood her. "You may not even be aware of the fact that you have moved at all, but the grass knows – if you see what I mean – the beer knows, and the bottle knows. They have all changed their relative position." Frutely rose to her feet and began to pace excitedly – gesturing with her hands as she rose to the finale. "The drum collects all this information, and the 'Brain' collates it and compares it with where everything was yesterday – which is when I did my last print."

"How far?" began Slobber, his question finished by another, "...Does the signal go?" said Frutely, "As far as it likes. If I left this thing in the ground for a whole year, it would reach every corner of the globe."

The doctor continued, regaling them with the tales of research difficulties and manufacturing problems, and her fears at one point that her idea had been stolen... "About three years ago," she expanded, "I misplaced vital research on my invention. I went frantic – tore my lab and my house apart. Ran through the streets, retracing every step I'd taken for two

days. I thought all was lost when, out of the blue, came a visit from a tall, pale-faced man. He presented me the unopened box of my research."
"Where did he get it?" asked Pot.
"The back of one of his cabs, he said. Mr Skint – my saviour, and owner of the cab company I always use. I had been to their lost property section of course, but nothing had turned up. Mr Skint told me that he had heard about how frantic I was from his secretary and had immediately ordered a thorough search." Frutely was now able to laugh about her ordeal but at the time she thought the worst. "Here's to Mr Skint", she offered as a toast.
"Mr Skint!" Pot and Slobber echoed as all three lifted their bottles in salute.

The three sat, drinking their beer and enjoying each others' easy company, until the Lectron Brain pierced the serenity with the delivery of three, short beeps – signalling the completion of its task. "All done", said Frutely, "Let's have a look shall we?"
"How accurate is that thing?" asked Potfondle.
"Oh, very", replied the doctor as she thoughtfully scanned a small printout, "For example…remember that rock Matchwood glanced earlier?"
"I don't think I'll ever forget it", replied Pot.
"He caused it to move to the left by over three millimetres."
"Blimey!" was the stereophonic exclamation of her two extremely impressed friends.

CHAPTER ELEVEN

Matchwood was starting to get a headache, or rather bow-ache, from the incessant chatter and questioning coming from Tree.

"You must have seen it! Come on partner, what aren't you telling me?" Tree's interest in the sea creature was bordering on obsessive. His plans for glory in showbusiness were expanding – a worldwide tour; posters with a picture of him on it, above a slightly smaller image of the beast. Tree had calculated a totally unworkable plan for capturing the monster, and had moved on to promoting the grand circus he'd created around showing it off to the world.

Matchwood was running out of ways to evade Tree's constant probing. He had convinced himself that what he had seen was indeed Nassian. Having reached this conclusion, he had also decided, with absolute certainty, that any attempt to capture him would be nothing short of suicide. He was therefore, extremely grateful that his interrogation was once more cut short by the appearance of the rest of the group.

"Don't think I have finished with you", hissed Tree threateningly, before Frutely, Pot and Slobber wandered within earshot. Matchwood was, of course, distressed by Tree's malevolence in absolutely no way whatsoever. He simply dismissed the little tree with one simple thought – *Pathetic little stick insect*.

The returning trio greeted their friends warmly, as though they had been away for days. Pot gripped Match's side and threw himself into the boat. "Hey Tree," he said, "you should see this cool gismo Frutely has."

Slobber clambered in and advised Matchwood of how far he'd moved the rock earlier that morning.

As they set off once more, Matchwood's curiosity for science was rewarded by Frutely who, on the back of Slobber's comment, explained to him how her Comparometer worked, with Slobber and Pot displaying their enthusiasm for the subject by assisting her in the explanation. They soon found themselves left behind however, as it soon became clear that Match, having spent considerably longer on the planet than them, possessed a scientific understanding for the subject that allowed Frutely to start using extremely long words.

Frutely and Matchwood were still deep in scientific discussion. Slobber, bored with being out of his depth, had returned to tinkering with his Vacuhat, while Potfondle and Tree chatted about this and that. Matchwood continued to effortlessly steer their course, while relating anecdotes of past seismic events he had witnessed or, at the very least, heard about from reliable witnesses.

Frutely listened – relaxed and content, her head resting on her outstretched arm, with the tips of her fingers permitted to gently break the surface of the water, as they moved through it. In this dreamy state, she allowed her thoughts to drift.

It was Tree who eventually broke the serenity of this picturesque scene. He had been sitting silently as Potfondle chatted about...well actually, Tree had no idea what he was talking about since he had actually stopped listening some time before. However, Tree suddenly posed a question to the

group, causing all to prick up their ears and listen. Even Match was forced to cease his chatter in order to reduce background noise. “Can anybody hear any birds?” he said, with a slightly enigmatic tone in his voice. The question was simple enough, the problem was that the answer was equally simple. No. No one could hear anything. Not even the birds, whose constant twittering had been a solid companion during their voyage. Their sound so present that, like dull old wallpaper, its effect on their collective consciousness had become largely ignored. The fact that now that wallpaper had vanished is what motivated everyone to listen out as intently as they possibly could, in the hope that at least one sign of avian life would make itself heard through the silence.
“There are plenty of them in the trees”, observed Pot quietly.
“None in the air, though”, added Slobber in an equally reverential whisper.
“It’s not just the birds”, observed Frutely. She was right…there were sounds of nothing. No birds twittering, no insects chirping or buzzing, no Twit Rats swimming, not even a fish bobbing for flies.
“Creepy innit?” said Matchwood, breaking the deathly and extremely uncomfortable silence – hoping a little levity might reduce the tension, which had been growing rapidly since Tree’s initial comment.
Then, without warning, as though in reaction to an unheard gunshot, all the birds on all the trees suddenly, and noisily, sprang into action. The sounds of their screeching pierced the silence like a knife. Those travellers who were able, raised their hands to cover their ears as the deafening cacophony increased. The screeching masses rose from their perches and, as though with one single mind, took to the skies – darkening the heavens with their incredible number.
“Gods!” yelled Slobber, his words inaudible to his companions through the ferocious din. “What’s going on?”
Frutely observed his lip movement, and read their meaning. She glanced back up at the sky and offered Slobber a shake

of her head in reply, her mouth quite naturally and instinctively mouthing the words "I don't know."

Tree began to wish he had never said anything, as though not drawing attention to the silence would have prevented this hellish scream. It wasn't long before his customary cynicism rose up to protect him from his own fears, as images of a torrential downpour of bird muck filled his mind – *Crap!* he thought to himself. *An awful lot of crap!*
Slobber broke his gaze at the cloud of frantic flyers and glanced down into the waters below. Even the fish seemed to be panicking – furiously darting this way and that – altering direction without any apparent purpose, before all, quite suddenly it seemed, decided to make a run for it and head down river. Like a silver curtain they drew against the dark background of the Zintal rock bed. Slobber raised a single eyebrow – "That's a little strange", he observed quietly to himself.

The shrieking began to subside a little, enough at least for the group to become aware of the deep rumbling noise that had been hiding behind it. "Shine – my – torch!" offered Potfondle (his newly created replacement for 'Smack my Rodney', which he had decided to drop in the presence of Frutely – 'Rodney' being quite a rude word. His first thought had simply been to replace 'Rodney' with 'Richard' but had decided against that for obvious reasons.) The others heard this peculiar exclamation, and though they did not fully understand it, Potfondle's extended finger, at the end of his now firmly pointing arm, left no one in any doubt as to what his curious comment alluded. The trees on the left bank were swaying and shuddering. Until now, no one had really paid much attention to it, viewing it as the obvious side effect to all those birds rising from their perches. Leaves, weak branches and extremely unobservant birds fell to the ground as the vibration continued. Frutely moved her head all around, observing all that was taking place. The surprise of all this had caught her

completely off guard, which might explain why it wasn't until she observed the falling rocks from the canyons in the far distance, that it all clicked. "QUAKE!!" she shouted.
"Ya think!?" came Tree's sarcastic response. "Am I glad you're here! Thank you doctor for pointing out the bloody obvious!!!"

Although Matchwood had been aware of all that was going on around them, he had been using the majority of his concentration on keeping a central position in the river. Too close to the left bank and they might get hit by a falling tree. Too close to the right and they might be caught by mud slipping from the high banks. He too, had seen the avalanches of rock in the distance and had decided to try and maintain a stationary position for safety.
"This is incredible", cried Frutely. "It's got to be the biggest one yet."
"I think everybody had better sit down and grab on to something", suggested Matchwood very calmly. No one aboard responded; perhaps because his voice had been so calm as to be drowned out by the loud rumbling which continued, as though coming from some snoring beast that surrounded them; perhaps because they were already sitting, and firmly holding on to something – that being a generally natural reaction in people when terrified, and in a boat. Matchwood obviously hadn't given much thought to his suggestion, designed as it was to calm and pacify his passengers – enabling him to draw their attention, and gently alert them to the peculiar, and rather disturbing phenomena that was now advancing on them. He decided to try again – "People, people…" he said, his voice louder in volume but still unerringly calm.
"I don't wish to further alarm anyone, but if you would all like to turn your attention up river…" His voice began to drop away naturally.
It was Slobber who felt it necessary to add an obvious punctuation to Matchwood's subtle observations: "Holy crap!"

he said, his voice about as far removed from Matchwood's calm as it is possible to be.

Frutely's eyes widened and her jaw dropped. She rushed to Matchwood's bow, "Is that what I think it is?"
"Probably," replied Match, "you are very intelligent."
Intelligent she was, but something about what everyone now stared at in pure amazement, didn't seem quite right to her. "Don't bores usually travel up river?"
"As far as I know", came Match's reply, his voice still eerily calm.
"What the hell is it!?" cried a terrified Tree.
"A bore", said Frutely, turning to face her companions.
"Doesn't look very boring to me", mused Slobber, his attempt at humour designed to mask his obvious terror.
Before them, in the far distance, could be seen a white line. A wall of white water, several feet high. A bore – a wave that occupied the full width of the river.
"A burst dam?" suggested Slobber.
"No dams on the Twit", replied Potfondle quietly. "What could have caused it?" he added – a question aimed at no-one in particular.
"Bores are caused by a high tide", said Frutely.
"Uh, Professor, the sea is behind us", observed Tree, offering yet another unhelpful contribution.
"Where it came from," said Match, "can be discussed later...assuming we don't drown, that is."
Matchwood quickly considered his options. He couldn't head for the banks... their continued shaking made it far too dangerous. He couldn't outrun it...already moving at quite a speed, and quickening all the time. All he could do, he decided, was treat this waterwall as though it were an ocean wave. He told everyone to secure themselves and their belongings – "Lie as low as you can!" he ordered. His passengers didn't need to hear the instruction a second time. Slobber grabbed most of the luggage, leaving Frutely – at her own insistence – to secure her own kit. Potfondle grabbed

Tree's bucket and wrapped his arms around it, ensuring that one hand firmly grasped his mini trunk.

Matchwood's attention was firmly fixed on the charging foam moving towards him with increasing speed. He had, of course, a great deal of experience with ocean waves. They were different, peaks and troughs. Dangerous to be sure, but he always viewed them like a rollercoaster ride – up and down – easy once you get into a rhythm. This was something different. The water before it was, other than energetic ripples, relatively calm. The bore itself therefore, appeared as a sheer vertical wall of angry water. As it drew closer, the sound of the roaring wave matched the still present, yet dissipating rumble of the quake. *Well,* thought Match, *at least the quake's over*. He found small comfort in this fact however, since positioned as he was on the river, the quake held little danger. That which was now before him was going to be tricky, to say the least.

He watched, stationary in the middle of the river, waiting for his moment. "Wait for it", he said quietly to himself, as though about to issue himself with an as yet unknown instruction. "Wait for it", he repeated. "And… Now!" With that he began to exhibit forward motion, steadily gaining speed. "Fast enough, Match?" he enquired of himself. "Yip!" came his own reply. He maintained this velocity, now concentrating all his efforts on ensuring that he hit the wave head on – his intention being to allow his bow to slice through the waterwall like a knife. The roar of the wave grew louder as Match's speed permitted the time of their battle to be reduced. "HERE…" he said.

"Well," said Tree, "time to kiss your ass goodbye."

"You're not helping", sobbed Potfondle. "If you're so sure we're going to drown, perhaps I shouldn't waste my energy holding on to you."

"NO!" yelped Tree. "Sorry! You keep your furry little hands right where they are."

"WE…" continued Matchwood, after a very pregnant pause.

"Looking forward to your third soaking of the weekend, Slob?" said Potfondle – trying to break the tension.

"Yeah," replied Slobber, with an attempt at laughter, "I was actually thinking of just jumping overboard to save time. Anyone got a surf board?"
"GO!"

CHAPTER TWELVE

"Well, Squit?" came the deep, precise tones, echoing from the darkness.

Festulas Squit raised his long, thin head from its customary floor-facing position and stared into the darkness with wide, soulless, black eyes. His hope was to catch a glimpse of the owner of this voice that never seemed to venture from the gloom.

"I'm waiting Squit", said the calm voice, displaying the merest hint of impatience.

"We *are* starting to make progress, sir", came Squit's eventual reply. The obsequious tone of his nasal voice dripped from his mouth as though it were a slug oozing its way out of a hole, as the tip of his nose lifted to allow his thin lips to curl at the ends, in a pathetic attempt at a smile.

"Starting to make progress, are you?" The voice in the dark, although as calm as ever, was clearly owned by someone who was not pleased by this report.

Festulas Squit knew this news was not likely to produce excitement in his Master's voice. He dreaded these twice-daily meetings. He clasped the rounded top of his cane with the long, skeletal fingers of his hands as his eyes, followed by his head, returned to their study of the cavern floor. He was about to offer yet more excuses to explain his lack of success to date, when the voice once more chose to offer its words of encouragement.

"My tolerance for you Squit, is not without end. However," the voice paused and Festulas waited uneasily for its resumption, "though a snivelling wretch of a man you undoubtedly are, it is difficult in this day and age to find a creature with your boundless capacity for deceit."

Squit's eyes and head raised once more, tilting to one side furtively – the pathetic curl of a smile trying even more desperately to create an impact on his leathery face. "Oh thank you sir", he said – in genuine appreciation of this wonderful compliment. He was about to offer more sycophantic utterances but the voice, tiring quickly of his servant's visage, chose to bring their meeting to a conclusion.

"Shut up you tiresome drip!" the volume of its words slightly increased.

"Yes, sir. Sorry, sir", was the all too predictable reply, as an almost grovelling Squit curled his head back down to the floor, and took a slight step backwards in submission.

"Get out of my sight, slug. Return in precisely ten hours!"

Squit extended his long, bony arms out from his sides and bowed – a position he maintained as he reversed his streaky frame away. After about eight steps, he began to turn…

"And Squit…" added the voice, calling an abrupt halt to Festulas's sly retreat.

"Sir?" replied Festulas, turning his head slightly in the direction of the voice.

"Have more encouraging news."

"For your service", came Squit's prompt reply, accompanied by the creaking of his deepened, snivelling bow. He turned to face the direction he had been using for his escape and sloped off, these final words echoing in his head – these words, delivered with soft tones that belied their actual meaning. Squit however, knew their meaning. Knew it all too well. With these four words, the owner of the voice had planted a seed of such fear in Squit's mind, that he now trembled with dread. Once safely out of his Master's sight he leant against the tunnel wall, allowing himself to slide down its rough surface – ending up on the floor. He produced a handkerchief from the inside pocket of his jacket, and mopped the newly formed beads of cold sweat from his brow. The item returned to his coat, he sat clutching his raised knees, and with his dagger-like chin resting on his chest, he closed his eyes and breathed deeply in an attempt to compose himself.

CHAPTER THIRTEEN

The long-legged birds, quietly sifting for food in the shallows of the Great Twit, suddenly found their peace disturbed by the spluttering of Slobber, slowly surfacing into consciousness. Until then, they hadn't paid much attention to this curiously coloured, and rather large piece of flotsam. The fact that it was now moving startled them somewhat – forcing them to disband noisily.

Slobber coughed and gagged, as an amount of river water was expelled from his body. He rolled slowly onto his side and breathed deeply. "Auntie's armpits!" he said, after a lengthy period of recovery. He rolled onto his back, forced the lids of his eyes to open and lay still, staring up at the clear, blue, afternoon sky. At length he decided to stand, and as he did so he suddenly found himself victim of a searing pain in his right leg. "AAHhh!" he shouted, throwing all his weight onto the other leg and toppling sideways, crashing to the ground. He clutched his head with his hands and screwed up his face in agony. "Aahh!" he repeated, with slightly less volume. He lifted his head and glanced at the offending limb. His eyes widened and his jaw dropped. A feeling of nausea drained all the colour from his face, as he stared in horror at the foot-long splinter of wood that was stuck in his thigh. He reached out and gently touched the tip, “Aargh!” came his cry, as his head thumped back onto the ground – his left hand clenched into a fist as it rose up, and was brought back down again to gently pound an extremely furrowed brow.

He lay there, his mouth wide open in silent screams of pain, the side of his fist rhythmically thumping his forehead. His right hand clutching an area of leg slightly above the wooden dagger.

“Nasty splinter you’ve got there!” chirped a familiarly cynical voice.

Slobber unscrewed his eyes and sat up abruptly, this unexpected observation putting his discomfort on hold.

“Tree?” he said, glancing all about him in search of the little plant.

“Behind you, Slobs”, offered Tree by way of location assistance.

Slobber turned the top half of his body to allow his head to swivel far enough around. “Tree!” he said excitedly, as he observed the plant, still in his bucket, lying on his side about three feet up on the river bank.

“How did you make it all the way up there?” quizzed Slobber.

“You threw me here. Remember?”

Slobber turned back to face the river and once more furrowed his brow, this time as a visual display of his attempts at recollection. After a quite lengthy period of thought, accompanied by several gentle shakes of denial from his head, Slobber suddenly found the memories flooding back.

Matchwood’s plucky attempt to successfully conquer the bore had seemingly failed. The brave boat had done everything right…theoretically. The wall of foaming water hit his bow with surprising force. He had done everything imaginable to remain afloat but, after what seemed like an eternity, the battle was lost. The bore picked them up and carried them with it for quite some distance before, as though it were an infant sick of

the game, tossing Match, along with his cargo, high up into the air. He had spun in flight, allowing his companions to shoot off in all directions.
The following panic had seen Slobber struggling to keep his head above water, as the continuous roll of the wave seemed to claw at him, trying to drag him under. He struggled with all the power he could produce in his arms and legs – occasionally breaching the surface, only to be dragged back down. It was during one such victory that his outstretched hand found itself clutching the rim of Tree's bucket – tossing violently within the wave's wake. As the rest of Slobber's body followed, breaking the water like a sea to air missile, Tree – held high like a trophy – had been thrown with all Slobber's might towards the bank. All Tree saw, as he sailed through the air, was his saviour vanishing back into the churning depths. Slobber continued to battle against his grasping opponent until eventually his victory was secured and, exhausted, he bobbed to the surface, his desire for survival forcing his tired limbs to find the safety of dry land, where he promptly collapsed into unconsciousness.

Tree advised him that he had lain there – immobile, save the gentle raising and lowering of his body as his lungs filled and emptied – for over four hours. The pair sat silently, before Slobber, who had been looking out over the water, suddenly realised that he had overlooked a matter of extreme seriousness. "The others?" came the eventual stark observation from Slobber, deeply ashamed that it had taken him so long to realise that he and Tree were alone. "Where are the others?" Panic starting to take hold, filling his stomach with its associated sickness. Slobber began to search all about him with his eyes, his head turning this way and that, as unwelcome but totally unavoidable fears started to fill his mind.
"Pot can't swim", said Tree solemnly, his voice so soft that Slobber barely heard it. These words filtered into Slobber's ears as though it were an unwelcome visitor forcing their way

into his private sanctuary. Throughout his battle with the wave, he could not recall coming into contact – visual or otherwise – with anyone other than Tree. He breathed out a shaky sigh, trying desperately to hold back the rising flood of emotion steadily building as a lump in his throat. In desperation he lifted his face to the sky and yelled out “POT!” – his wailing voice signalling his desperation – “FRUTELY!” – allowing himself the briefest of pauses to swallow down the rising tears – “MATCHWOOD!”

His list delivered he sat quietly, his ears straining to hear the most distant reply. Nothing! He cried out again. And again. And again. Nothing! He sat, gazing out over the gently flowing river once more. His breathing fast and shallow as his face dropped about as far as it possibly could, as the tears filled his eyes. He had no choice now but to stare down at the ground and permit his emotional dam to burst.

CHAPTER FOURTEEN

Festulas Squit reached for his cane and, using it for support, pushed himself back up the cave wall, sliding on his back until his legs straightened. He stood for a moment with his eyes closed, heaving one final sigh before delivering a single nod of decision. He stepped away from his stony support, straightened his tall, black, top hat and adjusted the cuffs of his white shirt, permitting them to offer their customary line of linen – separating the grey of his skin from the black of his tailcoat sleeves. With the top of his cane gripped tightly by the elongated fingers of his left hand, he strode down the slope of the cave floor, heading deeper underground, to where the warm glow of lanterns presented their invitation.

"Mr Squit, sir", offered Graith with a slight bow of his hairless head. His large eyes shielded from the lantern light by an eye visor.
"Graith", offered Festulas, turning his head slightly with all the speed of a thoughtful snake. "We have urgent matters to discuss", he hissed quietly, choosing to dwell on the letter 's' at the end of his sentence, beckoning, with a vague point of the tip of his cane, to a small table just a few feet away.

“Of course, sir”, replied Graith, as he watched the tall, slender man pass before him before following behind, his head still bowed.
Festulas Squit stopped and slowly reached out a bony hand, wrapping his long fingers around the back of a wooden chair. With slow, deliberate moves, he drew it away from the table before releasing his grasp and allowing his hand to move slowly to the brim of his hat – its next task being the removal of his topper. The rather battered object sailed in an arc through the air, before being placed gently on the table top, the left hand joining this synchronised performance with its cargo of Squit’s ever-present cane, which it lay carefully by the hat’s side. Squit stood still for a moment, as if to study the precision of this display, before seating himself – flapping out the tail of his coat, allowing its fork to dangle over the back of the seat, their frayed tips resting gently on the dusty ground.
Graith remained standing as Squit adjusted his chair, bringing his legs under the table. Satisfied with his position he gently rested his forearms on the scratched, wooden surface before eventually beckoning with a flat palm to the chair opposite – turning his head slightly in the direction of his servant. “Sit!” came the single command.
Graith quickly moved in accordance with his instruction. Taking far less time than Festulas to seat himself, the short, pink creature – naked accept for a pair of well-worn, leather shorts, secured by a proudly-worn tool belt – quickly jumped up on to his chair and, with arms tightly folded, eyes permitted to look no higher than his Master’s stomach, he offered one simple question: ”Your orders, sir?”
Festulas drew a deep breath and rested back in his chair. The fingers of his hands crossed one another as they knitted themselves into a triangle, his thumb tips gently resting against each other.
His head rose slowly allowing him to glower at Graith. His down-turned lips parted slightly as Squit’s nasal tones escaped from his mouth, dripping onto the table. “You and your idle group will give me more.”

"More!?" replied Graith – his eyes still unprepared to make contact with those of his Master – not entirely sure how to translate this rather cryptic order.
"More, Graith", hissed Festulas. "Increase the size of your little explosions. Have your men dig harder and faster…"
Festulas began to rise. His tall, wiry frame rose steadily, his presence increasing in harmony with the volume of his voice. Standing at his full height, he widened his eyes and extended a long arm, allowing its long line to end at an overgrown, gnarled nail of a pointing, bony finger. He drew a deep breath and in his deepest voice – attempting to emulate his own Master – allowed his obviously forced, deep, gravel tones to cut through the stale air like damp thunder. "Work yourselves to death if you must. For death from exhaustion will be far more preferable to the horrors I will visit upon *all* of you should you fail me!"
The unfamiliar precision of these deep, though still vaguely nasal tones, caused feelings of true surprise and alarm in Graith. For the first time in their association, Festulas Squit had actually produced feelings of true fear in him. He swallowed hard, and with a slight tremble in his voice, managed to squeak out: "Your word is our law, sir. You tell us how far you mean us to cut into this accursed rock and we will do it. Our lives are yours. To do with as you please. Our deaths are a small price to pay…" Festulas had to cut him short. The sound of Graith's high-pitched stuttering was beginning to grate. "Shut up you odious creature!" he commanded, his voice still maintaining its new found depth. "Get out of my sight. Instruct your minions."
Graith leapt off his seat and padded off, further into the depths of the caverns, his journey abruptly interrupted with his Master's voice bringing him to a speedy halt. "And Graith…"
"Sir?" he said, turning his body sharply about and standing almost to attention, his hands flat by his sides, his head up.
"Give me ten feet an hour or choose one of your men to die."

Graith had been so successfully intimidated by the forceful determination within his Master's voice, that he had been left with no doubt whatsoever that this was in any way, an empty threat. *Ten feet an hour!* he thought. *That's impossible!* He did not however, allow his defeatist fears to offer a trace of themselves in his words of reply – "We will not fail you, sir", and with a low bow, Graith turned on the heels of his bare feet and scurried off – chased only by the sinister laughter of his Master.

Festulas circled the cave, turning down several of the oil lanterns which hung from its walls, before skulking back to his chair, where he seated himself once more. From the inside pocket of his coat, he produced a small hip-flask, unscrewed the lid, and raised it to meet his dry, thin lips – taking a small swig of its contents. He then reached into his outside pocket, from which he exhumed a small leather pouch. He loosened the leather lace, holding its mouth closed and, with two fingers and a thumb, gently took hold of the contents and withdrew it. Festulas Squit then sat back in his chair, staring at his prize – a sinister smile scarring the lower part of his long face. *Such power you afford me,* he thought, as he stared into the gentle, white glow emanating from the egg-shaped stone, balanced at the end of his fingers.

CHAPTER FIFTEEN

Graith bobbled his way deep into the gloom, carrying his squat, pale-skinned frame as fast as his short legs would permit. The warm, orange glow from the lantern-lit domain of Festulas Squit, began to distance itself as he puffed his way into the darkness. As the gloom of the way ahead began to envelope him, he quickly brought himself to a standstill and removed the eye shield from his head, allowing time for his large, pale pink eyes to adjust to the comfortable lacklight ahead. Graith gave several lengthy and deliberate blinks of his eyelids, in an attempt to speed up their adjustment. In no time the blackness ahead began to steadily turn to vague gloom; then, as Graith concentrated on his future path, the outlines of the jagged, rock walls and ceiling became visible to him. “That'll do”, he whispered to himself before resuming his brisk pace.

Graith had been running for more than 20 minutes, before the subtle sounds of activity and voices began to trickle out of the darkness and into his tiny ears, the sounds giving welcome relief that his journey was soon to be at an end. This relief gave him an extra boost of energy and his speed, which he had successfully maintained throughout his journey, quickened. Ahead of him, clearly visible to his now fully adjusted eyes, he could see the tunnel walls opening out into a huge, dome-roofed cave. "Lads!" he shouted, managing to force a decent level of volume and clarity through his heavy breathing. "Lads!" he repeated as he approached the wide entrance – his vocal approach breaking the rhythmic sounds of metal hitting rock.

"Lads!" he said once more, as he made his unceremonious entrance, the urgency of his tone reflected in his now wildly flailing arms, that waved about like the wings of a distressed, and highly uncoordinated bird.

"Stop what you're doing!" he yelled, as his now uncontrollable rate of speed caused him to fly straight past the first worker he encountered.

"Stop what you're doing..." he repeated, moving swiftly past three others – his eyes seeming to reach out to them, pleading with them to end his forward momentum. "We must work harder!" he shrieked as all his men watched in statuesque amazement, their Guv pass by – his legs still moving as fast as ever, completely beyond the control of his brain; his arms waving frantically, although they did now seem to be serving some kind of purpose – a desperate attempt on Graith's part to flap his arms in an attempt to slow his rate.

"Stop what you're doing and work harder!" he continued, his lack of self control now seeming to have infected the speech centre of his mind, as his little legs, unwilling to stop, carried him straight through the middle of his crew – all now fully appreciating this farcical display.

All smirking faces watched with mischievous glee, as Graith's uncontrolled trek through the worksite caused him to head in one terrible direction. "WwwhhoooooaaAA!" screamed Graith, as his wide eyes suddenly alerted his brain to the dreadful prospect that now presented itself. With no-one rushing to his aid, and with little chance that his flapping arms were going to be of any use, the Clan leader tore straight into the gaping mouth of another tunnel. Down the steep slope of the latrine tube he went, his little legs reluctantly forced to quicken far beyond their design limits. Realising quickly that his haste could prove disastrous, Graith desperately began to reach out for the tunnel walls, hoping with all his worth that his claws might dig in and slow him down. His panic now at its height, he even tried to intentionally fall over, but his attempted 'trips' were easily foiled by his seemingly independent lower limbs. His workforce broke from their frozen poses, dropped their axes and shovels and rushed excitedly to the bog-hole entrance. All waited with childish impatience to hear the awful climax of their boss's inability to stop.

Graith's terrified eyes looked straight ahead, as his brain unscrambled the information it was now presented with. He desperately wanted to look away or shut his eyes tight, but his own morbid fascination prevented him from doing anything other than commanding his vocal cords to let slip one single observation…"Oh Cra…aargh…!" His intended comment was forced to change half way, as gravity suddenly made its presence felt, pulling the mole down – into a shallow pond of nightmarish filth.

"Yip!" said Chokkle cheerfully, "that's what it is alright", signalling to the assembled audience that the pending floods of laughter could now be permitted release. First a trickle of sniggering began, as the moles looked at one another. This sniggering grew into chuckles as nods and gestures were made. As the terrible sound of Graith landing in that terrible pool of raw sewage echoed up the corridor, chuckling gave way to laughter – full, howling laughter. The kind of laughter that puts you on the floor, your arms wrapping around straining stomach muscles. The kind of laughter that causes tears of delight and moans of pain as your jaw begins to suffer from the hilarity.

It must have been a full 15 minutes before anyone was in a position to answer Graith's angry cries for help. It was Chokkle – Graith's second-in-command, and catalyst for all this mirth – who was first to struggle to his feet. Desperately trying to control himself, he managed to hold back the continued giggling just long enough to instruct two of the moles to find a length of rope. “Make sure it’s long enough to be thrown from here…” he japed, “we don’t want to have to smell him until it’s absolutely necessary.” As his men scattered, searching every crevice of the huge space, Chokkle maintained his position at the toilet entrance, yelling out words of encouragement – occasionally stopping to allow a brief string of giggles to escape.

“I hear you laughing up there! Don’t think I don’t!” yelled Graith, the level of his temper heightened by the foul stench that assaulted his nostrils. “GET ME OUT OF HERE NOW!!” he shouted, opening his mouth much wider than is wise when you are up to your neck in effluence. Graith coughed, spluttered and spat, as a tiny amount of the watery ‘mud’ trickled over his bottom lip.

“You alright, Chief?” shouted Chokkle in response to his superior’s coughs – his voice, though giggle free, far more cheerful than Graith thought it had any right to be.

“Get me out of here now!” he repeated, this time through tightly gritted teeth. “We are in serious trouble!”

It was the way Graith said this final sentence that grabbed Chokkle. The Guv was, in general, a very relaxed person – not usually given to irrational exaggeration. He turned to the crew and, in a tone that demanded seriousness, urged them to get a move on. Very quickly a rope was located. Chokkle grabbed the hemp bundle and, having first pointed to three of his colleagues, issuing the instruction “Follow me”, he moved quickly down the toilet tunnel – making sure that his speed was not sufficient to duplicate Graith’s mistake.

At the cave’s base, the steep decline levelled out. Ahead, three wooden platforms, with a single hole in the end of each, extended out over a pit. Chokkle took one end of the rope and walked to the edge of the middle pier, while his three companions took up the other end, bracing themselves as though entrants in a tug-o-war contest. Chokkle quickly

located Graith – standing neck-deep in the foulest mud imaginable, head turned up in anticipation of aid, his eyes burning with an anger rarely rivalled in its intensity.
Chokkle said nothing as their eyes met. He quickly assessed the depth of the hole and drew up enough slack to make the distance – "Grab this", he said, as the frayed end landed with a gentle splat, in front of Graith's chin – the impact causing a tiny piece of 'mud' to jump up and hit Graith right between his eyes. "Sorry, Chief", offered Chokkle, withdrawing his eye contact and desperately trying not to smile.
Grabbing the rope with both his slime-covered hands, Graith hung on for dear life: "You will be", he muttered to himself, keen that no one else should hear. His time in the 'puddle of hell' had not been at all pleasant, and the last thing he wanted right now was for anyone above to be distracted from their purpose of removing him from it. "Once you're safely out, Graith old chap," he quietly mused, "once you're back on solid ground...I'll bloody show 'em not to laugh at me!"
"Pull him up lads!" Chokkle commanded, waving them back, urging them to retreat with the rope gripped tightly, rather than try and haul him up hand over hand. Chokkle was concerned that Graith might already be somewhat out of sorts. The effect of a slipping hand sending him back down there, was a thought too terrible for Chokkle to contemplate – the reprisals from their leader would be unthinkable. "We'll have you out of there before you know it", offered Chokkle, his tone of voice and facial expression trying desperately to display genuine empathy.

The three moles kept a firm grip on the rope as they steadily moved backwards, up the tunnel's sloping floor. Graith steadily rose out of the muck, the ooze making a squelching sound as it gave up its guest. Up through the foul air came Graith, dripping with mess, until finally he reached the wood of the 'squat piers'.

Chokkle issued his order to take it gently, assisting an extremely relieved Graith to pull himself up and onto dry land – finally reaching a point where, certain he was safe, he released his grasp on the rope.

“You alright?” said Chokkle, leaning over the brown, smelly pile that was his boss. Graith opened his eyes and grabbed the wrist of his subordinate. “Get me to a hose!” he hissed, his protruding upper two teeth remaining still, as his words leaked from the sides of his still clenched jaws.

A very reluctant Chokkle assisted his senior to his feet, trying hard to keep his long, whisker-covered nose as far away as possible from the foul odour that saturated his clansman. Once to his feet, Graith chose to fling his sludge- coated arm around his lieutenant’s shoulders, giving him a firm, one-arm cuddle. Exacting further revenge, he turned Chokkle to face him and, with a broad smile now dominating his face, drew him close, offering a full hug of friendship and gratitude. “You are my number two”, he said, placing his vile hands on both Chokkle’s cheeks before delivering a big kiss on his forehead. Still unsatisfied that enough revenge had been taken, Graith chose to even things up by giving his pal a second kiss, then a third – one on each cheek of his paralysed face. Graith then stood back to admire his work, his face dominated by a grin of pure satisfaction. Chokkle returned his smiling gaze, as a tear rolled down his cheek – an effect of the rotten stench that now enveloped both moles, causing a burning sensation in the throat and eyes. He began to choke and gag... “Does the smell bother you?” enquired Graith sarcastically, showing absolutely no sympathy whatsoever. “Come on,” he said, once the choking subsided, ”we don’t have time for this.”

Leaving his friend to wallow in his newly acquired stench, Graith caught up to the other three fellows – unaware that their quiet chuckling had been overheard. “Now,” he said, bringing his hands together in not so much a clap, as a splat! “I’m tired after my long run. One of you will have to carry me.”

The three stopped abruptly, looking at each other in fear. As they turned, Graith charged up and jumped on the back of Scoop, cowering in the middle. “You’ll do very nicely”, he said, locking his horrible arms around the neck and bringing his vile legs up to the waist, “Grip me tight now. You wouldn’t want me to fall off, would you?” he growled.
“No sir”, replied the reluctant donkey, wrapping his arms around Graith’s sticky, stocky legs.
“Good lad”, hissed Graith, locking his ankles together around Scoop’s belly – “Giddyup now. Lets go.”

CHAPTER SIXTEEN

Slobber wiped the tears from his eyes and stared up once more at the perfect afternoon sky. It was only when he glanced back to the ground, that he was reminded of the physical pain in his leg. With desperation still filling his heart, he grabbed the end of the large splinter, giving it a firm, sharp pull – freeing it from his flesh. Although this action caused significant discomfort, he did not scream...his soul was consumed with a different pain, the pain of profound loss. He drew the blood-soaked end of his tormentor to his face and looked at it for a moment before tossing it, thoughtlessly, over his shoulder.

"Hey!" came an indignant and strangely familiar voice. Both Slobber and Tree took startled note and scanned about them in search of the voice's owner.

"Matchwood!?" enquired Tree.

"Sounds a little like Matchwood", admitted Slobber who, like Tree did not want to jump to immediate, hopeful conclusions. The pair sat in curious discussion over whether or not the voice of Match had indeed just made itself heard.

"Well!?" came the unseen voice once again, displaying a little impatience.

"It is!" Slobber offered. "I'm sure it is. I mean…don't you think it is?"
"Give the man a bloody prize!" exclaimed the voice, angrily. "Who the hell do you think you are, discarding me like that. Do you have any idea who you're messing with!?"
Slobber frowned heavily before scrambling to his feet – grunting in painful discomfort as he put a little weight on his dagger-freed leg.

"Matchwood. You're alive!" he said – both relief and excitement fighting for dominance in his voice. "Thank all the Gods for their mercy", he continued, as he hobbled to the water's edge – scanning the surface for his friend. With no sign of him *on* the water, Slobber grunted his way onto his knees and thrust his head *under* the water, searching frantically for a glimpse of the little boat.
"What is the fool doing!?" said Matchwood.
"Where are you?" asked a puzzled Tree, realising that the sound was coming from the woods, not the river.
"How the hell should I know! I can't see!" came Matchwood's reply, his oddly cantankerous attitude growing more severe by the second.
Slobber eventually surfaced and drew in a huge gulp of lung-filling air.
"What's he doing in the river!?" snapped Matchwood, having been quickly briefed by Tree. "I'm not in the river!"
Slobber overhearing this, rose once more to his feet – hobbling back up the bank and standing, hands firmly on his hips, by the side of Tree – still lying on his side in his bucket.
"Keep talking!" shouted Tree, "We'll home in on your voice." Lowering his voice, he directed a question at Slobber – "How could he have gotten into the woods?"
Slobber stared straight ahead, offering nothing more than an extremely large shrug of his shoulders in reply.
Matchwood sighed, but did as was suggested – choosing to recite poetry until located…

If I were a man, I'd kick your bum.
I'd pull off your arms, it'd be such fun.

"Nice", offered Tree, sarcastically.
"Sshh!" hissed Slobber.

I'd sit on your legs, daring you to run.
As I thumped at your belly…
Using it as a drum.

The sound stopped. "What's wrong!?" cried Slobber, fearing that this had all been nothing more than a bizarre hallucination.
"Trying to think of another poem", replied Matchwood. "Hmmm…a-ha, I have it!. Here we go…"

Nassian sits, he sleeps, he waits.
He doesn't eat biscuits but he does like cakes.
He'll pick his teeth with the fingers of your hand…hand…hand….

Match paused again, struggling with his improvised verse. "Ha!" he eventually said,

Stick your bum in the air; bury your head in the sand.

"For the love of the Gods, Slobs. Find him soon, please!" pleaded Tree.
"I don't think I can stand much more of this!"

Does it tickle your fancy? Does it make you feel good?
Does it make you feel like a real woman should?

"Hey!" cried a jubilant Slobber, "I've found him…at least I think I've found him." Slobber stared down at the ground in

disbelief. “Matchwood, is that really you!?”
“Yip!” replied the foot-long piece of wood, blood staining one end.
Slobber stooped down and gently picked up the stick – the look on his face clearly reflecting the thought going through his mind: *I'm losing my mind. At least I hope I am!*
“Hey! Careful there bloke,” giggled the stick, “I'm ticklish.”
“Are you OK?” asked Tree, puzzled by Matchwood's extreme and sudden mood swing – seemingly drifting from ‘cantankerous old git!’ to ‘cheerful chappy’ in moments.
“Oh, I can't complain sonny”, came Matchwood's swift, albeit vaguely patronising reply.
Slobber rejoined Tree on the riverbank, sitting down by his bucket and placing the stick gently on the ground. He finally noticed Tree's position and carefully righted him – his apology for taking so long to offer his assistance, quickly accepted by the small plant.

Tree had been generally passive in his mood since Slobber had regained consciousness. The general cynicism that had dominated his attitude throughout the trip had been replaced by solemnity.
Although he liked to give the impression to all around that he simply tolerated the companionship of his small, furry friend, he did in fact have a genuine fondness for him. The belief that Potfondle was dead had filled every fibre of his being with true sorrow. As is customary on these occasions, Tree had been quietly consumed by grief and regret: *What will I do now? I wish I'd told him...* were just two thoughts he had, as regrets over time wasted, filled his mind. He had, since Slobber's emergence from deep sleep, forced himself to act at least a little like his usual self, but any attempts at dry wit had been half-hearted. Now – sitting with an injured, blue, drool machine, and a blood-soaked, talking stick – the absurdity of the whole situation suddenly grabbed him and the merest hint of a smirk crossed his mind. This smirk quickly turned into a

smile and was about to evolve still further into a giggle, when the humour was driven out by further thoughts of Potfondle – lying dead and alone.

Tree was still quietly wallowing in guilt at allowing himself to find humour, while his dead friend lay undiscovered somewhere, when the stick, who had been sitting quietly, suddenly spoke: "Pot? Dr. Gaiberond? Where are they?"
His question went unanswered for quite a long time, as an awkward silence replaced the general quiet of the group. Finally Slobber – with quivering lip – replied in a soft, sad voice: "Gone."
"Gone!!?" said Matchwood, his mood swinging back to 'cantankerous old git'. "Well obviously they've gone. If they hadn't *gone* they would be here, wouldn't they? The question is, where have they gone!!?"
The awkward silence continued to fill the space between words, before Tree – his anger at Matchwood's lack of consideration for his sadness – shattered the uncomfortable stillness, "They are dead! Understand? Potfondle! Frutely! Dead! Gone means dead and dead means gone!" His grief now chose a different path. The unsympathetic attitude of this clearly fuddled piece of wood, had given Tree the excuse he needed to turn away from feelings of his own guilt, and launch feelings of rage at Matchwood's failures. "You!" he said, his voice starting to shake with the powerful emotion of wrath. "You did this. You killed them. You damn near killed all of us!" His emotional rollercoaster had reached the top of the longest drop, and now gained momentum, building into an unstoppable, verbal assault.
"You pathetic, useless sod! You had to show off, didn't you!? Had to show us all what a great master of the water you are! You couldn't have played it safe and run away!? Oh no, not the great Matchwood!" he said, spitting through his temper, as his words rushed at Matchwood like a clenched fist through the air. Mimicking the boat's voice – choosing to paint a

picture of a character who was both arrogant and reckless, with a total disregard for the safety of his passengers – Tree continued, "Oh, I'm the mighty Matchwood. No wave can topple me. But it did, didn't it? You utter, utter, utter..." Tree began to falter a little, as the speed of his words began to overtake the speed of his thoughts. At this point, Slobber tried to interrupt. Tried to curb the tree's revenge on Matchwood.

"It wasn't his fault, Tree. It was no one's fault…"

"Shut your mouth, you giant, blue puddle of phlegm…" spat Tree, his anger now consuming him. Like a virus, it had been given a foothold and now like a virus, it dominated him, filling every nerve with its sickness. Slobber now found himself the victim of Tree's rage, as the anger contaminated his usual cynically passive attitude: "You! You could have saved him. You knew he couldn't swim. Knew he'd drown, and yet instead of saving him you chose to save yourself. You coward!"

"I saved you, didn't I, you ungrateful twig!" retaliated Slobber, "You think I don't wish I'd seen them!?"

Where Tree had fixated entirely on Potfondle, Slobber's thoughts included the lost life of Frutely. He gripped the ground in his large, tight fists as the tears once again emerged from his eyes. Slobber too, had courted thoughts of deep regret: *Why didn't I look for them? Why didn't I stay in the water – using every ounce of my strength to dive down and find them? I could have saved them. I could have done it.*

Self-pity – feelings of guilt and anger began to overwhelm the pathetic Slobber, inevitably causing him to break down once more. Tears now partnered by wailing, he opened his pain for all to see and hear: "I know it", he sobbed. "I know I could have saved them. I should have saved them", Slobber smashed the ground with his fists, "I let them die! It's all my fault, I let them…"

Matchwood, silent until now, interrupted Slobber's avalanche of anguish with three short words. Three words that brought everything to a stand-still. Three words that not only drew a dramatic halt to Slobber's sobs, but Tree's verbal onslaught as well. The birds too, seemed to silence their twittering, the animals, foraging in the forest, appeared to halt their activity, the fish stopped jumping, even the river itself seemed to silence its babbling waters…"They – are – alive!!"

CHAPTER SEVENTEEN

The eyes of the group of moles still gathered at the toilet-tunnel entrance, widened in disgusted disbelief. Nostrils closed and corners of mouths drooped as the group parted to allow Graith, still proudly riding his truly reluctant 'steed', to enter the larger cavern. Graith jumped from his mount and glared at the circle of creatures that now surrounded him – looking at each in turn, as he moved in a slow circle – the muck still dripping from his body. None could return his glance. All stood with their heads hung low. Their laughter long gone, they now stood in fearful anticipation of Graith's reprisal.

Graith, satisfied that the fear of the subterranean Gods had been well and truly put up his men, pushed through the circle – his path straight and true, leading him to a large barrel of water. He stood for the briefest of moments, his hands tightly gripping the barrel's sides before – with true athleticism – he leapt into it, fully immersing himself in its ice-cold water. One mole whispered a horrible observation that found itself quickly followed by a simultaneous 'Yuck!' from the others: "Isn't that our drinking water?"

Graith's head slowly surfaced from the now gloomy water.

The deep frown of anger on his brow had shallowed slightly, although his glaring eyes, shining like bright, white lights in the darkness, moved once more over the faces of his crew – moving from one to the other like search lights.
He drew himself to his full height and clambered out of the water – his exit far slower than his entrance. With his back to his men, his hands once more clutching the barrel sides, Graith, in a soft voice said, “Did you find that funny?” He expected no answer and he got none.
He continued: “Find it humorous that your boss was up to his neck in crud?” Again, no answer. Graith, now free from the disgusting goo that had clothed his naked flesh, turned slowly to face his fearful subordinates. As though a curious contagion, the deep, precise tones – used earlier to great effect by Squit – now found themselves being employed by Graith: “As deep in it as I just was,” he said, pausing slightly for added drama, “that is nothing compared to how deep in it we *all* are now!”
All heads were now upright. All ears, though small, were drawn by Graith’s quiet, deliberate words. The workers, Chokkle included, looked at Graith – his facial features: The long nose, wide eyes, thick lips and practically non-existent chin, were like stone – immutable, still and earnest. The moles looked at each other, hoping that at least one of them had observed some clue as to his meaning.
Graith allowed this uncertainty to linger for a while until completely satisfied that, following his comic entrance, his team’s attention was firmly fixed on the here and now.
“Our Master is displeased…”
The looks on the faces of the gang quickly changed upon receipt of this news, from curiosity to concern. Graith continued… “He sees nothing but failure in our efforts…” The group looked around at each other anxiously. Some muttered fearfully, echoing in whispers Graith’s pivotal noun – “Failure!?”
Graith waited silently for this disturbance to subside. He was quietly pleased with himself for the way in which he was

conducting this briefing. As happily surprised as Festulas Squit had been at the effect his change in tone and delivery had been. The group, realising that more information was to follow, turned their attention back to their leader.

"He demands more of us. He demands…" pausing once more, knowing that what he was about to say would not be greeted with applause, "ten feet an hour."

He was right, the whispers that had echoed around the cavern before were now replaced by shouts of disbelief – "Ten feet an hour!? Through Zintal!? That's impossible!" The volume of their words, which all amounted to the same thing, grew as the team whipped each other up – all in total agreement that such a demand was highly unreasonable.

Graith had lost the crowd. He knew he would, but their growing volume demanded he bring them all back to him. His initial attempts at drawing them all to order failed miserably. He tried shouting: "Quiet! I haven't finished!" That too, fell on deaf ears. He forced his way to the centre of the mob and, quite violently, began to force his men out – clearing a small space for himself in their midst.

His shouts for quiet, along with the violence of his shoves, eventually forced an uncomfortable hush over the group – dissected from time-to-time by occasional mutters of, "Stupid!" and, "Is he insane?"

Graith altered his approach. The friendly, understanding voice of their leader returned: "Lads, lads", he said, stroking the air – his hands moving up and down as though petting a large, invisible animal – as he gestured for calm. "He is our Master. Our lives are his to command. His word is our law", he reminded them. He continued, relieved that he had managed – for the moment at least – to quieten them down, "He is the keeper of the Egg of Gertrude and until his death, we have no choice but to obey his every command." Graith had successfully reintroduced calm – albeit a fragile one – by reminding his men of their sacred oath.

Directing his attention for a moment to the individual responsible for the 'Is he insane?' comment, Graith placed a

fatherly hand on the sloped shoulder of Wormil – the youngest of their group. Looking straight into his eyes, Graith asked: "Do you want *him* to hear your words of insult? Do you have any idea what he could do to you?"
Wormil, like all the others, was absolutely terrified of even the idea of *seeing* their Master, let alone have him speak to him. "Forgive me", he trembled.
Graith, once more, addressed the group: "We are the last of our kind. The last Clan. The last crew. He found us. He came with the Egg of Gertrude – our people's most sacred relic, given unto us by the Climpanion – most powerful of all the Gods of the lacklight." He moved among his Clan, hands tightly clenched behind his back. His expression sombre and sincere. His voice taking on the tones of a great orator, "He found us, deep underground, our lives almost at an end as we slept – consumed by a sickness that had prevented our awakening for decades. With the Egg, he healed us. He gave us purpose. Our lives belong to him, for they are lives we once more have *because* of him. He and he alone has the ability to call upon the power of Gertrude. As he once used it to give us life, so could he use it to take that life away again. *He* is the voice of Climpanion. *His* word is *our* law."
"His word is our law", repeated the others quietly, as they once more hung their heads – this time seemingly in prayer.
Graith drew a secret breath of relief. The loyalties of his Clan had been successfully reaffirmed. The strength of united purpose this faith delivered would, believed Graith, enable them to accomplish their task.
Quietly, he told them what their Master had said – calming his men with words of encouragement: "No one is going to die. We will do ten feet an hour."
He stood silently for a moment, hoping to find some further inspiration with which to feed his men. With a smile of absolute certainty in the truth of his words, Graith turned back to his crew: "How can we fail, my friends? We do the bidding of Climpanion."

CHAPTER EIGHTEEN

"What did you say?" said Tree, after a lengthy pause. He, like everyone and everything else, had actually heard what Match had said. His question, like so many questions, was asked more to give him time to think; time to doubt.

"They – are – alive!" repeated the piece of wood with staggered, deliberate delivery.

Slobber quickly looked all about him once more, sending tendrils of slime from his nostrils – shooting off like lime green spears. Apologising quickly to anything in the general vicinity, who he may have victimised with his unintentional attack, he looked down at the shard of wood. "Where are they?"

Tree, with the tiniest glimmer of hope rekindled in his soul, begged the next, obvious question. "How do you know?" he asked, with the probing approach of a seasoned interrogator.

Matchwood was silent for a moment before replying. With the calm intelligence the others had come to expect from him he said, "Precisely where? I don't know. Precisely how I know? I cannot say..."

Tree interrupted, dismissing Matchwood's words with impatience. "Argh!" he gruffed, "What does he know!? You heard him before, Slobs. He's mad as a brush!"

Matchwood, or at least what was left of him, retaliated immediately. His voice once more displaying authority, and the wisdom that only comes with age. "Listen to me, foolish child," he said, as though he were a parent scolding a youngster – "I'd like to see how much sanity you would retain if you'd just been smashed to pieces and tossed down a river like so much driftwood…right now," he continued, "most of me is lying on a small beach, at the mouth of the river. Other pieces are drifting out to sea, and some of me is, right now, fuelling a large fire."
Having successfully silenced his little critic, Matchwood explained that he knew what had happened to both Dr. Gaiberond and Potfondle, and that he had every reason to presume they were both very much alive.

As the wave hit, and the boat's best efforts to defeat the foaming waters were thwarted, he had watched with horror as his passengers – his friends – spilled out into the turbulent waters. As soon as he'd splashed back down, he had made every effort to be of assistance, but found himself powerless against the defiant wall of water. As he tossed about, pushed and buffeted by the rolling thunder of the wave, he had seen Slobber's struggle and valiant rescue of Tree. He had seen too, Frutely bravely risk her life – courageously struggling against the current to dive down and render aid to Pot. "*You* could do nothing, Slobber", he said, assuring his friend that in the grimy waters of the dirt-tearing hell they were all caught up in, he had no way of seeing very far. "It was a miracle that you saved Tree here."
Matchwood described how Frutely had obviously played a hunch. "She must have seen the bag Pot had been clutching when he went into the water", he offered. Perhaps hoping that Pot was still attached to the other end of its broken shoulder strap, she had managed to reach it. It was the bag she had rescued and fortunately, her assumption had proved correct – Potfondle was connected to the other end.

"So where are they!?" interrupted a frustrated Tree. "Are they with some of you on the beach?"
"No", replied Matchwood calmly. Appealing for Tree to remain silent, he continued… "Frutely brought Pot to her and together they struggled to reach the surface. Panic began to take over as they realised that, in the gloom, neither really had any idea which way was up. They kicked with their legs and pushed with their arms – desperately hoping the direction they had chosen was the right one. I watched with great relief as they slowly began to exact victory over the tugging currents and headed for the surface."
"So!?" said both Tree and Slobber, both at the edge of their 'seats'. "Cut to the chase!" they said in unison and with one echoing the impatience of the other, they added: "WHERE *ARE* THEY*!?*".

Matchwood was not going to be hurried. He had told them the practical outcome of his tale at the start – both Potfondle and Frutely Gaiberond were alive, he therefore saw no reason to deprive himself of explaining what he knew, in dramatic detail. Once more, as if this interruption had not taken place, he continued… "They fought and fought…"
"Auntie's armpits!" exclaimed Slobber. "Smack my Rodney!" added Tree, both realising that this irritating stick was not going to summarise his story. Both were reluctantly forced to accept the fact that they would have to listen to the whole damn saga!
This further invasion into Matchwood's dialogue caused him to stop. He remained quiet – giving the impression that he had childishly decided to deprive his companions of the rest of the tale.
"Well!?" barked Tree.
"Get on with it then!" added Slobber.
Matchwood remained quietly thoughtful for a moment longer – intentionally prolonging the agony. "They fought and fought," he eventually repeated, "clutching at the water above, gradually pulling themselves out of the depths." He paused

once more to ensure that attempts at further, unwelcome interruptions from his small, captive audience had been dealt with. Satisfied, he continued, "Suddenly, without warning or apparent reason, their efforts were halted by an external force of some kind. Their advance came to an abrupt end. Their thrashing ceased. I saw their faces, consumed with desperation, sink back into the gloom of the depths below. Down they went, deeper and deeper – dragged by some invisible force. This force… This creature…"

"*CREATURE!?*" cried out Tree. He had had more than enough. His emotions had been down, then raised up a little. Now he was being forced to listen to this annoying stick indulge itself in storytelling. "They are alive, yes?" he said, his anger clearly carried in his words.

"Yes", replied Matchwood, bluntly – realising that he had overstepped his bounds.

"Do you know where they are!?" asked Tree.

"Yes", replied Match.

"WHERE!?"

Matchwood was still and thoughtful for a moment. He had briefly considered a continuance of his full and detailed story but had decided against it. It was obvious to him now that he had been tolerated about as much as he was ever likely to be. He suddenly felt a pang of guilt about his selfishness. Realising that it was the life of his long-time companion that interested Tree, Match decided to submit to an earlier request and 'cut to the chase.'

"They are in a large, underground cavern. They were sucked into it through an opening at the bottom of the river…"

Tree and Slobber now sat, dumb struck by Matchwood's brief, precise description of where the other two were, and how they got there.

Pot and Frutely had been dragged into the submarine tunnel by something – Match hadn't seen what. Down and through they had gone, then up into an immense air pocket. Match hadn't seen what was behind the force that dragged them down and through the tunnel, but he did know that both Pot

and Frutely – though unconscious – were alive.
Tree and Slobber were once again silenced – both taking it all in. Tree, after some period of thought, and still preventing himself from being totally convinced of this momentous news, found himself immersed in one very simple and wholly reasonable question. "How exactly do you know all this? After all, when we found you…"
"Found!?" interrupted Slobber. "What do you mean, found!? The little sod was stuck in my leg!"
Tree was still suffering from the remnants of his anger virus, and his reply was a little less than sympathetic – "Who cares about your blasted leg! We are talking about my best friend here!"
Slobber, realising the gravity of Tree's feelings, quickly offered his apologies – allowing Tree to continue, this time without further interruption.
Tree's disbelief in what Matchwood had told them, was based partly on the fact that, in his mind at least, this news was far too good to be true – utterly welcome to be sure, but generally *too* good. Also, and this is where Tree felt he had conjured up a very valid point, was the very clear fact that, since their discovery that the large splinter was in fact a small piece of a talking boat, his general mental health had been questionable, to say the least!
"I accept that earlier my faculties were not completely within the realms of sanity", admitted Match. "I have explained the reasons for this clearly. I accept that it may have taken me a little time to, shall we say, find my bearings, but what I have told you has come from a fully-functioning and sane mind."
"A fully-functioning and sane mind would answer the question", pushed Tree impatiently.
Matchwood thought long and hard. "Alright," he eventually said, "I can see I am left with little choice… What I am about to tell you must go no further, understand?" With no acknowledgement one way or the other, Matchwood felt compelled to elaborate: "I'll tell you exactly how I know all this

but only if you *both* give me your solemn oath that it goes no further!"
Slobber agreed immediately. It hadn't occurred to him as to how Matchwood knew what he did – where the others were, how they got there, and why he knew where the rest of his body was. Tree, on the other hand, was less forthcoming. Eventually though – largely owing to Matchwood's patient silence, combined with Slobber's constant words of encouragement to agree – the little tree mumbled, "I suppose."
"That's not good enough!" said Matchwood. "This is important. I am breaking a sacred oath here. The least you can do, you arrogant twig," said Match – hoping to emphasise his point with a little abuse, "is give me a promise that I can trust!"
"If it's that important to you; if it will provide an answer to my question, then," replied Tree, "I swear on the roots of my forefathers that I will not repeat to anyone what you are about to tell me." This was quite some promise, Slobber thought – a little taken aback at the eloquence of his 'sticky' pal.
Tree continued… "May my branches be stripped of bark, and my…"
"Fine", interrupted Matchwood, a little concerned that Tree's promise could become a little extravagant, "Good enough."

It seemed an eternity before the stick spoke again. Matchwood had been silently weighing up whether he should divulge his secret – the secret of the Kia Willow as a race, as it turned out.
After careful consideration, he decided that he could trust Slobber…Tree, he wasn't so sure about, but for a Tanglepine to take an oath on the roots of its forefathers… All things considered, Matchwood, or at least what was left of him, decided to take a chance. "Kia Willows…" he said slowly, as though the words had to be physically ejected from him, "a*ll* Kia Willows are…are…"
"Are what!?" said Tree, his continued impatience finally getting

the better of him.
"Are... Telepathic!" said Match finally with a sigh of relief, actually panting a little, as though out of breath. As though saying one word was somehow, physically exhausting.
"Really!?" said Tree, with his typical cynicism.
"Only with other Kia's, of course..." said Match cheerfully. It was as if a huge weight – which he didn't even know he'd been carrying – had suddenly been lifted from his frame, "and pieces of ourselves, obviously", he chuckled.
"Telepathic!?" said Tree, almost with a feeling of contempt for this piece of deranged wood lying on the ground in front of him.
"Actually," said Slobber, his eyebrows raised, signalling that his mind was engaged in reasonable thought, "that makes a lot of sense."
"It does!?" queried Tree, "Why exactly!?"
Slobber considered the history of the use of Kia Willow in the ship-building trade, and the fact that its use was stopped for several reasons – one being that ships and boats would often, for no apparent reason, suddenly alter course and all meet up in the same place. "To catch up on all the gossip, presumably?" suggested Slobber.
"Basically. Telepathy is such a physically isolated method of communicating...at the end of the day, nothing beats a good old chinwag", offered Match.
Tree still wasn't convinced. After all he was a fellow tree – not the same species perhaps, but a tree nonetheless. *Surely,* he thought to himself, *such a secret would have got around. You can't keep secrets in a forest. All it would take is for just one Kia to mention it – perhaps talking in its sleep!*
"Telepathic?" he quizzed again, this time quietly. Thoughtfully. More to himself than anyone else.

With the veil of anger and general disbelief lifting from Tree's mind, combined with Slobber's further observations of Kia Willow boats' abilities in self-navigation, Tree found himself gently persuaded and his scepticism began to slowly subside.

“Telepathic, eh?” he said with the smallest hint of a smile in his voice.

“Yip. Telepathic”, replied Match, proudly.

“They’re alive?” said Tree, the relief of belief clearly detectable in his voice.

“Yip! They’re alive. Actually,” he said, adding a matter of general interest to the others, but sincere irritation to himself, “they’re currently being warmed by a fire.”

“A fire?”

“Yes. A lovely, raging fire… Fuelled by *my* bloody wood!”

CHAPTER NINETEEN

Potfondle coughed and spluttered himself into consciousness. He lay for a moment – on his side, his forehead resting on cold, hard rock – staring deeply into the lively, orange flames of a healthy fire.

"Are you alright?" came a friendly voice, startling Pot into further life. He sat up like a shot and saw, sitting cross-legged by his side, the sweet, smiling face of Dr Frutley Gaiberond.

"FRUTELY!" said Pot, his excited cry echoing loudly around the large cavern he now found himself in. "Frutely!" he repeated, this time in a whisper – his shoulders hunched as if attempting to avoid a further ricochet.

"Hello Pot", said Frutely, once the barrage of her name, echoing around the cavern walls, had diminished. "I'm glad to see you awake. How do you feel?"

Pot thought for a moment, as he glanced around, finally choosing to escape the confusion by languishing in the sight of the hypnotic flames. "Fine, I guess", he eventually replied, his voice offering testament to his fuddled mind.

Frutely smiled to herself. She had recovered very quickly. She hadn't so much passed out as collapsed from the exhaustion of her swim. Struggling against the current had been hard enough, but when she felt a force pulling her back, down into the gloom, the energy of blind panic had taken over and she had fought – albeit with no result – with all the energy she could muster.

Her memory after that was waking to find herself in an unfamiliar setting. Spotting Pot, she quickly ensured he was breathing – he was. Giving no real thought to her curious surroundings, she viewed the fire. Acting on instinct – not questioning who had set it, or even where they were – she brought the little Pillick to rest in its warm embrace, placing him on his side to recover himself. Only after she had sat down did she finally begin to take stock of their situation. Their entrance, she reasoned, must have been the pool: *must be a submerged entrance,* she concluded. The fire had been set at the top of a gentle slope, about 100 feet from the water. Sitting by the fire, Frutely had finally begun to looked around this large, dome-shaped cavern, cut into the living rock by some ancient force. She carefully studied the surface of its walls and ceiling – geology, after all, was her stock in trade. *They look smooth,* she thought, her brow furrowing with curiosity. She quickly rose to her feet and moved to an edge. As she gently ran her hand over the cold, hard surface of the wall, questions began to build, one on top of the other, in her mind. *What natural force could have possibly left this rock,* she pondered as her brow continued to furrow, almost covering her eyes with its depth, *this Zintal rock, so smooth?* "Smooth Zintal!?" she said aloud…very aloud in fact. So loud that her words forced her to duck instinctively, as the bullet of her enquiry shot around the vast space.

She couldn't believe it! Smooth Zintal rock! Not just a bit smooth – smooth enough but for the odd bump. This rock was completely, utterly smooth…like glass! She had never seen anything quite so beautiful. The veins of colour, normally just vaguely visible beneath its usually jagged exterior, were 'alive'. Blues, greens, reds, blacks all criss-crossed like the tracks of a busy rail depot. All snaking their own trail on a background of charcoal grey. She found herself almost lost in the tranquillity of its perfection as she gazed deeply into its gently flowing colours. She walked along the curved walls, trailing her hand dreamily over the stone surface, as though she were a child without a care in the world. Her head tilted to one side, as she immersed herself in the depths of colour, warmly lit by the friendly, orange glow of the fire. It was as though nothing else mattered. Nothing else existed. Frutely walked slowly around the gentle curve of this beautiful place without a single care in the world – humming quietly to herself. It was only when the smooth surface beneath her fingertips changed from glass to rough wood that she awoke from this dreamlike state. As her skin broke contact with the polished stone, the look of false tranquillity slipped from her face as though wiped away with an old cloth. She shook her head, as the reality of her situation reappeared with all the subtlety of a brick through a window. She fell against the large, wooden door – the touch of which had rescued her from the comfortable oblivion. She felt light-headed, unsteady on her feet. "What..? Where..?" she enquired almost incoherently. So dazed was she, that she could barely even manage to *think* in a straight line let alone talk or walk in one! Calmly, she took a moment to collect her thoughts, steadying herself against, what she now observed to be a very large, very heavy, closed door. With her chin against its surface, she looked up. The top of the door was so high as to be out of reach of the fire light. She retreated a little and found herself looking at one of two immense, black, metal hinges. Her disbelief clearly displayed on her face – all traces of childhood now gone – she stepped back even further. Then further still, her mouth open as her jaw dropped in wonder; her eyes wide with awe at this terrifying, mysterious sight.

Her mind raced with questions – *Who built it? When? Why?* As she continued back, stumbling on occasion, as what was before her was far more important than what was behind, she stared up – trying to make out where the top of this incredible

edifice was. As her eyes acclimatised to the gloom, she could just see where the door stopped. She tilted her head right back, straining her neck, to see that a perfect arch had been cut to accommodate the full height of this massive doorway – a massive arch for a massive doorway, carved to house a massive door – "By all the sciences", she whispered, believing it necessary to vocally display her feelings of respect and reverence at this truly magnificent place.
"Where are we?" asked Pot, once he had recovered himself enough to glance around at his new surroundings.
"I don't know", replied Frutely, her voice lowered as if in a library. "I've seen plenty of caves in my time but nothing that even comes close to this."
Pot followed her hand as she gestured for him to look about him. He followed her trail around the walls and then up to the heights of the ceiling. Only when her hand pointed in the direction of the door, did Pot find his tongue: "Blimey!" he said, "That is a seriously big door." Words then failed him as he, reflecting Frutely's earlier reaction, sat dumb-struck – jaw dropped in sheer awe. Only when he noticed the position of the large, round handle – hanging, like a giant knocker, about thirty feet from the foot of this large creation – did he once more, find the ability to articulate himself. "Giants!" he said, his voice echoing the trembling of his small frame.
"Not necessarily", said Frutely, in response. "Look at this place. Look at its beauty. The size of the door may simply be to add to the grandeur – This could be a place of worship or something. The Gods of the world usually require a lot of space, after all." Dr. Gaiberond had been so consumed – once her initial shock had subsided – with thoughts and theories as to the purpose of such a place, that she hadn't noticed the location of the handle on the door. It was only when Pot pointed at it, in order to provide a little background to his suggestion, that the idea of giants allowed itself to enter her mind.

Pot, consumed with images of large, hairy men, left the fireside to wander around and take a closer look at things. Cautiously, still trembling a little, he approached the door, running his hand over its rough surface – reaching as high as he could, in an attempt to touch the lowest of the large, perfectly distanced, equally spaced nails that occupied its surface. With one hand successfully grasping its rounded head, he reached up with his other hand and latched on. Once fixed, he heaved – trying to pull himself up. It was no good, his strength was not sufficient to lift him more than a few, measly inches from the ground. Pot stepped back and looked at the foot of the largest door he had ever seen, or even heard of. There was a gap between the foot and the floor, but a closer inspection – provided by Pot lying on his stomach – showed that it was too small to slither under.
"Can you see anything?" asked Frutely.
"Just darkness", replied Pot rising to his feet and brushing the dust from his front. "Cold, deep, scary darkness", he added, muttering under his breath. He stared up at the handle, "Looks like the handle to a latch, don't you think?" He moved away, aiming for the wall – "Lucky you were able to light a fire", he said, his attention still far removed from Frutely's direction.
Frutely stared into the energetic flames: "I didn't light it!" she said, her reverential whisper showing signs of quiet concern, "It was blazing away when I woke."
"WHAT!?" shouted Pot, causing another volley of loud echoes to fire around the walls and ceiling. Concerned that his involuntary shouts might arouse curiosity from the giants, he ran back to Frutely's side and quickly returned to a more sensible whisper. "Who lit it, then!?" With his adrenalin levels now peaking, he grabbed the end of a piece of wood and, clutching it like a sword, began to wave it around, searching out the invisible strangers he knew were hiding in the gloomier parts of the cavern. Frutely sighed to herself, *Better let him have his moment of masculinity,* she thought.
"You might as well come out!" he yelled, fear stripping him of

all sensible reason, as he stood with his back to the fire, waving his torch frantically. “Come on! we know you’re here. show yourselves!”

“You’re wasting your time”, said Frutely – offering the gentle voice of calm reason. “I’ve looked all around this place. There’s nobody here but us.”

“What!?” said Pot, continuing his irrational torch waving, “You looked around? On your own!?”

“Obviously on my own. You were asleep!” replied Frutely, her voice tinged with a little irritation at Pot’s inference that she was incapable of carrying out such a task. “Whoever set this fire…” she continued, “whoever brought us here in the first place, obviously means us no actual harm.” The logic of this statement was lost on Pot who, realising he had inadvertently given offence, stopped waving his stick around. Thinking for a moment, whilst staring into the colourful walls of the cavern, he eventually asked why Frutely thought they weren’t in any real danger.

“Whoever…” she stopped herself. She was about to say ‘whoever brought us here’ but decided against it. Pot was already a little shaken. *Introduce the notion that they had been deliberately delivered into this place and he might flip out completely,* thought Frutely. Such a prospect did not, however, bother her. Her mind was one consumed by scientific curiosity. Where she was, what force moulded it – built it, was far more important than who had delivered them up. Returning to the topic at hand, she continued: “Whoever lives here,” she quickly said, “could have easily killed us when we arrived…we were, after all, unconscious. They didn’t though…no, instead they brought us to this fabulous, wondrous place, lit an excellent fire and left us alone.”

“Ah!” said Pot, wishing to suggest his own theory at this point. “What if those who live here are giants?” he said, pointing at the door. “What if we were found by their evil servants. A bit of luck, they probably thought! Yeah, that’s it. They found us here in this place of…of,” he began to falter, looking for a word that he eventually, unfortunately found, “sacrifice!” His imagination begun to get the better of him, as his trepidation began to create a peculiar 'truth' concerning their environment and recent history. "That's why we are alone. That's why they quickly cleared off. They don't want to become victims themselves. After all…two small Pillicks? Not much of a feed for a giant!" At this point he realised exactly what it was he was actually saying. As the remaining colour began to drain from his face, he swallowed deeply as the sickening fear rose: "For the love of toast!" he simpered, "We're sacrifices to a giant. A giant with a taste for Pillick." He sank to his knees with a thump and stared at the ground, desperately trying not to cry in front of the good doctor.

Bringing a halt to his trembling chin, he drew a deep breath and slowly pulled himself back onto his feet. He stood, looking vaguely heroic, for a moment, gathering his fading courage. "Well," he said, placing one hand on his hip and pointing his still burning torch at the door, "if he thinks this light snack is going to give up without a fight, he's got another think coming!" His volume increased once more and his tone deepened with defiance, as he attempted to add weight to his words. He moved out, striding around the cave, waving his torch, cutting and stabbing the air. He glanced quickly at Frutely, who looked up at him with just the merest hint of a smile.

"I will place myself in harm's way, fair maiden", he said, standing with legs apart, attempting his most heroic stance yet. "I will fight him and pay for your escape with my own life." Striding forth as a hero would, he allowed a dramatic silence to descend before returning to motionlessness. "Then," he said, continuing his 'masterful' speech, "with your departure assured…" pausing yet again, for even greater effect, "I'll give that swine the worst case of indigestion he's *ever* had!" and with that he delivered a dramatic nod of his head – a visible display of his determination – before leaning back against the wall, where he now found himself standing.

Frutely had been sitting, listening to Pot's heroics – a smile slowly beginning to grace her face. She had found it all vaguely absurd but thought too, that Potfondle had looked strangely attractive as he strutted about, vowing to protect her with his last ounce of strength. She snapped herself out of the dream state she had permitted herself to slip into and, with some small sense of embarrassment, wiped the girlish smile from her face.

She looked over at Pot, checking more than anything else, that he hadn't noticed the glimmer of admiration that had begun to appear – albeit without her consent – in the eyes and lips of her face.

She looked at Pot, and Pot, leaning against the cavern wall, looked back. His face was still, serene; a smile of contentment on his lips and a look of bliss in his eyes. *Oh no! He saw me,* she thought. *He saw me and now I'm going to have to come up with something pretty fast.*

Frutely did like Pot, but she had absolutely no intention of declaring anything more for him than passing friendship. She decided to return his looks of longing with a simple smile. *Look into his eyes,* she thought, *and smile back. Then quickly look away and pretend to be interested in something else. It's just a smile of friendship. That's all, nothing more.* Not entirely convinced, Frutely performed her mentally rehearsed smile and looked away. Quickly choosing to study the door once again, she jumped back into a past conversation: "Besides," she said "I've never met a giant. There's nothing to suggest they're hostile..." Receiving no comment from Pot, she forced herself to deliver a fleeting glance in his direction, before fixing her eyes back to the door. "Have you ever met one?" she asked, for some reason finding herself stuck for words. With still no response of any kind coming from Pot, Frutely looked at him again – for longer this time. He was still standing against the wall, motionless, his face still occupied by a look of total contentment. Frutely waved her hand. Nothing. She stood up and walked over to him – "POT!" she yelled. Nothing. It was then that it suddenly dawned on her – "Oh Gods!" she uttered, "He's drifted off!" She grabbed his hands, hoping to pull him away but he locked his legs and stood firm. She hit his arm but got no response. She slapped his face but only made his cheek red. *There's nothing else to do,* she reluctantly concluded. *Right. Here goes,* she told herself in preparation, before pressing her lips to his and delivering a gentle kiss – her eyes wide open, anxious for signs of consciousness. Observing no reaction, she allowed the gentle kiss to grow into a snog. This, she noticed, did cause a glimmer of reaction. There was nothing else for it. It had to be done and Frutely knew it… The snog became a 'Frenchie'!

Frutely found herself carried away. Upon Pot's full recovery, the kiss became a full and mutual embrace. The pair moved away from the wall and Frutely opened her eyes, which quickly widened into a display of horror. She pushed Potfondle away and, coming quickly to her senses, apologised... "It was the only way to bring you out of the trance", she said, not that Pot required any form of explanation.

"What trance?" said Pot, a smirk of self satisfaction on his face.

"This wall. This rock. Maybe it's this whole place. I don't know…" said Frutely, seeking solace in scientific supposition and patting the air near the rock, ensuring her hand didn't make contact, "There's something in the rock perhaps," she said shaking her head as she tried to make sense of it, "you went into a trance as soon as you touched the rock. The same thing happened to me while you were sleeping." It didn't make sense to her. Zintal rock didn't possess such a power. True, this was the first time she had seen some that looked like this… *It doesn't make any sense at all!* was the single, repetitive thought that ran through her mind.

"Quickly," she said, grabbing Pot by his shoulders, "what was going through your mind during your encounter?"

"You're a good kisser", replied Pot, the smirk on his face transforming into a boyish grin.

"No!" snapped Frutely, "During your trance! What was going

through your mind?"
"What trance?" said Pot, a small frown of puzzlement crossing his brow.
Frutely released him and sighed to herself – "I forgot about mine too. Almost immediately."
"Sorry", said Pot "I really don't know what you're talking about..." Attempting to make Frutely feel better, Pot decided to offer some positive words – "It was a very good kiss, though. I don't know about bringing me *out* of a trance but it could very easily put me into one...a very nice one."
Frutely shook her head, partly in embarrassment, partly because she couldn't think up a suitable reply. In actual fact, she had enjoyed it too. The enjoyment she felt had left her with feelings of vague anger, and her inability to formulate a suitable reply to Pot's compliment merely served to exaggerate her frustration. It was with a strange sense of relief therefore, that their joint attention was suddenly interrupted by the sound of someone, or something, opening the door.

CHAPTER TWENTY

Slobber tore some cloth from the bottom of his trousers and used it as a bandage on his injured leg. Getting to his feet, he stood silently for a while, looking out across the water. “Right!” he said decisively, “Let’s find ‘em.”

Matchwood, his mental powers now fully restored suggested a direction. Though not large enough to posses the power of sight, he did have a generally sound knowledge of the area. His telepathic abilities – linking him to the pieces of his larger body, now fuelling the fire that warmed Potfondle and Frutely – had given him a very real sense of where they were.

The plan was simple. Slobber would dive into the Twit and swim about until he located the submerged tunnel. Once done, he would return to the bank and retrieve Tree and Match.

The big, blue chap waded in until the water was up to his armpits. Then, first allowing his drool to empty out, he drew a deep breath before disappearing under the now tranquil surface.

The two wooden, life forms sat on the bank, Tree providing detailed descriptions of what he could see – this really

amounted to nothing more than a list: Fish jumping, twig floating, Twit Rat cleaning itself, and so on. One minute passed, followed by another, then another. It was following this third minute that Tree began to feel pangs of anxiety.
"How long can a Slobber hold its breath?" he quizzed with quiet concern.
"Not sure", was Matchwood's brief reply. "Seen any bubbles?"
"Lads?" came the unseen shout from Slobber. He'd lost his bearings a little and had surfaced further down river.
"This way!" cried out Tree, by way of assistance.
"Found it yet?" shouted Match.
Slobber's first attempt had been unsuccessful. He swam back to the area of bank occupied by his two friends – "Perhaps a little further up?" he offered.
"Of course!" cried Matchwood, "How could I have been so stupid!?" Match was not best pleased with himself. To his shame, it hadn't occurred to him to factor in their original rate of drift during their little tussle with the curious bore. To make amends for this unforgivable oversight, he quickly calculated roughly how far they would have been carried down the river.
"By my reckoning," he said after a period of quietly muttering to himself, "we need to go about 100 yards up-stream."
Slobber climbed back onto dry land. He carefully placed the small piece of Matchwood in a pocket and tucked Tree, still in his bucket, under one arm. Then – still limping slightly – he set off through the trees, heading further up-river.

"Sorry about your leg", said Match, feeling the gentle lurch of Slobber's limping.
"It's OK", replied Slobber cheerfully "You didn't do it on purpose."
"I don't know quite how to tell you this…" said Match, his voice laced with embarrassment and a little guilt, "Actually, I did…Sorry!"
Slobber waved off this further apology suggesting that Match shouldn't feel guilty about it – "It really wasn't your fault, Match. Just an accident, that's all."

"No", said Match, desperately needing to clear his conscience. "You don't understand, Slobs…" pausing, he tried to formulate a suitably apologetic explanation – "Me being stuck in your leg…it wasn't an accident. It *was* intentional." He waited for a moment, expecting shouts of outrage – none came.
"Actually," he continued, needing to fill this uncomfortable silence, "me being broken off in the first place wasn't an accident either."
Slobber frowned to himself but still said nothing. It was Tree – unsurprisingly – who decided to add something to the, so far, one-sided discussion. "What!?" he said, "Why on earth would you intentionally damage yourself!?"
Slobber seemed to be a couple of steps behind in these proceedings – "You stabbed me on purpose?" he said quietly, the creases of his frown deepening. "You actually stabbed me in the leg on purpose!?" There was still no detectable anger in his voice, his questions though, did seem to be gaining something in the 'slightly cheesed off' area.
Tree's question had slipped past without much notice. Since he was now far more interested in observing the result of Slobber's intensifying irritation, he chose not to repeat it.
Slobber stopped, reached into his pocket and pulled out the offending stick, holding it up for inspection by his now glowering eyes. "Let's get this straight…" he said, his voice starting to show signs of sarcasm and irony – something Tree spotted straight away, "This morning you intentionally damaged yourself, ripping away this dagger I now see before me..?" the level of detectable cynicism in Slobber's voice had Tree almost laughing with glee although, for his own safety, he managed to keep his pleasure from becoming audible. Being something of a devotee of the art of sarcasm, he was well aware of its power, along with its habit of spreading out to anyone who happened to be nearby.
"Tell me something Match - Wood. Had it been your cunning plan all along to stab me? Are you serving some psychopathic need? Was I the original target for your insanity, or did my leg take the place of Frutely's arm or Pot's

buttocks?" Slobber was really in his stride now. "Please, my dear twig, explain to me how long ago this curious plot began..." his voice beginning to change a little, as a hint of anger started to creep in, "Really, do tell...I'm curious to know exactly when you decided it was necessary to launch a physical assault on me!?"

Tree desperately wanted to clap but could manage no more than a gentle shaking of one of his branches.

"Well!!?" said Slobber, genuinely angry at this point.

Matchwood sighed deeply. "I knew this morning that my part in this adventure would be at an end before long. My intention, in letting myself get injured, was to tear off a small enough piece to be easily carried in one of the bags..." he offered another deep sigh before admitting, "I really wanted to come with you. I'm old, not long for this world... I just wanted one last bit of excitement."

Neither Slobber or Tree spoke for a time – both quite touched by Matchwood's admission. Realising that he had their ear, Match decided to continue... "When the wave hit and I realised that my capsize was inevitable..."

"Yes?" said Slobber, curious as to how this story ends.

"Well, I was concerned that something like this would happen – the group being separated, I mean. I believed that my telepathic ability might prove useful...and you have to admit it has. I'm afraid that jabbing myself into your leg was the first thing that crossed my mind. The only way I could guarantee that I would remain with at least one of you."

Slobber was thoughtful. "So," he said, "it was just pot luck that it was *my* flesh you ended up in?"

"Afraid so", admitted Match, "Yours was the first body I made contact with. I am sorry. If I could have thought of another way, I would have."

Slobber was inclined to be forgiving. He could see the logic of what Match was saying. He was right, his knowledge, experience, and abilities had served a very great purpose. He'd got them this far and had confirmed that Pot and Frutely were still alive – not only alive, but also a general idea of

where they were. Tree too, had to admit that as attacks go this one was motivated by good intentions.
"Did you really hit that rock on purpose?" asked Tree as the party set off once more.
"Of course!" replied Matchwood, "I'm far too good a sailor to have not been aware of its presence."
"Not too good with waves though, are you?" reminded Tree, borrowing some of Slobber's earlier sarcasm.

They had walked about 100 yards up river. Slobber stood surveying their surroundings, which did look familiar. After describing what he could see to Match, they concluded that this was roughly the place. Slobber set down his cargo and limped back into the river – disappearing once more beneath the calm surface. He dived down several times before eventually achieving success. His head breached the surface, preceded by a raised hand, clenched into a fist of victory – "YES!" he shouted, turning quickly to make a mental note of exactly where, in relation to the bank, he was.
Swimming back to where his companions sat, he congratulated Match on his powers of navigation – "Talk about blind faith", he quipped.
Quickly picking up the stick and returning him to his pocket, Slobber was surprised to find that Tree was actually keen to get back in the water. "You really do care for the little guy, don't you?" he said, with a gentle laugh of understanding.
"Well..." said Tree, dropping his tough front, "He is my oldest friend."
Tying Tree's bucket handle to his belt, Slobber once more emptied his drool pouches and jumped back into the Twit. He took a very deep breath, checked that everyone was ready and dived down – heading straight for the tunnel opening.

CHAPTER TWENTY-ONE

The large, circular handle jiggled and jostled before slowly moving – rotating anti-clockwise. Pot suddenly found his hand in Frutely's – their combined grip on one another tightening as the fear of uncertainty began to dominate their minds. Both watched, wide eyed, jaws dropped about as far as it is possible for a jaw to fall. Both were frozen – hypnotised by the slow movement of the tremendous handle. Pot managed to eke out "Giants!" his voice trembling as his imagination conjured up pictures of the truly grotesque. Curiously enough, the early heroics of which he had recently described engaging in, didn't seem to materialise themselves. His blazing sword of fire was not suddenly slicing the air, and his body had managed to move itself slightly, so that he was actually just behind Frutely rather than in front – guarding her 'escape.' Frutely herself hadn't noticed this absence of bravado as her mind (contaminated by Potfondle's description of Pillick sacrifice) was busy trying to free itself from the image of a hairy giant bursting through the door, its intent firmly fixed on the notion of a light snack before dinner. As a scientist, her thoughts were desperate to offer some other explanation for who might now appear before them. *Perhaps,* she thought, really clutching at straws, *the corridor beyond this portal is different. Perhaps the handle on the exterior is smaller and lower down. Perhaps a system of gears and pulleys allow someone of a more usual height to simply twist a small knob at the foot of the door…* Even she had to admit to herself that these ideas were a tad naive. The harsh reality she had to face was that the handle on the other side was most likely a duplicate of that which held her attention so strongly.

CRUNCH! came the sound as the ring suddenly halted its movement – its task of lifting the latch done. Pot and Frutely began to shudder – for Frutely this was extremely embarrassing and her logical mind cursed her for it: '*What do you think you are doing!?*' it said. '*You are a woman of science and yet here you are shaking like a child!*' Reasonable thought was, at this juncture, utterly pointless, and Frutely's words to herself went completely unnoticed as the psychology of fear took over completely. The choice of running away had not even allowed itself to be presented, as both Pillicks found themselves powerless to do anything but stare before them, as the enormous slab of wood slowly swung out, offering a deep, drawn out, yawning creak.
Potfondle and Frutely stared – eyes almost out of their heads, utterly terrified by the vision which now presented itself to them. The smooth hair that coated their bodies, stood to attention and all the colour drained from their exposed skin. Potfondle wished he could just pass out, and he wasn't alone. Frutely too, if truth be known, also wished that the protective veil of unconsciousness would wrap itself around her, its gift of ignorance allowing her to suffer the torment of what she believed was at hand – unconcerned and more importantly, unfeeling.
Unfortunately for the two Pillicks, the fear creature, which had so successfully set up home in their hearts, minds and mouths, had added a new, sickeningly ironic twist… Morbid fascination!
The doorway, now fully exposed, offered no further insight into

what lay beyond. Almost the full space, hidden by the door, was now occupied by a giant. Not a big, hairy creature – dispossessed of much intelligence and claiming the worst smelling breath on the planet – as Pot's mind had conjured. No, what stood before them was far more terrifying…
The creature stood motionless, looking not at its appetiser on the ground but straight ahead – it's lifeless, black eyes barely visible to those on the floor. Frutely suddenly found a little composure, as her scientific curiosity – a trait which had been with her all her life – suddenly emerged from its hiding place, making a little space for itself in a body otherwise consumed by fear. She looked up, studying this creature of myth. Its eyes, large and black, seemed not even to permit reflection as they sat motionless under the shelf of the beast's horn-rimmed brow. Scanning her eyes up a little, Frutely gazed upon the crown – two small ears set in front of two large, curling horns. To the side of these, concluding the symmetry at the top of this dull-grey head, were two small horns, which stuck out like tiny mountains. The creature remained utterly still, as though inviting examination, offering a statuesque pose – allowing its meal to view the terrifying splendour of its full, fantastic presence. Frutely's eyes trailed past its long nose – the nostrils flaring dramatically at its tip – down its smooth, dull-grey neck. There were no shoulders to speak of, as its long arms flowed out from this streamlined body – one clawed hand resting against the side of the doorway, the other still holding the handle prisoner in its mighty grip. Its sleek, dark-grey scales, which coated the surface of the monster, changed little in shade except for on its snakelike belly. Here, as though bored with the lack of colour, they changed – presenting a long ellipse of deep, dark red. This display of colour ran from the middle of the chest, down to where its short, powerful legs protruded, connecting the body to the ground. Finally, its feet found themselves in Frutely's view. They were large and flat – they looked webbed. There were no toes to be observed, just large, hooked claws. Though still terrified, Frutely's re-awakened scientific mind, concluded that

there must be a tail. Sure enough there was, though obstructed from her view by the towering leviathan. She theorised, quite calmly considering her circumstance, that such an appendage would be long and most likely forked, its tip ending in two, perhaps three, large spines. Since the only thing that even came close to this monster were childish descriptions of sea creatures, Frutely presumed the tail would include some form of webbing – enabling the thing to move swiftly through the water.

Pot sat as though frozen while Frutely continued her ever more considered visual examination – seeking out the detail. Her eyes rose once more then widened, her jaw dropping once more, her subtle head movement brought to an abrupt end as she met the life-sucking gaze of the creature's emotionless eyes. Slowly it moved its head down, studying its extremely small meal. It offered no expression, no sound, before suddenly lunging towards the Pillicks. The last thing Frutely saw, before her eyes – totally without her consent – screwed tightly shut, were two long fangs. Glistening white, they hung like stalactites from the upper jaw of the creature's long snout.

Pot, still motionless, watched – too terrified even to close his eyes – as the creature's head threw itself forward. Its teeth and neck heading for the couple like a runaway train. The vision of this terror was so striking that it didn't even leave room for Pot's life to flash before his eyes.

The beast's sharp movement cut through the air. All was lost. All was about to end. Pot, accepting that his life was about to come to a dreadful and final conclusion, suddenly found himself feeling a warm sense of calm. Gently closing his eyes, Pot suddenly felt like he was floating – up and away from the torment about to deliver itself upon him. His consciousness left his doomed body and drifted up towards the ceiling. All the troubles and cares of his world departed as dispassionately, he watched the events below. With little concern now, he witnessed the creature's head lunge towards

his body, and the body of Frutely. He glanced around, hoping that her consciousness too, had decided to vacate, before the gnashing of teeth and the crunching of bone began.
Oh! thought Pot's floating self, with the surprise one experiences when coming across some forgotten money in a pocket, *that's curious*. The creature had stopped, its still-flaring nostrils just inches away from the two bodies. It snorted and sniffed, the force of the air from its nose nearly knocking the duo onto their backs.
The consciousness of Pot gave a silent scream as it suddenly found itself sliding back down into its body, landing with a bump. He opened his eyes as Frutely opened hers and both looked, through half-closed, fearful lids at this giant nose that now sniffed at them. Their eyes once again widened as the nose drew itself away, back up into the heights. Pot and Frutely exchanged brief, terrified glances – frowns of wonder at why it was they were still alive – before directing their view back to the object of their inevitable destruction.
The creature reared up once more and then brought its head, slowly this time, back down to Pot and Frutely's level. With its chin hovering mere inches from the floor, it glanced at Pot and then at Frutely – who both stared back, like rabbits caught in the headlights of an oncoming vehicle. The creature raised its heavy, overhanging brows – allowing its face to suddenly look far less frightening – and its huge mouth opened, allowing the Pillicks to see its impressive display of sharp, white teeth…
"Oh splendid!" it said in very precise, accurate tones – much to the dismay of Pot and Frutely. "You're both alive…Not only alive but awake. How marvellous. Oh I am so very pleased!"
Pot's frown was echoed on the face of Frutely as both looked at each other quizzically. "Yyyyou pppprefer your fffood to bbbbbe alive, I suppose?" stuttered Pot – surprised that he actually had the guts to speak in the first place.
"Food!?" said the creature, its head quickly drawing back – seemingly startled by this suggestion. "You think I want to eat you!?" it added, seemingly both startled, and insulted, by the idea.

"You're not going to eat us, then?" offered Frutely quietly, not entirely sure that she had read the situation correctly.
"Good heavens no!" replied the creature with a slight chuckle in its voice, a small smile creeping across its long mouth. "Eat *you*!? The very idea!" The creature raised up again as if wishing to distance itself further from this clearly embarrassing and distasteful subject. "What on earth would bring you to reach such a dreadful conclusion?" he asked, but before either had the opportunity to suggest a possible answer, the creature, quickly analysed his entry and general appearance. With a single snort of laughter, the beast dismissed his own enquiry: "Scratch that", he said, obviously aware of his own image, "Silly question. Please forgive me. I certainly didn't intend to frighten you." The creature took a few moments to adjust itself, choosing to lie on its side, propping its huge head on one hand in a very casual manner. "I must say, it was something of a surprise to find visitors in my hallway. As you can imagine, I don't receive too many guests." Its manner was very informal, as though it were chatting with old friends who had just popped by. "I'm so glad you recovered", it said, fixing its gaze on Pot in particular, "Honestly, I was in something of dilemma over what I should do with you." The creature sat thoughtfully for the briefest of moments. "I mean, mouth to mouth was rather out of the question!"
Pot said nothing, a little confused as to whether he should still be scared. *After all,* he thought, *this could all be a con. Lulling us into a false sense of security before suddenly gobbling us up.* The creature waited for a reaction from Pot to its observation. Receiving none, it concluded that the joke was lost – an explanation was clearly due. "Mouth-to-mouth…" he repeated, smiling and reaching across to give Pot a very gentle tap on the shoulder with one of its claws, "I mean, you might have stuck in my teeth or drowned in my saliva. Worse still, perhaps," he said with a chuckle, "what if you'd woken up…reached the wrong conclusion? Honestly! Can you imagine the embarrassment!?"
Realising that Pot's silence was induced by continued

apprehension, the creature decided to try and put everyone at their ease. It explained that they had appeared from nowhere, in what he advised them was the front hall of his summer home. Not entirely sure what he could do to offer the most assistance, he had lit a fire – hoping that its warmth would bring them around. That done he had left them in peace.
"How long have you lived here?" asked Frutely, curious that she had never even heard of anything like him before.
"Oh several hundred years, on and off", said the creature. "I have several homes around the world. This is where I like to hang my hat so to speak...here for a month or so, during the summer months. Gweep is so perfect in the sunshine, don't you think?"

As the creature continued, gesturing wildly with its free arm, describing the splendour of its home – once the Summer Palace of the Royal Family – he suddenly found his lecture rudely interrupted by a loud shriek of surprise coming from the entry pool. This shriek was then followed by extremely rude shouting – 'Get away from it!' and 'Quickly, before it eats you!' The creature, and indeed the two Pillicks, turned to see the cause of the commotion. The creature frowned with concern and then smiled with delight as it observed a large – or rather, from its perspective – a small, blue person emerging from the water, waving his arms about and shouting very loudly.
"More visitors…" it said excitedly, "How marvellous!"

Slobber ran, still limping, towards the group, his arms flailing about – "Get away from it! Come on you two, this way! Out through the pool!" he shrieked. "Ya! Ya!" shouted Slobber, as though he were trying to frighten away a herd of sheep, "Shoo! Shoo!"
"Is *he* with you?" asked the creature of Frutely from the side of its mouth. He really wanted to laugh but chose not to, fearing his outburst may insult this absurd individual.
"I'm afraid so", replied Frutely, who had become quite comfortable in the company of her startling, new companion.

She quickly rose to her feet and ran towards the approaching Slobber, her arms raised in an attempt to pacify her frantic friend. "There's no danger", she assured him. "The creature means us no harm…"
"Creature! What creature?" asked Matchwood. "Quickly, describe it!"
Frutely, upon hearing Match's voice looked around to see him but could not. "Match?"
"Yes, yes I'm here!" he replied sharply.
"Where?"
"Never mind that now", he snapped. "Quickly, describe what this creature looks like."
Frutely was quiet for a moment – puzzled by the request to describe something that was pretty difficult to miss. "He's blind..." offered Slobber – his eyes now displaying the same look of general apprehension that still existed in the face of Potfondle, "...I'll explain later."
Frutely still didn't fully understand but decided to do as she was asked, giving the invisible Matchwood a complete description of the mythical animal. She was then about to explain the circumstances of how they came to be there, and what she had discovered about the beast thus far, before Match cut her short.
"We must all leave here immediately! We are in terrible danger!"
"No we're not!" said Frutely dismissively. "This creature…" she stopped abruptly and turned her head, looking up at the giant with a gentle frown – "What is your name?" she said, "We can't keep calling you 'The Creature!'"
"Quite right", agreed the monster, jumping to its feet – causing the ground to tremble slightly. "I'm dreadfully sorry! How terribly rude of me…" it said, scanning its eyes across the faces of its increasing number of visitors.
"I am…"
"Nassian!" interrupted Match, rather impolitely. "You are Nassian! The Destroyer."
"You know him!?" quizzed both Slobber and Frutely.

"Oh yes. I know this beast." All remained silent, even the creature whose face dropped with shock at the story Match now imparted to the group as to who, and what Nassian was.

Stunned, Frutely looked up at Nassian, delivering a look of sheer disappointment. "Is this true?" she asked. "Do you wreck ships and eat sailors!?" She was horrified at the idea. She had begun to relax in the easy company of this charming creature and now, here she was facing the prospect that he was nothing more than a monster after all.

Nassian too, seemed disappointed in his turn. Ashamed by the tale and hurt that people whose lives he had saved now questioned his integrity. He drew a deep breath and seemed to swallow a lump in his throat. "Firstly," he said, "may I be permitted to see the face of my accuser?"

With Matchwood's consent, Slobber drew the wooden shard from his pocket and held it out in front of him for the creature to study.

"Hmm!" said Nassian calmly, lowering his head to take a long and considered look at his judge and jury. "Kia Willow, I presume?"

"Matchwood!" replied Matchwood abruptly, "Kia to the core, mate!"

"Obviously", said Nassian, with a quiet chuckle – making reference to the noble boat's current appearance. Thinking better of it, and since no one appeared to be sharing the joke, the creature apologised: "Forgive me, my friend, that was rude of me."

"Save it for the judge!" snapped Matchwood. "You don't fool me with your posh voice and false courtesy. You're a killer!"

The huge creature looked across their faces, his eyes resting on Frutely: "A little knowledge is a dangerous thing, wouldn't you say", he said, again with a vague chuckle in his voice although, his eyes – Frutely noticed – quite clearly displayed the look of a being whose feelings had been hurt. She was about to offer an apology when the creature continued:

"Nassian," he said, directing his words at the stick, "is the name of my *species*. Its actual meaning in the ancient tongue, is 'Lord Of The Depths' – not Destroyer!" He paused for a moment to permit time for feelings of regret to become apparent in Matchwood. With none forthcoming he continued. "*My* name, for anyone who is interested…" this time looking into the faces of Potfondle and Frutely specifically, "is Sebastian…" pausing again as he raised his nose into the air – offering a pose of obvious pride, "meaning 'Reverence' in the language of my forebears." Moving his head back down, he once more stared firmly at Matchwood. "My appearance has, over time, caused many inaccurate – and I might add – slanderous stories about me to circulate." He turned, taking great care not to swipe anyone with his lethal tail, and walked slowly and silently towards the door. Frutely for one, felt the sharp jab of shame. She was, once again, about to offer words of apology for being so quick to believe Matchwood's tale, when Sebastian stopped and turned back to face them. He raised his arms and lifted his head high – "Keltremancian," he whispered, and as he did so the room suddenly became bathed in a warm, white light which seemed to emanate from behind the glassy surface of the colourful walls.

The eyes of the group widened with surprise at this truly magnificent spectacle. The colours Frutely had observed before were now far more intense. She could see that the lines of blue, green, red, and black did not actually cross one another – one breaking the form of the other. No, the lines ran behind and in front, creating a beautiful three-dimensional pattern.

"This is the entrance to the ancient Palace of Mantura", announced Sebastian loudly – drawing everyone's attention back to him. "Once the great rooms, which lay beyond this understated door, were alive with the sounds of laughter and conversation. Hundreds of my people would congregate here, to talk of the world and speak with our noble and wise King and Queen." The group gazed around at the walls and ceiling, much impressed with the glory of it all. Sebastian had fallen silent, he turned his head to the floor and lowered his arms to his sides. "Alas," he said with obvious regret, "that was all so long ago. I was just a pup…" his voice trailed off and tears appeared to form in his eyes, as thoughts of happier times filled his mind. The five explorers felt compelled to move towards him; join him in an offering of apologetic sympathy. Sebastian stared down at his feet as the group congregated at his ankle, offering pats of empathy to his scales.

"My people," sniffed Sebastian, "began to die out…slowly, over hundreds of years. Our ability to reproduce seemed to vanish overnight…I was one of the last."

"What happened?" shouted Frutely. "What killed them?"

"Men!" offered Matchwood quietly, thoughtfully.

"We killed your people!?" said Slobber, his face filled with regret as he somehow felt responsible for the actions of his gender.

"Men, and indeed women, were no threat to us", replied Sebastian upon hearing Matchwood's suggested explanation for his race's near extinction. "Bipeds at this time were limited in their intelligence", he continued, delivering a look of apology to those bipeds present. "They shared our homes. Acting as cleaners, they kept our halls free from discarded scraps of food and such. They lived on what we threw away."

"You lot were mice, then!" smirked Tree, who until now had been uncharacteristically silent – his comment directed at his companions.

"Well, I suppose one could make that analogy", answered Sebastian, his small ears belying acute hearing. "Personally, I like to think of those early men as…" he struggled to think of an inoffensive description.

"Pets?" offered Tree.

"As companions in life", he eventually said, finding something suitably pleasant and honourable. "We gave them large, safe homes in which to live and they…"

"Lived in filth and ate garbage?" offered Tree, truly enjoying the cynical images running through his mind.

"Whilst I wouldn't put it quite so indelicately," said Sebastian, "that's basically it… In any event," he quickly added, directing his words to Match, "we most certainly did not eat them! My diet, and indeed the diet of my people, consists largely of fish."

Sebastian continued with the history of his people and their eventual demise. Since Nassians were so long-lived, they apparently didn't notice the lack of youngsters for some time. Sebastian explained that his race choose a mate once they reach their 500th birthday – an age it was thought, where enough time had been spent living to 'put away childish things' – as he put it. By the age of 500, a Nassian would have formed many friendships and associations, and it would normally be the case that a male and a female would have already decided whether or not they were right for each other. The marriage itself was an extremely simple affair. The King or Queen would simply call a prospective couple to their audience chamber and ask: 'Do you decide to be together from this day forth?' If the answer from both of them was 'yes', that was that – they were married and expected to stay true to one another for the rest of their lives.
Once a decision to have offspring had been reached, the couple would go off to a far away place and alone, bring physical expression to their commitment. "And because raising children," said Sebastian, "is such a demanding job – particularly when you're talking about a pregnancy that lasts for over three years, and an infancy which last for about 120 – a couple would normally only have one pup in their lifetime."
It was for these reasons, it had been suggested, the Nassian race had been slow to realise, that nursery places were somewhat easier to come by than in the past.
Frutely in particular was fascinated by what Sebastian was telling them. An hour ago, she hadn't even heard of Nassians. Now, here she was receiving a history lecture from one! She desperately wanted to interrupt and enquire as to the actual reason for his people's departure, but didn't want to intrude on his account of an obviously painful period in his own personal history.

Sebastian described how the King had called together all of his wisest advisors. "My mother was one", he said proudly. "She was one of my people's most respected physicians."
Not a particularly observant doctor! thought Tree, preventing his cynical observation from manifesting itself into audible words – now aware of Sebastian's fine sense of hearing.
This Council debated the problem for years. Tests were carried out and envoys went out into the world, searching for a possible reason – all to no avail.
"The millennia rolled on and our…'Garbage Men'," said Sebastian with a nod to Tree, "evolved and left our homes. As time passed, they forgot about us…not that there were many of us left to remember…" He fell silent once more. When he had recovered himself he continued his lecture, explaining that those who were left, a mere handful – the last to be born – disbanded. "I have a cousin who lives in the north. A peculiar land, where the men wear skirts and for some cruel reason, torture these colourful, multi-legged animals that seem to live there!"
"Torture!?" squealed Pot.
"Yes. Its rather a curious thing actually. The men blow down the creatures' noses, inflating their stomachs with air. Then they squeeze their air-filled bellies, forcing the air out through their hollow legs!"
"How cruel!" said Slobber.
"I suppose so", replied the giant. "Actually, the sound becomes quite harmonious after a time. My cousin tells me that he has never seen the animals out in the wild. His theory is that they are bred specifically for the purpose of being inflated. Either way, there's no obvious evidence that the creatures are unduly concerned by their treatment."
Frutely could contain her scientific curiosity no longer – "What actually happened to your people!?" she said, somewhat impatiently, quickly apologising and repeating her question more sympathetically.
"It was never discovered," replied Sebastian, thoughtfully, "possibly a sickness brought to us by a large chunk of outer

space, which apparently hit our world. Perhaps it was just our time to go."
"And the others...?" pushed Frutely.
"Others?"
"The others who still live... Your cousin... Have you tried to have young?"
"Curiously enough," said Sebastian, his brow raised high, "since my cousin is male..."
"No!" interjected Frutely – desperate to find an answer to her query – "You said there were others. Did no females survive?"
Sebastian advised her that two females were among those who remain. "Several attempts have been made to produce young," he said, "but with no success." He then stated that since bringing up the young was such a commitment of time, none of the survivors were of a suitable age to properly perform the task. "I myself, only have a couple of hundred years left."
This news, said with such resignation, caused an uneasy silence to descend over the group. True to form it was Tree who asked the question all the others were thinking: "How old are you, then?"
"Three-thousand, four-hundred and twenty-two", came Sebastian's swift reply.
"Bloody hell!" said Pot, without really thinking.

"Well," said Sebastian, changing the subject and causing a sound like a clap of thunder as he struck his webbed, clawed hands together, "if you'll excuse me, I'll fix you something to eat. I hope you enjoy fish." With that he swiftly turned about and walked out of the room, reaching for the door and closing it behind him. So keen did he seem to remove himself that he very nearly trapped his long, snakelike tail in the closing door.
"Great!" said Pot, his observation initially lost on the others. "Locked in again!"

CHAPTER TWENTY-TWO

Above, the ground shook harder than it ever had before. The group of people that had congregated around the broken hull of Matchwood, struggled to stay on their feet. The few houses that lined the shore shook and shuddered. Roof slates slipped, fences fell flat, and windows cracked, although, curiously enough, none of these dwellings actually fell completely apart. This wasn't because the build quality was so good, quite the opposite. The quality was in fact so bad that the houses merely rocked from side to side like reeds blowing in a gale.

The crowd of people – who had been alerted to the presence of the talking bits of wood by a little Pillick, who had been out walking a very reluctant and uncooperative Twit Rat – fell about, some screaming in fear. In time the shuddering ceased, and the growing crowd stood quietly listening to the details of Matchwood's adventure – the near drownings, mythical creatures and such. As often happens in situations like this, one member of the group – a large Pillick who hadn't really been listening to the underlying moral of Match's story (not that there actually was one) – quickly raised up a large and very lumpy piece of driftwood and shouted, "Lets kill it!" Matchwood found himself powerless to prevent the peculiar, and utterly illogical bloodlust spreading throughout the small-minded group, as one-by-one hands reached for whatever weaponry they could grasp, and joined in the shouts of, "To the forest!"

As the group rushed through Flintlewood, others – who had no clue what anyone was actually talking about – found themselves unable to resist the temptation to follow the herd. Shopkeepers tore off their aprons and charged out into the growing rush of hot-heads. Farmers, observing the chaos, left their ploughs and, with pitchforks in hand, ran to add their voices to the shouts of destruction – of which they too had no real understanding.

Matchwood – or at least what was left of him – sat on the beach, his pleas for calm going unheard, his assurances that the creature was actually quite charming and, moreover, innocent of the crimes he had laid at its feet, falling on the deafness of ignorance. "Bugger!" he said to himself – for he was now totally alone – "I really should have told the story better." Quite rightly, he was now feeling more than a little guilty at being the spark which lit this particular fire.

The lynch mob, now expanded to include most of the townsfolk, jumped into carts and leapt onto horses. No one really gave much thought as to the rightful ownership of the modes of transport selected – their desire to cause harm to… well, by this time pretty much anything – had become all powerful. By this time there were only a handful of people who knew what had set the whole thing off. No one cared why everyone had suddenly begun to behave so strangely, all they knew was that if everyone else was involved, they wanted to be involved too!

Before long, Flintlewood was deserted – apart from the odd dog, or elderly Pillick who, having seen as much of life as they needed to, either lacked the energy or inclination to be bothered with what most described as 'a load of old nonsense.'

The group charged out of town, off the well-worn roads and into the woods. Shouting and waving weapons about, they headed off – one following the other – no one really having much idea of where they were going since Matchwood hadn't been overly specific, and no one had thought to ask. Since Matchwood was a boat, the lead idiot – the Pillick who had started this absurdity – in a moment of uncharacteristic clarity – chose to follow the river. The others of course, were simply following him. Their advance was soon halted by yet another quake, this one worse than ever. Trees fell, people scattered in terror. The screams of "Let's get it!" were quickly replaced with shrieks of '"Let's get out of here!"
Before long, the shuddering ground had a pacifying effect on the mob. Dazed and confused, the amassed Pillicks picked themselves up and re-grouped, discovering quickly that, miraculously, no one was injured. Regrettably, this instance of pure luck rather encouraged the riotous hoard, and it took no time at all for the desire for chaos to return. Once again, the waving of weaponry began. "This way! Let's kill it!" Pillicks all, returned to the indiscriminate chase.

CHAPTER TWENTY-THREE

Dust and rubble flew out in all directions. Graith peered out from behind his rock, the appearance of his head quickly followed by several others, then, like quickly-sprouting flowers, others popped up from their respective hiding places. "Well?" said Graith, rising slowly to his feet. "If that ain't shifted it, I don't know what will." He turned to face the two closest moles, pointing at them, and ordering them to go down the advancing tunnel to confirm the level of progress that this – the largest of the two explosions they had set off since their work had resumed – had achieved.

The two 'volunteers' ran down the dust-filled shaft, skilfully avoiding late-falling rubble. Coughing and spluttering their way through the dusty fog, they reached the marker which indicated the point where the charges had been placed. Expecting the newly-exposed dead-end to be just a few feet away, they cautiously groped around, stumbling forward in the blinding dust. With no wall apparent, they set about marking the distance from the marker. "One, two, three, four…" they counted as they moved gently, using their feet as rulers and their hands as guides, along the rough surface of the newly-created walls. The dust and smoke prevented even their eyes from seeing beyond the edge of their noses. “Five, six, seven…” they continued on, through the choking atmosphere – “Eight, nine…” they still hadn’t found their course impeded by the back wall. “I reckon we’ve only gone and done it, Squirt!” said one with excited surprise that their goal had been achieved so soon. “Ten!” they shouted in triumph.

“Ten feet, plus the six from the last go…” calculated Graith back in the base cavern, “that makes…” quickly counting up the amount on his eight fingers – four on each hand, “10, 11, 12…erm?”

“Sixteen, guv”, offered Chokkle who had moved from his cover rock and now stood by Graith’s side.

“I know that!” snapped Graith. “You think you get to be boss without knowing how to cou…”

“Hold on!” interrupted a voice, shouting from the work tunnel. Graith stood, eyes wide in the darkness.

“Blimey Squirt, there’s more than ten feet!” The pair squinted and strained as the dust and smoke began to clear a little – enough at least for them to be able to see that the newly-formed end wall was not yet at hand. “11…” they started walking again, still slowly, still steadily, “12, 13…Blimey! 15, sixt…ooof!” The discovered end wall brought an abrupt finale to their mathematics, as it made its presence felt.

“Well!?” shouted Graith.

“Fifteen and a half feet!” shouted back the explorers, with true pride in the group’s achievement.

Graith dropped to his knees. “Did you hear that!? Fifteen and a half feet!” he whispered, barely able to believe his own, tiny ears.

“By the grace of Climpanion,” said Chokkle, “that’s over 21 feet, guv. 21 feet in two hours!”

“Twenty-one feet!” echoed Graith.

“Over 21, boss!” came the shout from the two moles, as they emerged from the still-dusty mouth of the work cave.

Graith helped himself to his feet by climbing up the leg of his Second. “You lads…” he said, his chest pushed out in pride, “you lads are the best. Our ancestors thought they knew how to dig. Ha! They were beginners." His words of praise were quickly followed by a rousing cheer from his men, who followed this verbal nod to their efforts with plenty of hand-shaking and back-slapping.

At length, Graith felt the need to tear himself away from all the self-congratulation. "Right, lads!" he said, clapping his hands to gain their attention. Once all eyes were on him, he stood, rising and falling on his toes – "I'd better go and tell the Master the good news." With that he grabbed his eye-shield, and headed off up the tunnel that he had so clumsily entered the cavern by, just a few hours earlier – the jubilant cheers of his men sending him on his way.

Festulas Squit broke his gaze into the glowing stone, still held in his long, bony fingers and turned his head in the direction of the sound of gently, flapping feet. He carefully returned the stone to its leather pouch, and stashed it in the pocket from whence it came. Quickly, he rose to his feet, almost knocking his chair over, and busied himself with turning up all the lanterns – reproducing the same warm, orange glow that had existed at Graith's earlier departure. Satisfied that the light was bright enough, he returned to his seat – carefully adjusting his position so as to appear that he hadn't moved an inch.

Graith wandered into the larger space, his eye-shield firmly secured about his head.

"Well, Graith?" said Squit with eerie calm, his head unwilling to turn and face his subordinate.

"Well, sir," said Graith as he moved round the table and stood before the wiry figure, "you asked us for ten feet, and we have done ten feet – twenty in the last two hours." Graith had made the conscious decision, as he travelled the connecting tunnel, not to divulge that they had in fact, surpassed their target. *Tell him that, Graith my boy, and he'll expect twelve feet an hour*, he had thought.

Festulas skilfully hid his sheer relief that the goal had been achieved, choosing instead to simply offer Graith a sneering

smile. "Very good, Graith", he said – his voice now vacant of its earlier strength and instead, returning to its nasal drip. "Congratulate your men. Tell them I am pleased. Tell them to continue." He then lifted a hand and flicked it as though brushing away a tiresome fly, dismissing Graith without a further word.
"Thank you, sir", replied the mole, bowing low. "I'll tell the men of your pleasure, sir."
Festulas, irritated that the flick of his hand had not produced the desired effect, slowly rose to his feet and glared at the little creature. "GO!" he shouted, in his forced authoritative tones.
"Yes, sir. Right away, sir", bowed and scraped Graith as he moved backwards down the tunnel once more.
The slithering insult to life watched – waiting for Graith to fully remove himself before sitting back in his chair. Crossing his fingers behind his head and placing his feet up on the table top, he relaxed – permitting the disturbing sight of a genuine smile to distort his face.
His moment of relaxation was short lived. His closed eyelids opened as though he were startled by some unfamiliar sound in the dark – *"Squit"*, whispered an unseen but familiar voice. *"Squit"*, it repeated. *"Come."*
Squit stared into the non-existent distance as his eyes glazed over, giving the appearance that he had escaped the dinge and slipped into the world of daydreams. This catatonic state lasted but a moment, before Squit shook his head and blinked himself back to his rather disturbing reality. He leapt to his feet, this time knocking his chair flying behind him. He picked up his hat and cane and headed off at speed, up the stony corridor which lead to the lair of his Master – his gangly legs striding out with all the grace of an uncoordinated stumble.

Upon reaching his destination, Festulas stood, his hat carefully positioned on his head, his hands nervously gripping the top of his cane, which he held in front of him. Here he stood, stationary, awaiting the unseen voice of his Master. "Well Squit..?" he said to himself, quietly rehearsing his participation in the forthcoming conversation – starting with his Master's customary 'greeting'. This time he would not feel like a scalded child. This time he had good news to impart...

"Well Squit?" came the voice, interrupting Festulas's train of thought, its tone and pitch as deep, precise, and intimidating as ever.

"You sent for me, Master?" said Squit, shuffling slightly on his feet.

"Yes", came the solitary reply.

Festulas waited for a moment, expecting the sentence to continue. He felt uneasy – more so than usual. It was rare for his Master to send for him, their meetings were normally set to a rigidly observed timetable. "Well, Master," said Squit, desperately needing to fill the silence, "we have achieved ten feet!" he said, offering a pathetic smile – hoping perhaps, for some small measure of praise.

"I know", came the unexpected reply from the dark. "We have visitors, Squit."

"Visitors!?"

"Yes Squit, visitors."

"I had no idea!" This news made Festulas tremble. Not because there were people where people should not be, but that *he* was the one being presented with this information – not the one with the information to present.

"Clearly", replied his invisible Lord. "On this occasion," continued the voice, "I am inclined to be forgiving. You had other matters to attend to, I'm sure." The words themselves may have been forgiving, but Squit could not help but fear the sentiment was not entirely sincere. His Master had not, in the time he had known him, been terribly concerned with forgiveness.

"It is of little concern," the voice continued, "they are contained for the present."

"Would you like me to take care of them?" offered Squit, keen to make up for his mistake in permitting their presence in the first place.

"No. There are other matters for you to concern yourself with."

"Other matters, Master?"
"The good people of Flintlewood it seems, have been somewhat shaken by the most recent side effects of our little endeavour."
"Master?" asked Squit, puzzled by this news.
"A large group has allowed itself to become somewhat emotional. They come even now – trampling through the woodlands, creating little quakes of their own with their undisciplined advance."
Squit desperately wanted to appear calm in the face of this news, but the thought of rampaging hoards discovering that it was he and his moles who were the cause of their grief, didn't bear thinking about. "What are we to do, Master?" he whimpered.
"I have given you your instructions. You have the plan", the calm voice beginning to display a hint of anger, "You will find what I seek... Understand, you pathetic worm!?"
Squit now found himself on the horns of a terrible dilemma – who to fear more, his Master or the mob?
"Forget about those foolish Pillicks", said the voice. "They are of no concern. Be about my business, Squit. Fail me and an eternity of pain shall be yours."
Squit bowed lower than he had ever done before, as much because he felt sick with fear, as it was a display of respect. Bent almost double, he carefully shuffled backwards before turning, his legs shaking so much that he barely managed to take himself out of sight, before collapsing into a sobbing, simpering heap.

CHAPTER TWENTY-FOUR

The handle once more jostled and the door swung out, issuing its low, moaning creak as Sebastian, carefully holding a large tray filled with food, slowly moved into the room. Setting the tray down on the floor, he looked first around the room, then at his unexpected guests, "Sorry about the wait," he said politely, "I had run out of Quipper Weed, and fish without Quipper… Well!"

Neither his entrance, nor the sight of this enormous platter of food produced a reaction from the assembled diners. His words too, seemed to cause no response. Sebastian placed his hands on his hips – or at least where you would normally expect hips to be – and stared at his guests, all sitting, cross-legged in a circle around the fire. All eyes present were fixed, not on the flames, which continued to crackle and burst their way upwards, but on the area of wall they faced. The expressions, from those who had facial expressions to observe, were blank; vacant. Tree was silent, Matchwood – as much as any stick can be – was quiet too. Sebastian raised an eyebrow and smiled – "Hmm", he said, as though in agreement with a thought he had just had. He raised up his

massive arms and pointed his nose towards the vast ceiling, "Getheren!" he whispered.
Obeying his command the lights dropped, leaving – once more – the warm, orange glow of the fire, the only form of illumination in the room. Sebastian took one more look at his guests, still blank and motionless, before turning, collecting his tray and leaving the room – closing the door behind him and standing, waiting on the other side.

Frutely gently surfaced from her catatonic state. She looked at the wall opposite, on which her gaze had been fixed for the last two hours, then scanned across the faces of her circle of friends – who themselves were doing likewise. In unison, they looked up and, again in unison, looked over at the door as the large handle jostled and rotated. The door swung open to reveal Sebastian, standing with a congenial smile on his face and a large tray of food in his hand. "Blimey. That was quick!" said Pot, rising to his feet and fixing his eyes and nostrils on the large metal tray, which slowly descended to the ground. Slobber and Frutely joined Pot at the side of the large, oval platter, filled with grilled fish, fruits and vegetables.
"Please," said Sebastian with a grin, "tuck in. I'm sure your ordeal has sharpened your appetites."
The group didn't need a second invitation and, as they tucked into the feast, all complimented Sebastian on his fine, culinary skills. The chef gratefully acknowledged their thanks before slipping, unnoticed out of the room once more, gently trailing the door behind him.
"Oi!" shouted Tree – one of only two present not filling their face with fish – drawing attention to Sebastian's stealthy exit. His mouth full of fish, Slobber spat out a protest…
"Dessert!" said Sebastian, without turning. "I forgot the dessert", his clawed hand quickly slipping out through the shrinking gap of the closing door, before it slammed shut.
"Great! Locked in again", sighed Tree once more.

Tree's resignation to the situation had not been echoed by the three bipeds since they could see what he could not. The door had slammed with sufficient force to prevent its successful closure – jumping its enormous latch. Slobber, wiping his mouth with a sleeve, walked across to the narrow strip of space between door and frame. Squeezing his fingers into this slit he heaved – nothing! He tried again, adjusting his body to give him greater leverage.

This time the structure moved, just slightly. Frutely and Potfondle's eyes widened and, motivated by this small achievement, joined Slobber to assist. The door moved a little more – enough for Slobber to slide his arm along the edge and grip the other side – offering him even better leverage. The three struggled and heaved, their exertion displayed on ever-reddening faces – faces which twisted and crumpled, as the desire to explore the area behind this obstruction forced them to give their all to accomplish the task.

The crack grew larger, large enough for Frutely to squeeze through, then large enough for Potfondle – who was slightly bigger. Eventually the gap was of sufficient size for Slobber to attempt an exit. He scraped and scuffed his large body – forcing himself through the gap. Once on the other side, he ushered the others to help him push a little further, opening the door just enough to make it easier for him in particular, to dance from corridor to room.

Job done, the three now stood, surveying that which had previously been denied them. The corridor was, like the room they had just escaped from, immense. It had no light of its own, but the gloom was reduced by a pale glow, coming from its far end. There were large chunks of fallen stone on the ground, and its walls of Zintal were rough – a total contrast to the finely-crafted work observed in the entrance hall from whence they came.

Frutely looked all about her, frowning. She found it curious that here was visible the decay one would expect from hundreds of years of neglect. Yet just a few feet away, guarded by its colossal door, there stood a room seemingly untouched by the passage of time.

A shout from Tree – concerned that he and Match may be left behind – produced speedy reaction in Potfondle, who jumped to their retrieval.

"Grab a couple of torches too, can you", whispered Slobber loudly as Pot's small, hairy body disappeared through the gap.

In no time Pot returned with Tree, Match and…well…a few more pieces of Match – burning brightly at one end. He handed one to Slobber and one to Frutely, keeping the third for himself.

"What can you see? Come on somebody, tell me!" said Match with quiet frustration.

"Sshh!"

"Don't you Sshh me!" replied Match, unclear as to whom he was actually replying. "Where do you think the wood came from to light those torches!?"

"Sorry!" said Slobber, looking at what he held in his hand. "Does it hurt?" he asked, feeling a little guilty.

"No. It's dead wood, don't worry about it. Quickly now, what can you see?" he repeated – clearly frustrated at being unable to see for himself.

Slobber obliged and began, in as much detail as possible to describe what lay before him.

The corridor extended for some distance ahead, large boulders and other rubble littering its length. Down its walls, from time to time, there were the remains of arches, blocked now by fallen rubble – a visible reminder to the length of time this grand Palace had stood idle.

Slobber went on to describe how rough the walls were, how simple the floor appeared – in contrast to the room from which they had escaped.

"Well," said Tree, "I suppose there must be a kitchen or something around here. Sebastian must have cooked that fish somewhere!"

Slobber agreed, Tree's point was well made.

Frutely busied herself with inspecting the overall structure of this corridor. She had stroked its walls, hoping to find some reason for the apparent lack of continuity between this area and the entrance hall. As the narrow confines of her torch-light moved about the place, she noticed, from the corner of her eye, a gap. A triangular space – big enough to crawl through – within the fallen rocks of one of the grand arches. She got down on her knees and pushed the burning end of her torch into its darkness. "Hey!" she said, "There's a way through here!"

The others, in response to her calls, gathered around her – staring down the tube, straining to see more than her torch would allow.

"There's a way through…here", said Frutely, half her body swallowed by the small tunnel. On her hands and knees, she carefully negotiated her way through – the others standing, watching her disappear from their sight.

"You OK!?" said Pot in a concerned, shouted whisper – his head deep in the open mouth of the triangular gap. Finding his question without reply, Pot allowed the rocky mouth to consume him further. Pushing his torch ahead of him, he repeated the question, this time a hint of panic in his voice, displaying greater need for positive reply. Fear began to hold court in the rest of the group – Frutely had still given no response. Potfondle moved further into the tunnel, ignoring his racing heart and steadily drying mouth – "Frutely!" he shouted, the panic in his voice growing by the second.

"Frutely!" he repeated, his voice becoming more of a shriek.

"What!?" came the spat whisper of irritation.

"Thank the Gods!" said Potfondle, as his head emerged into the room where Frutely now stood. Pot, aggrieved that his display of genuine concern had been rewarded with nothing more than an impatient reply, returned to a whisper: "Are you OK?" he said, as he wriggled out of the hole and onto his feet – his torch shining in Frutely's eyes.

"I'm fine", she replied vaguely, forcing herself to participate in a conversation in which she had little interest – her words directing themselves toward Pot, as her torch and face remained fixed on a nearby wall, "Look at this!"

Slobber, Tree and Matchwood heard no reply to their repeated whispered shouts. Slobber, concerned for the well-being of his two companions, picked up Tree and stuffed Match into a pocket – which didn't please the stick at all. Already fed up that he had not been given the visual details of what was going on, the fact that he was now imprisoned by fabric, without so much a 'by-your-leave', had really irritated him. Loaded with the woodwork, Slobber squirmed and slithered – pushing both his torch, and Tree before him – down the rocky throat that had consumed his friends.

"Oi!" shouted Tree, as he emerged into the open space of the other side, "Have you suddenly developed hearing problems!?"

"Sshh!!" hissed both Frutely and Potfondle, their heads not even bothering to turn and look in his direction.

"They're OK!" shouted Tree, directing his words behind him – into the tunnel.

"Sshh!" hissed back both Slobber and Matchwood as they began to emerge into the room – subconsciously of the opinion that nothing louder than a whisper should be offered in this curious, and extremely echoey place. Slobber squeezed himself out of the rocky tube and picked himself up, with torch in hand he joined the others: "What's wrong!?" he asked, his eyes following the light from the torch as he looked this way and that.

"Nothing", said Frutely, her eyes still fixed on the wall. "Look at this."

Slobber's attention moved from her face, following the line of her outstretched arm to the end of her torch, and onto the wall, upon which her own attention was firmly fixed.

Carved out on the rough surface were pictures and writing, at least Slobber assumed it was writing, since he couldn't make out a recognisable word. "What is it?" he asked quizzically – his mind filled with curiosity.

"Writing", replied Pot, his mind consumed with the images.
"Obviously!" said Slobber, dismissing Pot's input. "What does

it say!?" he asked, eager for Frutely's rather more informed response.
"It's writing!" she said, sending Slobber's eyes skyward. "It's history!"
"History of what?"
"Look..." she said, the light of her torch redirecting Slobber's attention back to the wall – forcing him to focus on the object of her amazement once more. "Can you read this stuff?"
"Some of it", she replied. "Most of them are just simple pictographs, but this," pointing her torch at a mass of peculiar shapes, "is writing, ancient writing!"

The story the wall told was almost mythical. An ancient tale of how people and Nassians had shared the caves of the Palace. Just as Sebastian had said, those early people were almost like rodents – living in comparatively small holes, and surviving on what the Nassians saw as nothing but scraps. Frutely drew Slobber's attention to several, larger carvings, whispering to herself as their meaning became clear to her.
"Amazing!"
"What is? How do you know what all this means?" asked Slobber – whose only interpretation of these so-called words was that they were nothing more than elaborate squiggles.
Frutely explained that her grandfather had been an archaeologist – spending most of his life in caves, studying old bones and ancient writings. "I used to spend hours at his home. He taught me quite a bit about..." her words trailed off as she became absorbed by the work. She sighed to herself – "He never found anything like this, though. This is incredible. Listen..." All ears became attentive as Frutely, struggling at points, tried to relate the story crudely carved out on the hard rock of the walls.
She began with a large image, showing a group of Nassians standing around a large globe...thin lines connected each

creature to this apparently glowing orb. At the bottom left of the design, there was a doodle of a person peering from a hideaway, a small line connecting him to his closest Nassian. As they looked at the images, Frutely told of their meaning – using the writings to explain their significance… The man, somehow enlightened by the power of the orb, moved among his people – everyone he touched found their minds affected, and in a short space of time, their race grew in strength of body and of mind. Further images showed little stick figures attacking the Nassians with spears and swords, smashing eggs, and murdering the young in their beds. Frutely's eyes filled with tears as she found herself having to face an ugly truth. She turned away from the wall and stared at the floor – "It was us!" she said to herself. "We did it! We killed them!"
"It was a matter of survival!" said Slobber, who had been wandering around the room, looking at other pictures on the wall.
"Was it?" replied Frutely, her watery eyes still fixed on the floor.
"Look at this", beckoned Slobber. His grandfather had known nothing of archaeology; he hadn't been to university; he hadn't even read many books, but Slobber had learned enough from him to know that what he was looking at was a vision of death. The story he had discovered, showed another aspect of the Nassian world – a depiction of life before the chapters Frutely had been reading from. They told of exactly *where* early people fitted into the world of the Nassians.
"We were cattle!" said Slobber; his mouth turning down in disgust.
The pictures they all now viewed with horror, showed images of people in cooking pots, of banquets comprised of arms and legs, of heads on sticks – served as appetisers at parties..! Frutely took it all in, as did everyone else, scarcely able to comprehend the terror of it all.
Returning to her wall, Frutely began to try and make sense of it. She walked herself through the tale, adding it to the history she knew from her grandfather, books, myths, even fairytales.

As she walked the wall, her torch illuminated a picture showing the curious Stone of Power once more. This time *men* stood around it, bathing in its streams of powerful light. The only Nassians visible were on the floor – dead.
The final picture showed another globe of light – this time it was the sun, as viewed by people as they left the caves and explored the surface. “A bloody rebellion, then”, she said, again more to herself than her companions – “The mice rising up against the cats!”
“Sebastian lied to us!” suggested Tree. “Why would he lie about a thing like this?”
The group were more than a little startled to find that Tree’s utterance was answered by a very well-spoken, and now familiar voice – coming from the corridor: “Wouldn’t you!?” said Sebastian, his quietly sombre voice echoing through the small tunnel and into the room.
Frutely crouched down at the small entrance they had recently squeezed through. “You knew about this?”
“I knew”, replied Sebastian, lying on the ground, his ear pressed up against the crack in the wall.
“Funny, you didn’t think to mention it!” remarked Tree.
Sebastian sighed. “Won’t you please come out. I’d like to explain everything.”

Having seen the carnage carved out on the walls around them, no one was in any particular hurry to place themselves within easy reach of Sebastian’s mouth. This fact apparent to the creature, he resigned himself to the necessity of holding a conversation with a crack in the wall.
It was true that his race, being generally carnivorous, had eaten most living things around them, and this obviously included people. “You must try to understand…” he said, “back then your race wasn’t as it is now. Those early people had no language, no art, no obvious signs of real intelligence...” Drawing upon an obvious comparison, he remarked: “How much thought did you give to the future ancestors of those fish you recently tucked in to?”

"Good point!" said Tree, able to feel quite smug since he didn't eat the fish – being a tree of course, he didn't eat meat of any kind.
"The fact is that *I* don't eat your race. So far as I know, none of those who still survive do!"
They all thought hard. Eventually Slobber piped up – "OK," he said, "point taken. I suppose we believe you."
Sebastian seemed visibly relieved by this, although this look of relief was short lived.
"What about this orb thingy?" Tree's question was met with silence.
The question was repeated, this time by Frutely: "What can you tell us about the Stone of Power?" she quizzed, theorising that 'orb thingy' might not have been understood.
"It's a myth", came Sebastian's eventual reply. "Supposedly the Stone of Power, or as my people knew it, The Orb of Skeltenna, gave its owner great power."
"Power!?" said Tree. "What kind of power!?"
"Power of life and death, for one. Power of immortality for another. The legend has it that if one stood in the glow of its light, the knowledge of the Universe would be theirs. Nothing would be impossible. All things would be understood."
"Really!?" said Slobber. "Cool!"
"What exactly does power of life and death mean?" asked Frutely, her concerns a little more adult than how to make the perfect apple crumble.
"Well," said the creature, "legend has it that the Orb fell to our world from above. At its heart was a God – Skeltenna, imprisoned there by other Gods for…well…actually, the reason for his apparent imprisonment was never truly explained. Anyway, while the Gods could incarcerate his body, they could do nothing about his power..."
"So you're saying this thing has the power of a God!?" Pot could scarcely believe it. "I think that answers your question, Frutely. After all, how much power does a God have?"
"Anyway," said Sebastian, keen to clear up the whole eating people problem, "the truth is that my people *did* eat your

ancestors...Sorry about that! It is true that your ancestors *did* contribute to the general demise of my race...for that *you* should be sorry! However," he continued without a pause, preventing anyone from jumping to apologise for the actions of their past, "our race had begun to die out long before the origins of your species developed the ability to fashion metal into spears and swords."

All fell silent once more as everyone thought on the subject of extinction and magical stones.

"Perhaps," said Frutely, her head reappearing in the great corridor – closely followed by her body, "the slow deterioration in the numbers of your people allowed mine to develop."

The others filed back through the gap, all parties feeling generally guilty for their race's part in the misery inflicted on these giants. Sebastian apologised for making his guests feel like prisoners, but advised them that, with the Palace being in something of a state, they should – for their own safety, and his peace of mind – refrain from wandering around. "Besides," he said, leading them back into the entrance hall, "there really is nothing very much to see."

Standing at the doorway, and satisfied everyone was accounted for, he uttered "Keltremancian", to re-ignite the hidden lighting.

"Weren't the lights on before?" quizzed Tree, his question – as did the absence of light when they escaped – going completely unnoticed.

CHAPTER TWENTY-FIVE

A head appeared in the entrance pool, followed by another, then another. These heads quickly became bodies, as they rose from the water and charged for the monster, waving clubs and recently fashioned spears. Their shouts and speed of advance startled the group of explorers.

Sebastian narrowed his eyes at this latest intrusion into his privacy. "Good heavens!" he said quietly to himself. "They got here rather fast."

"What was that!?" shouted Slobber.

"Nothing."

The number of Pillicks grew as still more emerged from the entrance pool – "Kill the beast!" shouted some. "He's the cause of these quakes!" followed others.

Sebastian decided to remove himself from the situation and headed out through the door, pulling it shut behind him. His original visitors saw his plan and quickly followed, barely managing to scrape through before the door slammed shut – this time not jumping the latch.

Safely on the other side, Sebastian fell down onto all-fours and 'galloped' as fast as he could down the corridor. The others followed but quickly found themselves out-paced.

Turning to see their safe exit was more than guaranteed by the securely fastened door, they stopped to catch their breath.
"Who, in the name of my rosy-red buttocks, were they!?" puffed Potfondle.
"I believe," said Matchwood, his voice almost apologetic for knowing the answer, "that those are the good people of Flintlewood."
"What!?" said Frutely. "How did they get here!?"
"Um..." Matchwood had to force the guilty explanation from his small body, "I'm afraid I told them."
"*You* told them!?" exclaimed Pot. "How could *you* have told them? You've been with us the whole time."
"Not me here," announced Match, "me on the beach."
Pot and Frutely exchanged looks of utter confusion.
"You'd better tell 'em", said Tree.
Match, again found it necessary to break his sacred oath and explain to non-Kia about his telepathic ability.
Both Pot and Frutely sat dumbstruck by his admission.
"Bloody hell!" said Frutely, much to the surprise of her companions.
Matchwood now had more news for them. All sat opened-mouthed as he advised them that the quakes had got worse. Not only stronger but more frequent.
"We've felt no quakes!" said Frutely, "A quake doesn't just shake the surface. We would have felt them." She was quite obviously concerned. Concerned and more than a little confused. The others made several utterly implausible suggestions, as they continued the journey down the long corridor, all dismissed by Frutely's silence.
Pot, grasping at straws in a vain attempt to impress, suggested that perhaps the Zintal rock was acting as some kind of insulation against the shaking. His reasoning was simple: "This whole area is Zintal rock – until now believed to be impossible to cut, right?"
"The Nassians managed to cut it", said Tree.
"And whoever did those carvings on the wall..." added Slobber, whose words suddenly drew him to a complete

standstill. “I can’t believe it!” he said, delivering a single slap of his hand to an unsuspecting forehead.
The others now joined him in his lack of movement, all looking at him silently – all with one, unannounced question on their mind – *What!?*
“The cave…” he said. “The carvings…” He’d lost them. The obvious question that had been quite happily left unasked, now surfaced: “What are you on about, spit factory?” said Tree – his enquiry shared by the others, though perhaps put less delicately than they might have wished.
Slobber, realising that he was talking in riddles, shook his head as though to draw back the curtain of obscurity: “That entrance hall place was displayed in that cave back there”, he said excitedly.
“What!?” said Frutely, her single word delivered in a shouted whisper – an attempt to quietly display her alarm that Slobber had not thought to draw her attention to it earlier. The beauty of the cave, along with the method used in creating the carvings, had never left her mind. She grabbed Slobber by his wrists and, staring earnestly up into his eyes, insisted he give her a detailed description of what he had viewed.
The room was described, its walls with their mesmerising glow surrounded a large number of little stick figures – all standing with arms by their sides and heads bowed. There seemed to him to be a disturbing eeriness about the carving. Frutely’s eyes remained glued to his as she virtually demanded that he remember details of any writings.
Slobber closed his eyes and drew a deep breath, going through the memory of what his eyes had captured. He could only give a vague description of a couple of the symbols – the words appearing alien to him, he hadn’t paid them much attention.

Frutely released her grip and began again to move down the snaking path.
“So?” said Pot, catching up to her.
“I’m not sure”, she admitted with a deep sigh – regretting that

her attention had not been called to it earlier. "I think the room serves a specific purpose. You and I both experienced some kind of trance when we came into contact with the walls..." She stopped in her tracks once more, reaching out and grabbing Pot's shoulder – Tree's earlier remark about the lights suddenly filtering into her consciousness. "The lights were on when Sebastian left to get food, yet when he returned the lights were off", her words drifted into a whisper, "Why would he turn the lights off?" she enquired to herself.
"I don't trust him!" said Matchwood, still inside the pocket of Slobber – who had by now, joined the duo. From the silence his remarks forced, Match believed all eyes were upon him – awaiting further explanation. "I may be blind," he said, "but I can still smell a well-cooked fish...Smurdon fish, unless I'm very much mistaken?" The murmurs of general agreement, confirmed the accuracy of his olfactory senses. "To bake a truly perfect Smurdon, takes approximately 90 minutes, yet to our recollection, Sebastian was only absent for a fraction of that – ten, maybe fifteen minutes, at best."
"Perhaps the light amplifies the trancing effect", suggested Pot, in a moment of extraordinary clarity of mind.
"He could have been gone for hours!" suggested Tree, unclear as to what trancing effect Pot was talking about. Slobber and Matchwood too, had no idea what Pot was talking about, but the idea of losing time required an explanation and this was as good as any. The details of *how* seemed less important to them than *why*.

It was with a new sense of unease that the group continued their exploration of the corridor. Questions of what the room was for dominated their collective thoughts. The idea of it being a grand entrance to a wondrous palace had somehow never rung true. The room itself, with its unique walls, did suggest it was intended as a great display, but the heavy, rather plain door smacked more of a prison than a palace. The puzzle of the door increased as their careful steps took them past several other entrances – all collapsed and none

with doors. The room served another purpose, of that they were becoming certain.
“Pleasure?” suggested Tree.
“A trap!” said Slobber. “Like a honey pot for trapping insects.” His words sent shivers down the backs of those who had backs to shiver. Tree, having no spine, gently shook his branches. Matchwood, having neither a spine nor branches simply issued a verbal display of what they were all feeling: “Yeesh!”
The chilling notion of the true purpose of the room, where bits of Matchwood fuelled the fire by which they had all warmed themselves, consumed each of the travellers as they continued their careful march down the stony tube. As they approached the white light that had guided their approach, they could see that the rubble-filled passage opened out into a larger area. Not a room, certainly not the sort of room you would expect to see in a palace. No, this was what you would expect to see underground – a cave. A plain, ordinary, rough-surfaced cave – cavernous indeed, but a plain old cave nonetheless.

As if with one mind the group slowed to a steady creep – almost tip-toeing up to the entrance. With voices hushed and eyes wide with uncertainty and fear, Slobber – who had grudgingly accepted the front position, which the others had cunningly moved him into without his realising – carefully edged his head out into the light. Like a sloth surveying a new branch, he slowly turned his attention to the left and then the right. To the floor and to the ceiling. Turning back to face the others he whispered “Looks safe enough.”
“Well?” said Potfondle, after a lengthy period of glance swapping.
“Well what?” replied Slobber, knowing full well that the expectation of his companions was that he proceed with a more detailed search of the cave. His question, much as he expected, drew no verbal response. Instead his friends, even Frutely – which did surprise him a little – simply offered him

raised eyebrows, and the curious head-nodding which, without words, said 'Go on then. What are you waiting for!?'
Slobber sighed, acknowledging to himself that as the largest, the dubious pleasure of getting killed first was his. He turned his back on the others and reluctantly crept out into the obvious light of the cave.
Although desperate that his footfalls made no sound, each step seemed to send a clashing echo around the space – a ricochet that seemed to yell out 'I'm here. Please come and hurt me'.
Cringing with each loud, hammering footstep, Slobber carefully made his way to the centre of the room – his head twitching in all directions, his eyes wide and unblinking, keeping watch for the smallest hint of movement, his ears keen and sharp, ready to alert him to any sound other than the deafening collisions of his feet on rock. Every muscle in his body was geared to turn tail and run like the wind – from what exactly, he knew not. Quite simply, and quite understandably, Slobber was approaching a state of extreme fear, so much so that even his saliva factory had chosen to shut down. Since waking up, the previous morning – *Gods, was it only yesterday?* he thought, desperately trying to give his mind other things to dwell upon – he had met a talking boat, been terrified on the ocean by an unexplained seizure, fallen into a river, capsized and fallen into the river *again*, thought his friends dead but then discovered they were alive, tried to fight off a monster, eaten fish in a giant flytrap, and then run away from a blood-thirsty mob… All in all, the last couple of days had been somewhat more eventful than his usual weekends!

Slobber stood still, allowing the sound of silence to thunder through his ears. To his left there was another corridor, this one leading down in a gentle slope – a warm, orange glow emanating from its depths. Ahead of him was a large, dark hollow in the wall. This area made Slobber very uneasy for some reason – its darkness seemed intentional somehow. Slobber slowly turned in the direction of his watchful friends, raising his hands and shrugging his shoulders, 'There's no one here', he mouthed, careful to make no sound.

Frutely tightened her grip around the remaining torch and scuttled to join him, closely followed by Pot and Tree – all four quick feet treading carefully.

Looking around the cave, Frutely frowned. "Well where did he go?"

"Don't know", replied Slobber. "That passage looks too small…" he said, nodding his head in the direction of the glowing tunnel.

"Oh this is ridiculous!" announced Frutely, her voice still a whisper. "He must have gone through there!" she added, as her legs suddenly took her body in the direction of the darkness. Pot and Slobber swapped looks of concern but followed her nonetheless.

The dark space was much larger than the opening suggested. Its ceiling was very high, the torch revealed that much, but how far into the depths the darkness went was a question the flames were powerless to answer.

The area where they all now stood revealed nothing. They now faced a dilemma. Should they follow Sebastian – sure that this was the only direction a creature of his size could have taken – or choose independent exploration of this increasingly curious place.

Once Slobber had taken the trouble to update Matchwood on the detail of their surroundings, the five debated the matter…very quietly. Charming though Sebastian was, there was something about him that was not entirely trustworthy.

"Well, he didn't eat us", was Pot's offering, as they tried to weigh up the pros and cons of following this passage, rather than the smaller, lit one.

Tree huffed a single, cynical laugh: "No one I have ever met has eaten me", he said. "That fact doesn't make me automatically trust all of them!"

"He did build you a fire", said Slobber.

"Using me!" said Matchwood.

Frutely was quiet, thoughtful: "OK!" she said, taking control of the conversation. "He didn't eat us, that's true, and although we think we were in what seems to be some kind of trap, he didn't activate it – he didn't turn it on…at least not straight away." Her words were slow and deliberate as she tried to make some kind of sense of his actions thus far. She continued her logical approach to the problem, uninterrupted by the others: "The carvings on the wall were small and low, as though carved by people more of our size than his. He said he was young when the slow demise of his race began…" She stopped again and began pacing around within the confines of an invisible fence. "I don't think he knows about the carvings, or the purpose of what he called the entrance hall…" Looking at the faces of Pot and Slobber, and aware of the silence from Tree and Matchwood, she realised her argument was being viewed as less than convincing. "Look," she said, turning to face her audience, "you saw his reaction to those people. He appeared genuinely scared…" She stood with pleading eyes and arms reaching out in an attempt to guide the others to her viewpoint.

"He did run off…" said Slobber in agreement.

Frutely decided to approach the problem in a different way, as much for her own benefit, as to make a more convincing argument. Still facing the group, the torch-light of flame illuminating their faces, she began to count out the points of her opinion.

"One – he didn't eat either Pot or myself…on its own not a reason to trust someone…" she added, acknowledging Tree's earlier observation on the level of trust that should automatically be placed in someone, simply because they *don't* eat you.

"Two – not only did he not eat us but he lit a fire…admittedly using pieces of Matchwood, but he couldn't have possibly known that.

Three – he didn't eat Slobber who, it has to be said, originally behaved in such a manner as to provoke some form of retaliation.

Four – he made us some food…"
"Five…" interrupted Matchwood, "he turned on the trap to prevent us from leaving! Explain that!"
Frutely thought for a moment. She could explain it. To her it was becoming clear. Admittedly, she did have to give Sebastian something of the benefit of the doubt, but her argument was relatively simple:
By the way he ran from the mob, it was fair to deduce that he was scared. Add to that the fact that until that day, she – a scientist – had never heard of such a creature walking the planet. There were no records, no fossils… "No fossils?" she muttered to herself. *If so many once lived, why are there no fossils?* she thought. It was a question upon which, at that point at least, she did not permit herself to dwell. "He ran away. Why?" Her question was rhetorical, and even if it hadn't been, she didn't allow anyone time to answer. "Few people run away from mice, and to him that's as much a threat as those people would have posed…"
"Lots of people run away from mice!" interrupted Tree quietly. With his witty and quite accurate comment drawing no retort, he rejoined the others in silence – hopeful that his point had nevertheless been made.

Tree's observation notwithstanding, Frutely's reasoning seemed to be having a positive influence. The eyebrows of Pot and Slobber slowly began to rise in appreciation of her reasoning. She continued: "I truly believe he either doesn't understand the original purpose of the entrance hall, or he has forgotten over time." Frutely's argument was compelling, but even she had to admit there were gaps. Why did he turn the lights on the first time? Was it to prevent them from leaving?
"He must know that the light affects people in some way", said Tree, wishing to add to the discussion once more.
"Agreed," said Frutely, "but to him it may be nothing more sinister than an incredibly effective and humane defence system. A way of preventing mobs like that from doing him, or even themselves, any harm…or a way of preventing unwanted

guests – burglars, for example, from wandering about the place."

"You don't think that bloomin' great door might do the trick then?" asked Tree, once again, his salient point going totally unheard.

The group stood, all thinking the same thoughts. All working systematically through the evidence. Was Sebastian a carnivorous monster, ready to eat anything with a heartbeat or was he, as he seemed to be, a slightly effeminate, timid giant – scared and, for the most part, alone.

At this time, the Jury was still out.

CHAPTER TWENTY-SIX

Graith's stumpy little legs moved faster than they had possibly ever moved before. Up the tunnel he once again came, up into the cave where his regular meetings with his Master took place. The light from the lanterns, though low to normal eyes, blinded him. Shielding his face with his arm, he fumbled about the top of his head looking for his eye-shield. "Dammit!" he exclaimed, upon the discovery that they were not present. Squinting through nearly shut lids, his hand raised to block as much of the light as possible, he peered around the room. "Master?" he shouted. "Master?" Certain that he was alone he started up the next tunnel, tripping and stumbling up its path – his eyes still registering spots of light, preventing him from seeing clearly.

"Aaarrgh!" yelled Squit, as the mole's foot connected with his shin – lying as it was, along with the rest of him, on the floor. Graith's surprise at this talking lump, prevented him from recapturing his balance and he tumbled over, crashing to the ground and rolling like a ball – eventually sliding on his belly and hitting his head against the wall.

Squit quickly recovered himself and scrambled to his feet. "Graith!" he growled angrily, limping his way up the path to confront his assailant.

Graith quickly got to his feet and moved to intercept him. "Sir!" he shouted. "Something incredible! Something terrible! Something…"

"What are you babbling about!?" spat Squit, his temper not improved by the mole's collision.

Graith stood, panting – trying to catch enough breath to permit an unbroken sentence. "30 feet…" he puffed.

"What!?"

"30 feet, sir. 30 feet with the same amount of explosive."

"Really?" said Squit, his pathetic eyebrows rising to express his pleasant surprise. "I'm impressed", he offered, his grey face insulting the world once more with its attempt at a smile.

"No sir," panted Graith, his face not reflecting the pleasure of his Master's, "you don't understand, sir. It ain't possible. It ain't us!"

"What do you mean it isn't you!?"

"Zintal don't cut that easy. We were bloody lucky to get ten feet an hour", the concern on Graith's face was more telling than his words.

Festulas looked into his subordinate's frightened eyes and heard words of fearful concern. "You pathetic worm!" he sneered. "You find a way to cut through this accursed rock as though it were soil, and it scares you." Festulas stooped over the cowering mole, his mouth turned down, his nose suddenly seeming more pointed, and his eyes more devoid of life than ever before. He jabbed at Graith's pink body with the end of his cane – his action punctuating every slithering, slavering word: "You pathetic, snivelling wretch…" he jabbed, leaving Graith with no option but to step backwards with every painful prod. "You weak, feeble, creature of the darkness. We have success. We achieve our aim and all you can do is charge about like a frightened child."

Graith continued to step backwards, closely followed by the slow, creeping steps of his sadistic tormentor. Back he

went…back and eventually out into a bright and open space. His blinded eyes didn't see the high walls of the corridor to his left. Nor too did they acknowledge the existence of a gaping, dark void – now framing three figures.
"Hey!" shouted Slobber, as he charged across the open space, the continued level of adrenaline removing from his mind the still present nag of his wounded thigh. "You there, stop that!"
Squit looked up with total surprise, his soulless eyes fixing on the image of this large, blue man, stampeding towards him, reactivated drool glands spraying gob-juice left and right. He had but a moment to think – fight or flight?
The surprise of Slobber's appearance had left him with little ability to run, and the size of his opponent, now flanked by two small Pillicks, prevented him from finding much motivation to fight. The fact that his hand lifted his cane up high into the air, was a matter of pure animal instinct…Squit was far too weedy a man to be able to inflict much damage to someone of Slobber's dimensions.
Slobber's charge continued, gaining momentum over the albeit short distance. His anger at witnessing the injustice of a tall man bullying a little one, had surprised him – bullying was a matter that had always bothered him, although he rarely had occasion to step in – but the rage he currently felt was out of character. Later, he would attribute it to the fact that the events of the last couple of days had left him tired, confused, scared, and generally pretty cheesed off!
Festulas Squit braced himself, as every muscle in his lanky frame prepared to do battle…or rather, get beaten to a bloody pulp.
"Stop!" shouted Graith, stepping into Slobber's path – placing himself in harm's way – one hand raised, its palm flat and forceful. Graith squinted through screwed up eyes – his other hand attempting to create a shadow of protection for his sight – "Stop right there, mate!" he ordered.
Slobber did as he was instructed, though he was unsure exactly why the victim should be protecting his attacker. Pot

and Frutely too, came to a standstill, and all three stared with a mixture of confusion and anger – the former directed at this odd-looking, pink creature, the latter reserved for the stick-like wielder of the cane.

Festulas lowered his weapon, adjusted his attire – straightening his hat and straining his neck in his collar. Taking back command of this now vaguely calmed situation, he took a small step forward, brushing Graith aside with the bony fingers of his grey-skinned hand. He stared at Slobber who, in turn glowered back. Taking comfort in the curious protection Graith had afforded him, Squit cleared his throat, lifted his head and allowed adversarial words to dribble from his grotesque mouth: "You are trespassing here…"

"That's right. You are interfering with official PEA business", added Graith, his ties of loyalty tightly bound by the stone Squit held in his possession.

Squit looked down at his companion and snarled "Be silent, worm!"

Slobber clenched his fists tightly, and renewed his glare of anger to this slither of skin-covered bone that stood before him.

"You're with the Port Establishment Agency!?" asked Frutely, her mind now finished with its task of searching through her memory – seeking an answer as to why this man looked so familiar to her.

Turning to face the inquisitor, Festulas sneered a smug, repellent smile and offered out his hand: "Festulas Squit. Nice to see you again Dr Gaiberond."

Those in the group who had heads to turn and features to express dismay did so as, giving expression to their collective dismay, Slobber said: "What! You know this person?"

Frutely stared into the eyes of Squit, her mind filled with feelings of deep disappointment and betrayal. "Oh we've met alright, only you mentioned nothing of the PEA!" she said through gritted teeth. "Festulas Squit?" she asked, noticing the expressions on the faces of her companions – demanding of her, some explanation of how she came to be familiar with

such an odd looking fellow, "I thought your name was Mr Skint."
"Skint!?" said a confused Potfondle. "That bloke from the taxi firm?"
"What?" added Slobber, "the man who returned the plans for your…whatever you call it…the quake finder thingy?"
"Comparometer. Yes." Frutely looked Squit up and down, her full expression that of a person who is in utter disbelief at their own gullibility. So relieved had she been to get her plans back those three years ago, that it hadn't occurred to her that this Mr Skint was anything other than that which he claimed to be. Fixing Squit's lifeless eyes with her own, she allowed her anger to surface: "You stole my plans!"
Festulas smiled a smug smile, displaying his blackened teeth. "Prove it!" he said – his words dripping from his mouth in such a way as to turn even the strongest stomach.
Slobber had heard enough. Pot had heard enough too, but felt it more prudent to wait for his larger companion to make the first move. If Slobber hated bullies, he hated lying, cheating bullies even more. Regardless of the wishes of the curious, pink creature, he was going to kick this Squit's bony butt. He lunged forward, reaching out to grab the scrawny, leathery, grey neck of the odious streak of unpleasantness that stood with a smirk still crippling its already grotesque features. His speed took everyone by surprise, and his anger caused his hand to grip tightly around Squit's neck.
Pot smiled a wide smile, taking pleasure in the fact that this deceiver was about to meet a very painful – and due to Slobber's now fully active dribbling – a very wet kind of justice. Frutely also took some pleasure in seeing this thief and bully struggle and strain – choking for air as Slobber's grip continued to tighten.
Graith rushed to Squit's aid once more, though his reasons for trying to protect this creature baffled all who looked on. All that is, apart from the group of pick-wielding, eye-shielded moles who now charged into the bright, open space.
All eyes widened with fearful surprise at the sudden

appearance of this small army. Graith smiled and looked up at Slobber, who replied with a frown of total bafflement as his jaw dropped and his grip relaxed a little. Squit turned his head as much as he was able, his eyes rolling as far round as they could in order to witness the sight already reflected in the eyes of his attacker. The vision of all his men, ready to defend him with their very lives, produced on Squit's face, a crippling smile – the kind of smile that only appears when a person realises that they have their opponent hopelessly outnumbered. The kind of smile that presents itself when, all at once, the tables are well and truly turned.

Slowly, he moved his head around to look once more into Slobber's eyes, and allowed his mouth to part slightly as a sinister, gurgling chuckle forced its way out. A genuine display from Squit of smug satisfaction: "Well?" he said confidently.

CHAPTER TWENTY-SEVEN

Deep underground, a room with no doors found its dimly lit, and highly polished walls steadily brighten, as the colourful strands which criss-crossed under their surface, began to glow. Their rhythmic undulation, causing ripples of coloured light to dance around the still-gloomy space, quickly found themselves accompanied by a pulse of repetitious, white light – its steady beat acting as the guiding percussion for this beautiful orchestra of soundless rhythm.

In the centre of this bell-shaped container sat the conductor. A shimmering, pulsing stone. Its rounded surface distributing the white pulse, guiding the lines of red, blue, green, and black in their performance – which now quickened as the beat grew faster.

The perfect sphere – save for a small scar on its underside – began to rotate slowly. Its pace of movement eventually catching up with its own repetitious glowing as, in time to the visual music, it slowly rose from its elaborately carved plinth, allowing its spinning form to hang in mid-air. Its quickened rhythm interrupted briefly by a single, blinding, flash of light.

CHAPTER TWENTY-EIGHT

The moles busied themselves, putting the finishing touches to the complicated knots, binding together Pot, Slobber, and Frutely. Tree and Matchwood had rather cunningly chosen to remain quiet, their perceived threat viewed with no more consideration than anyone would normally give to a little tree and a stick of wood.

Festulas Squit rubbed his neck as he strutted back and forth, his face now carrying an inscrutable grin. He stopped and looked down at his newly bound captives, as they struggled with the ties that restrained their hands and ankles. He moved slowly towards them, his direction aimed squarely at Slobber. Drawing up his cane, he delivered several sharp jabs to Slobber's injured leg: "So..." he said, revelling in the courage his moles now afforded him – "Not so powerful now are we!?" Observing his captive's angry expression and fidgeting arms, he added: "Struggle all you want, you drooling freak. Those bonds are..."
"Triple tied, sir", offered Graith.
"Triple tied", ended Squit, with a slight snarl in Graith's

direction – an indication to his slave that his assistance was not welcome.

"What's going on here!? Who are all you people!?"

Squit curled his top lip as an attempt at charm began to assault his face. He pondered for a moment before choosing to answer Frutely's question. Pacing back and forth once more, punctuating his searching stares into the dark cave with the occasional glance at his prisoners, he chose to make the stereotypical blunder that all villains seem doomed to commit...

"Well, my good doctor. Obviously I'm not the owner of a taxi company..."

"Really!?" replied Frutely to this rather obvious admission.

Stopping near the dark entrance, Festulas waited for some sign from his Master that he was not to proceed. With no such symbol forthcoming, he felt comfortable in revelling in his cunning.

"I am with the PEA", he said, leaving such a pause that it seemed that would be an end to his confession. Eventually though, he continued, gesturing towards Graith and his fellow moles: "My...shall we say companions and I are on the brink of completing a very special project. I wonder...can you guess what that is?" he snivelled patronisingly. "We," he continued quickly, denying Frutely a chance to respond, "are, right now, at this very moment, doing the impossible..." He paused again, this time for dramatic effect. "We are in fact..."

"Tunnelling through Zintal!" announced Graith proudly, unintentionally stealing Squit's moment of triumph, bringing his ego trip to a grinding, shuddering halt.

Festulas slowly turned his head and delivered a long, hard glare of total, abject hatred to the little mole.

Attempting, as much as he possibly could, to ignore this innocent blow to his ego, Squit continued. The plans he had stolen from Frutely three years before had been used to construct a version of her machine. Only this one not only read data, but allowed its user to emit false readings to any other mechanisms of a similar ilk.

"What!?" shrieked Frutely, appalled by the notion that her very own creation had been perverted into a mechanism for deceit, rather than truth.

"Not quakes", said Squit his eyes widening with satisfaction. "Explosions! Big, beautiful explosions!"

"Explosions large enough to shake the ground for miles around!? What the hell are you using?"

"Pobble Strikes!" announced Graith with pride, producing a small, round object from a pouch on his belt, and nonchalantly tossing it into the air before safely catching it again.

"Pobble Strikes!?" said Frutely. "How many!?"

Receiving a nod from his Master, Graith answered, his chest sticking out further still as his pride in their accomplishments could finally be passed on: "To begin with…ten…"

"Ten!!?"

"Is that a lot?" asked Potfondle

"A lot!?" replied Frutely, "Two are enough to cause a crater 30 feet deep and 70 feet wide!" She stared at Graith, "What do you mean, to begin with?"

"Well," said Graith, "ten weren't doing the job. Nor were fifteen…"

"Fifteen!?"

"Yeah, I know. You'd think fifteen would be enough to destroy most of Gweep," said Graith, choosing to view Frutely's very sincere concern as true applause for his team's work. "You'd have thought that twenty would do the trick, but that only allowed us five feet a day in this bloody stuff", he said, kicking the base of a nearby wall. "I tell ya, you've got to take your hat off to whoever carved out this place."

"How many have you been using?" repeated Frutely.

Allowing a dramatic pause, and looking with pride at the visored faces of his men, Graith first looked at his Master, before replying: "98."

"NINETY-EIGHT!!!???"

"Don't worry, Dr. Gaiberond," said Squit, "the Zintal acts as a

perfect cushion against the very blasts we are using to cut through it." His total lack of concern for the chaos they were causing on the surface left Frutely, and for that matter the others, cold.
"See," said Pot, "told you so, didn't I..." referring to his earlier, half delivered theory, "Zintal insulation." Pleased with himself, he sat smiling. Shortly, however, his smile found itself replaced by a frown, "But why go to all this trouble to create a few tunnels?"
Squit stared at Potfondle for a time, before turning to face the dark cave once more. Raising a bony hand, he scratched at his pointed chin. "The tunnels are simply an experiment", he said, keeping his back to his doomed hostages. "We needed to see if we could do it before announcing our intentions to develop this part of the Twit."
"Develop the Twit!?" exclaimed Potfondle. "You mean ruin the Twit!"

Festulas, still receiving no sign to halt his explanations, went on to describe at least part of their cunning plan. "The PEA have, as I'm sure you are aware, wanted to exploit the Twit for decades. This damned rock however, prevented us from doing anything other than drawing up plans and quietly purchasing land..." Squit quietened himself and quickly turned to the moles, instructing them to return to their work. In response to the order, they shuffled about – delaying their retreat, concerned that their assistance may yet be further required. Eventually though, they grudgingly did as they were ordered and slowly began to file off, back down the tunnel from whence they came.
Squit watched for a while until he was certain all the moles were out of earshot, before turning and stooping over the 'soon to be dead' trio.

Convinced that his future words would be carried no further, he lowered his voice to a whisper. First glancing again at the dark cave, he confided in those who he was sure would soon

be dispatched by his curiously silent Master.
"What those fools don't realise," he said, nodding in the direction of the retreating moles, "is that I have a secret." He quietened himself again for a moment, hoping to produce an enigmatic pause. Much to his disappointment, no one rose to the bait, leaving him forced – with some small measure of further disappointment – to continue anyway. "My work for the PEA happily coincides with the needs of a greater power. I…" he said, a frown crossing his brow – his voice silenced by the curious smiles, broadening on the faces of his audience. Squit stared into their eyes. Eyes that looked at him, then glanced over to the dark cave, then back at him…
"Hi Sebastian!" chirped Tree – an event in itself that caught Squit's attention.
Festulas slowly turned his head to meet the recipient of the tree's greeting.
He watched, motionless, rooted to his spot as his eyes took in the terrifying vision of the creature.
Sebastian quietly rose up and extended his arms, allowing a soul-clenching roar to blast from his mouth.
"Mr Squit…" said Frutely, the smile on her face displaying the same level of satisfaction that Squit's had earlier. "Meet Sebastian."
Squit found his muscles completely beyond his control as Sebastian struck. He managed a quick turn of the head and – an action which seemed very odd to all who saw it – a smile. Sebastian's eyes flashed with anger and his nostrils flared. Squit looked around just in time to see a display of huge teeth, before Sebastian's mouth closed around him.
"That was a bit extreme, don't you think?" said Slobber, staring up at the swallowing Sebastian – his face twisting, as the thought of being eaten and digested created disturbing images in his mind.
"Oh, my dear boy. Don't think I didn't give this whole matter a great deal of thought. Frankly, I fear that meat as tough as his will give me terrible indigestion…possibly even make me physically sick."

"But why eat him?" asked Frutely, her feelings for Squit far removed from friendship, she did however, feel that devouring this evil man was a little on the harsh side.
"It seemed like a good idea at the time", answered their saviour.
Sebastian realised that the visual impact of seeing someone suddenly picked up and swallowed may be a little difficult to take. He realised too, that what he had done would, to the casual observer, seem to be a tad over zealous. True, he could have just terrified the awful man, but there were other factors of which his guests were unaware. "Tying you up and threatening your lives…" he said, "not at all the way a host should treat his guests, in my view… Besides that," he added, choosing to explain, at least partially, why his anger with this man went a little deeper than simply a lack of manners, "that frightful man and his minions have brought nothing but disaster to the usual peace and quiet I enjoy here."
"It's not that we're ungrateful," shouted up Pot, "it's just that we feel eating him was perhaps a little unnecessary."
"Not at all unnecessary!" replied Sebastian. "This is the first time that horrible toothpick of a man has been within my reach. Normally he stays down there, hiding out in tunnels far too small for me to successfully traverse..." Sebastian went on to explain that his unwelcome visitors had been there for months – "Causing terrible dust and frightful shudders, with their hideous explosions… My modest little abode," he said, nodding over in the direction of the dark cave, "is in a shocking state thanks to him and his ilk." He had, he said, gone down the original tunnels as far as he was able, but could not quite manage to slither down the smaller, new tunnels Squit and his moles had created. "Really," he said, displaying as much sincerity as he could muster, "I would have much rather discussed the matter like a gentleman…perhaps over a cup of tea, or a gin and tonic. I called and called, pleaded with them to come out, hoping that some compromise could be reached…" he paused to observe the expressions on the faces of Pot, Frutely and Slobber. They didn't look convinced

– still choosing to see his action as unreasonable. He placed his hands on his 'hips' and said with true indignation: "It is technically *my* Palace! He was trespassing!"
"Right on Sebo", said Tree, his view being somewhat less sympathetic than the others.
"Finally!" said Sebastian, "Thank you, my friend of the foliage."
"Ah well!" said Slobber, dismissing a situation that he was powerless to influence. "Shall we see where those moley fellows got to?" It was only when he tried to move that he realised his bonds were still very much tied.
Sebastian apologised for not attending to their ropes earlier and, with surprising dexterity, bent down and extended a razor sharp claw – cutting through each of the ropes with the very tip. The three rose to their feet, rubbing their wrists and looking up at Sebastian with polite smiles of gratitude; smiles that did their best not to betray their shared concern over the ease of Mr Squit's despatch.

Slobber, still intent on following the moles, started off down the tunnel. Realising that he was alone in his adventuring, he turned to beckon the others, "Well!?" he said, "Don't you want to see an end to this tale?"
"Of course!" said Frutely, whose concern over the true nature of Sebastian's character had caused her to drift into a dream of logical conclusions. She gently shook her head, forcing herself back into the reality of here and now, and moved to join her drooling companion. Pot picked up Tree's bucket, and tucked Matchwood into his belt. He would follow Frutely. The kiss she had delivered dwelt on his mind. He was still unclear as to why she had kissed him at all, not that he was complaining, but he did feel that some explanation was required. Did she mean it? Was it likely to happen again? Did she enjoy it? What sort of wedding would she like? And so on…
"If anyone's interested…" piped up Tree, "I don't particularly want to go." His comment went unanswered, the others clearly dismissing it as typical cynicism and a general lack of

the spirit of adventure. In fact that wasn't it at all, as his next utterance served to point out – "How many moles were there? Did anyone count?"

"Ah", said Frutely. "Yes. Good point."

"Step aside," said Sebastian, "I'll come with you. I doubt they'll attempt to do harm to you with me looking on."

Despite their nagging doubts over his reliability, the five travellers had to admit that Sebastian's presence would deter any would-be attackers, particularly attackers armed with pickaxes and Pobble Strikes.

"Good point", said Slobber, after a brief period of thought. "Move aside fellows, let the man go ahead." His words were greeted with frowns from Frutely and Pot, as they bobbed their heads, and raised then lowered their eyebrows, desperately trying to quietly suggest that having Sebastian up front was not a good idea.

Slobber watched the giant creature lower himself onto all fours and slip down the passage. Much to everyone's surprise, his large body fitted snugly into the circular space of the snaking tunnel.

Reaching up and removing a fresh torch from its metal holder, and watching Sebastian's tail snake past, Slobber whispered "Maybe you want to walk ahead of that many teeth but I don't!"

Down the tunnel they went, their pace dictated by their rather large guide. As they moved down the stony corridor, Pot made several attempts to broach the subject of the kiss with Frutely. His efforts however, did not pass beyond the point of opening his mouth to ask his carefully rehearsed question, only to quickly shut it again – deciding that his words needed more thought.

As he jogged down the corridor, he offered a decisive nod: "Got it!" he muttered to himself, speeding the movement of his legs in order to catch up to Frutely, who – being somewhat fitter and free from the luggage of a small, sarcastic tree – kept pace with the longer legs of Slobber.

"Frutely," he puffed as he sidled up to her, "there's something I need to ask you..."

"I DON'T BELIEVE IT!" shouted Frutely, forcing Potfondle's question, along with his body to come to a sudden halt.
"What!?" said Pot, his eyes fixed firmly on Frutely's face – completely oblivious to their shared surroundings.
"I don't bloody believe it!" spat Frutely, completely ignoring Pot in favour of striding across the open space of Squit's meeting room, halting in front of the result of her stolen plans. Standing in front of the curious construction, she immediately began assessing it. Tutting to herself and shaking her head: "A perversion of science!" she muttered, through angrily gritted teeth. "A debasement of the basic principles of the search for knowledge!" she continued, her irritation at what Squit had used her design to produce, rose and grew, culminating in her grabbing the table on which this 'Lieometer' – as she termed it – sat, and pushing with all her might until the table, along with its offensive contents, crashed onto the floor. Not content with seeing this contraption break into several pieces, Frutely – just for good measure – kicked and stamped at each fragment. Viewing her vandalism for a moment and clearly concluding that this was not quite enough, she hurled each piece at the wall, shattering it still further.
"Can we go now," asked Tree, "or is there anything else around here you'd like to vandalise? By the Gods look! There's a couple of pesky chairs over there!"
"Shut it, sticky!" came Frutely's angry reply, "before I find the urge to do a little light pruning!"
"To think…" offered Pot, hoping to calm a potentially tricky situation, "we drank to the health of that rancid man."
Frutely chose not to dwell on the matter since it was she, and her naiveté that had precipitated the raising of beer bottles in the first place.

Feeling that their work in this particular place was done, the group continued on, with Slobber and Potfondle undecided as to which posed the greater danger, Sebastian's spiny tail or Frutely's explosive temper.

As their journey continued, Tree found a curious question fill his mind. A question that though utterly logical and really worth everyone's attention, once more went completely unnoticed: "I thought he said he couldn't fit down here."

As they moved down, deeper into the darkness, the glowing, flickering torch flame soon became their only source of light. Down and down they walked, until the walls of the tunnel suddenly gave way into a large, dark, open space.

"Blimey!" announced an extremely surprised Chokkle, as his eyes acknowledged the visage of Sebastian's head, as it penetrated the room. In response, all eyes turned, most moles forced to issue some expression of surprise and alarm – many unrepeatable.

As the enormous figure glided further into their presence, all eyes stayed fixed until, quite suddenly and without any form of warning, the small pink creatures burst into action. Without apparent purpose, they scattered – running this way and that, their panicked dashing about so devoid of direction or aim that many crashed straight into one another – their shrieks of terror suddenly coming to an abrupt end as they collapsed, unconscious, onto the floor. Pot and Slobber found the humour of this sight too great to resist, as bursts of laughter erupted from their bodies. Tree allowed a pause in his chuckling to describe the scene to Matchwood who, in turn, joined in with the hilarity. Frutely too, found that her still present feelings of anger were no match for the moles' frantic, energetic and utterly pointless rushing around. Even Sebastian, who had at first tried to calm the situation with gentle assurances that he wouldn't eat anyone, found it hard to prevent the occasional chuckle from escaping.

The laughter increased as panic was soon joined by confusion – quite literally blind confusion – as the light from Slobber's torch suddenly made its presence felt, reflecting off the smooth, glassy surface of the cavern walls.

"What in the world is going on up here!?" shouted Graith as he emerged from the new tunnel, the glimpse he caught of Sebastian before Slobber's torch burnt his view, fully answering his question. Every bit the leader, Graith shouted "Put that damn thing down! Can't you see what it's doing to us!? We won't hurt you, if that thing don't hurt us...My word on it!"

"Don't worry," said Sebastian, his words intentionally loud enough to be easily overheard, "if anyone so much as spits at you, I'll eat them!"

Slobber, realising that the light was actually causing the moles very real pain, ceased his laughing and quickly turned about, using his body to block the crippling glare of the flame, while the moles groped around for their eye-shades.

"Is that where you've been blasting?" questioned Frutely, pointed to the fresh scarring of the newly formed tunnel entrance.

"Yip!" said Graith proudly. "That's the second stage."

Pot sniffed the air: "Cor! What's that awful stink!?"

"Ah," said Graith sheepishly and glancing in the direction of the toilet, "that's Stage One... You get used to it after a while."

Graith looked around, mainly at Pot, Frutely and Slobber – his eyes, though hidden by his visor, were still reluctant to place themselves in the direction of the giant monster which stood, arms folded, quietly surveying his surroundings. "Hang on", he said at length. "If you're here, where's the Master?"

The three adventurers looked at one another from their separate areas of the room. "I think he means the streaky fellow", suggested Tree.

"Ah!" said Slobber, striding through the now gathered and recovered moles, "The big fellow ate him", he said nonchalantly. "Got a problem with that, talk to him."

Graith looked at Chokkle, and then at the faces of the rest of his men. The expressions of shock and grief were curiously short-lived. "Ah well!" said Graith, with a deep shrug of his shoulders. "Didn't like the chap very much, anyway."

"Yeah," added Chokkle, "we only followed him coz of the Egg."
"Egg?" inquired Slobber, a tad confused.
Graith, showing signs of being more than a little irritated that his Second had allowed these strangers into a Clan secret, without any obvious thought, explained the details of 'those who follow the Egg of Gertrude'.
"The egg of who!?" asked Match with a slight chuckle, breaking his silence at last.
"Gertrude", said Chokkle, directing his reply at Potfondle – understandably believing it was he who had asked the question. "Master Festulas possessed the Egg, so we followed him."
"Well…" continued Match, as Pot lifted him from his belt to sounds of amazement from the assembled moles, "wait around a while and you can witness a Nassian lay an egg…your egg, to be precise."
The moles looked around at each other, as the slow dawn of understanding shone its light into their minds. Suddenly, as if with one mind, they all sank to their knees in praise of their new Master. That Sebastian had obtained the Egg by swallowing the previous owner was not a factor for consideration. That he now had it at all, was.

CHAPTER TWENTY-NINE

Slobber stood at the entrance to – or, depending on your point of view, exit from – the cave, his ears straining as he attempted to verify a sound he thought he'd heard. The others were unaware of his absence as they all busied themselves in various ways. Sebastian, surrounded by his new, loyal subjects, surveyed the room. He knew this place. He had been here before. Frutely and Potfondle came to him as he shared his memories, describing it as a meeting place – a place of great significance as he recalled. As he continued, Frutely broke away to inspect the freshly exposed face of the new tunnel. With Sebastian's tales echoing around the large, bell-shaped interior, she found her mind once more consumed with questions: *The Zintal protected us from the explosions!?*, her thoughts repeating Squit's earlier words. *What rubbish!* "You!" she said, interrupting Sebastian, and pointing in the direction of Graith.

"Graith!" said Graith abruptly, angry at the rudeness of this person.

"Whatever. What exactly were you doing here?"

"Told you, finding a way to cut through Zintal", he said, nodding apologetically to Sebastian and moving to join her at the tunnel entrance.
"No. That's not it. I know it and you know it, so I ask you again...What – are – you – doing – here!!?" she said, with a deep scowl scarring her face, distorting her complexion.
Graith looked puzzled. He turned to face his Clan, hoping that one of them might have some understanding as to what this woman was on about. He looked back at Frutely, offering nothing more than a silent head-shake, accompanied by an obvious shrug of his bare shoulders.
Frutely huffed impatiently. It was obvious to her – at least it was now – that much of what she and the others had been told, was complete and utter nonsense. Her irritation that none but her had reached this conclusion, was somewhat diluted by the fact that she – the only seismologist in the group or indeed, the country – was only just now realising that she, let alone anyone else, had been mind-numbingly slow to wake up to the facts. Firstly, as her earlier thoughts had indicated, the idea of the very substance they were blasting, acting as some kind of insulation against the vibrations of those very explosions, was impossible. The effect of a blast, created by nearly 100 Pobble Strikes on the surrounding rock, would have caused such a degree of shaking as to bring down the roof of any subterranean cave – the shockwaves felt on the surface were example enough of that. Secondly; she found it inconceivable that Graith – a mole, a 'Master Digger' – would consider it a worthwhile exercise to create a tunnel, when it was clear from Squit's confession that his, and the rest of the PEA's intention, was to use his skills to deepen, and widen the Great Twit. "Why a tunnel?" she eventually said, in response to Graith's confounded visage. "Your Master – that Festering chap. He worked for the PEA. They aren't interested in tunnels..." she allowed her inquisition to tail off, hoping that her assistance would allow a moment of blinding reality to shine through the mole's ears, illuminating his brain. She

watched hopefully as Graith's facial expression began to shift and change. The image of cogs turning was so graphic in her mind that an audible scraping of rusty metal was almost detectable.

Graith looked at Frutely, her head tilted to one side, a curious smirk on her face and her eyes wide, hoping to somehow telepathically assist him further. He looked at Chokkle who, having been privy to Dr. Gaiberond's words, was himself desperately searching for an answer to her inferences. The two then searched the faces of the rest of their Clan, hoping that some vital piece of evidence would suddenly present itself. This glancing around continued for what seemed like an age. Frutely's face grew redder, as the visible strain of mentally projecting the finale to her point was beginning to tell. The pair looked at her, their men, the tunnel entrance, everywhere in fact, before finally both Graith and Chokkle suddenly had that 'eureka moment' Frutely had been so desperately hoping for. There it was! That wondrous moment! Frutely was of course, prevented from seeing Griath or Chokkle's eyes but she was certain that behind those visors, they were wide – echoing the vision she could perceive – as two jaws slowly dropped open!

"Well?" she said, feeling that now was the right time to drag their conclusions out into the open.

"Bloody hell!" said Graith, in a classic moment of true understatement.

"Of course!" blurted Chokkle – this at least, as far as Frutely was concerned, was a little more encouraging.

Graith and Chokkle stared blankly at one another, as the utter stupidity of their blind obedience and unquestioned loyalty, was realised. It was obvious, at least it was now. The techniques required to tunnel were completely different to the disciplines employed for dredging – even dredging a riverbed of near solid Zintal.

Frutely picked up a broken pick handle and tore off a piece of her clothing to wrap around its tip. Borrowing a flame from Slobber, she 'permitted' Graith and Chokkle to lead her down into their freshly excavated hole.

"Funny thing is," commented Graith, as they navigated its gentle slope, "this dig was becoming strangely easy."

"Easy?" questioned Frutley.

"Yeah, we were shifting more rock than we had any right to."

Frutely left this point without response. Her general feeling after all, was that they had no right to go shifting any amount of rock in the first place.

Upon reaching the tunnel's end, Frutely gently touched the wall, stroking it as though it were a favourite pet. It was warm, not only warm but offering a strange, gentle vibration – almost purring.

She found herself lost in the moment once more, a little like the experience she had had at the entrance cave, when first her hand had come into contact with its walls. This time however, the feeling was different – similar, but different nonetheless. In the strange entrance hall, it was as though she had surrendered her will. Here it was different, she couldn't quite put her finger on it...here she was surrounded by a feeling of great wisdom and peace. At the same time though, there was a sense of foreboding and unrest, which she found curious. Graith and Chokkle watched as this strange woman carried out her peculiar examination of their tunnel. To them it was rock, nothing more, nothing less.

CHAPTER THIRTY

Slobber turned to face his companions, the remainder of which were sitting, happily listening to Sebastian's tales of the past – tales that were almost intentionally incomplete but quite entertaining all the same. "They're coming!" he announced, his face echoing the clear concern in his voice.
"They?" said Sebastian, turning his head gently. "Who are they?"
"The Pillicks!" replied Slobber, moving quickly to join the group.
"I thought you'd trapped them!" said Tree.
"Hardly trapped, old boy. I just decided to hold them until they forgot why they had all congregated in the first place. I assure you my dear, tiny plant, there was never any danger to them…not the sort of danger they were intent on placing at my feet, at least."

The moles quickly picked up their instruments of excavation and moved to guard the entrance, while Potfondle, concerned for Frutely's safety, rushed down the dark corridor to warn her of the imminent attack.

Sebastian sat silently, staring into the entrance of the new tunnel. Only when Frutely, Potfondle and the others returned did he speak up. "He can't have seriously thought..." he said – almost to himself, seemingly as though an idea had just crossed his mind – allowing his sentence to remain unfinished.
"Seriously thought what?" obliged Potfondle.
Sebastian stared into space for a moment, as though mulling something over in his mind. "I'm terribly sorry," he said, in reply to the question. "I was just thinking aloud."
"Thinking what!?" pressed Pot, his and everybody else's attention now divided between keeping a watchful eye on the entrance, and eager to hear what Sebastian was referring to.
"Well," said Sebastian, taking far more time to respond than seemed appropriate, "the thought occurred that our Mr Squit who, as I speak, is giving me terrible indigestion, might have been attempting to locate The Orb of Skeltenna."
"That mythical power ball, thing?" said Pot.
"Yes. That's the chap", replied Sebastian, his voice calm, his general demeanour far more relaxed than it had been during their first encounter with the townsfolk.
"Can't say what Master Festulas was after, assuming he was after anything at all," offered Graith, "but Mighty One, I'd have to say that he had us tunnelling in the right direction."
"Oh?"
"There is something down there," aided Frutely, "I felt it."
Sebastian quickly requested an update as to how far the hoard were. "Still a way off!" came the stammering response from one of the moles.
"Alright," he said, looking down at the original 'interlopers', "if it is the Orb, and half the stories about its power are true, it might prove to be of some assistance in our impending predicament."
"Assistance?" said Slobber hastily. "How?"
"Well if you, and a few of my new mole friends here, could quickly locate it and bring it out here..."
"Yes?"
"I might be able to use it to...oh I don't know, send the angry

mob back whence it came."
"It can do that?" said Frutely, a little panic detectable in her voice.
"Possibly."
Slobber and his friends wasted no time, ushering to Graith and setting off down the tunnel. "When we get to the end," said Frutely as they ran down the corridor, "that Pobble Strike you were chucking about earlier, might prove useful."
"You got it, lady!" replied Graith, retrieving said item from his belt in readiness.
As soon as the group arrived at their immediate destination, Graith placed the Strike in a small groove while Chokkle quickly set up the detonator. Pot, Slobber and Frutely stayed back – at Graith's suggestion – and waited for the tiny explosive to do its job.
"Are we quite safe?" asked a concerned Slobber.
Graith simply nodded casually before depressing the tiny plunger, offering little opportunity for further distance to be acquired...***KKKRRROOOOOOSH!***

"By all the Gods!" whispered Slobber, slowly rising to his feet through the swirling dust, as he stared straight into the brilliant light emanating from the chamber, which their efforts had uncovered. He was soon joined by the others, as all five stood in awe of the sight of the Orb, as it spun and pulsated.
"I can't move!" said Frutely, her attempts at forward momentum prevented somehow. The others too, found their ability to progress into the chamber itself, strangely impeded.
"Look!" said Graith, noticing further movement from the walls themselves, as hundreds of colourful strands of bright light flowed out into the tunnel.
Their hypnotic, undulating motion allowing them to flow gently beneath the surface of the rock, causing it to shine, as their gentle caress caused the material to smooth and gleam.
All turned to watch as these beautiful tentacles snaked their way past them, up the corridor. All still powerless to move their limbs.

CHAPTER THIRTY-ONE

The moles braced themselves, as the sound of shouting voices grew louder and louder.
Sebastian crouched down by the new tunnel-mouth – his head nearly twice the width of its opening: "You must hurry!" he shouted. "Our guests are almost upon us." Looking back at the entrance and his new-found servants, his eyes flashed and his lip curled: *I can't possibly kill all of them by myself,* he thought, *one always manages to escape!* – his voice to himself, somehow different to that which had been heard aloud.
Turning back to the cave, concerned that no reply had been forthcoming, Sebastian once more pleaded for their return: "I really do wish you'd hurry it up down there. Our circumstance is about to become rather uncomfortable, I fear."
"We can't move, sir", shouted Graith, struggling to free his legs from the invisible force that tied them to the ground. "We've found the Power-ball your Honour, but something's stopping us from getting anywhere near it."
The snaking strands of light continued up the rough stone – their course clear, their path obvious, as their pace quickened. Sebastian saw them as they neared, his brow furrowing deeply as his lack of understanding dawned. His reaction was

to move away, something deep within him found the sight somehow disturbing.
As the snaking strands made their way towards him, he backed away – his face powerless to prevent the reflection of the thought in his head: *No!*
The moles stepped away from the cavern entrance and stood, tense – awaiting the imminent arrival of the rampaging mob. The Pillicks burst in, shouting and waving their weaponry and newly-fashioned torches – their shouts, which had allowed their momentum to remain constant, suddenly left them, as though it were a bird frightened from its perch. The Pillicks stopped dead and stared at the slithering, flowing lines of colour, as they spread out and across the domed ceiling; over their heads and down to the floor behind them.
The moles too, stood in wonder – all thoughts of battle seemingly removed by the beauty of the display that danced and flowed about them. No one really noticed, as the criss-crossing lines knitted across the void of the entrance – turning the hollow space into very solid stone, preventing anyone from leaving.

Back at the chamber, the pulsing, floating stone began to throb and vibrate ever more intensely – the lines of colour keeping pace with the rhythm, as their own colour pulsed and glowed in response to the Orb's initial action. Slobber, Pot, Frutely, Graith and Chockle watched, their mouths open wide in wonder and amazement as the Orb suddenly, and without warning, sent out a final, blinding flash of pure, white light. Its brilliance consumed them as it washed over them – through them. Up the tunnel the radiant wave went. Up and out into the freshly-sealed cavern, washing all present with its glory. Then, still maintaining the attitude of a wave, the brilliance retreated – leaving behind it a virtually bare and empty cavern, clear of Pillicks, Slobbers, Tanglepines, Nassians, and Kia Willow fragments. Only the moles remained, the action which had sent everyone else away, had transferred them from their respective places about the cavern, to the Orb chamber itself.

Here they all stood – still, motionless – staring blankly into the softened light of the resting Orb, its glow somehow causing them no discomfort, as it softly flickered and pulsed – its curious activity seemingly conducting a beautiful and silent conversation. In response, the moles simply nodded at points, as though signalling their consent to some unheard request or suggestion.
Once again the glowing sphere began to rotate, as it lifted itself once more from its decorated plinth. Once satisfied with its position, it once again issued a brief and gloriously brilliant flash before vanishing, taking the moles with it, and leaving the chamber still, dark and utterly deserted.

At the mouth of the Great Twit, there sat a small group of very dazed and extremely confused people. Slobber, Frutely and Potfondle silently looked at one another, their faces a picture of total and complete befuddlement. Even Tree found that his voice had no expression to adequately articulate their curious situation. Slowly scanning about them, they noticed, sitting still, high on the beach, a small but perfectly constructed wooden boat – its name proudly displayed on a plaque at its bow: *Matchwood.*
"What's going on?" said Slobber, as soon as his confusion would permit his jaw, tongue and vocal cords to synchronise. Frutely picked herself up and walked to the water's edge. Staring out to sea, she attempted to find some explanation that could answer such a simple, but deep and searching question. Everyone looked in her direction, hoping that her scientific mind could offer some rational explanation to what had taken place. Their shared wish perhaps, to bring a suitable end to their journey, and make some kind of sense of it all. Dr. Gaiberond turned slowly and looked deeply into searching eyes. "We went where we did not belong. We saw that which we were not meant to see…" she paused, knowing that her answer was substandard and uncharacteristically philosophical…not to mention totally unfounded, "someone

politely showed us the door."
Slobber heard these words but did not truly understand them. He looked at Pot and smiled. "Well," he said, "at least we did what we set out to do."
"We did..?"
"Yeah, I suppose we did", agreed Pot, "More, in fact. Not only did we find the cause of the quakes, we probably stopped them too."

In a land far from Gweep, a large creature carefully set a fire and placed a freshly caught fish on a spit. It extended its long neck, and began to cough and gag, as it forced a lump out of its stomach and up its throat. As the regurgitation reached its mouth, the creature bowed its head, allowing its cargo to spill out onto the grassy ground. A further, sharp cough and the creature spat out a cane and a hat.
Festulas Squit lay motionless but alive, near the crackling fire – his hat and cane lying nearby. Sebastian looked over the pathetic creature he had been carrying in his secondary gut. Gently, he reached out with the tip of a very sharp claw, and carefully plucked a small leather pouch from Squit's coat pocket, and shook the contents out into his large, webbed hand. He looked at the small, smooth, egg-shaped splinter from The Orb of Skeltenna, before lifting it, and placing it carefully into his mouth.

Festulas Squit, in the dull haze that exists between the night and day of consciousness, found his ears plagued by the sound of an all-too-familiar voice. A voice that at first had him convinced that he was indeed dead, and that his duplicitous and miserable excuse for a life, had led his abrupt disagreement with mortality to one unavoidable end...He was in Hell!
It was the deep and precise tones of his Master that pervaded his consciousness. The unseen voice, still unseen by him now, as he struggled to prevent morbid curiosity from opening

his eyes, and taking a peek at the creature that had devoured him, and had now, rather disgustingly, vomited him up again. "A snivelling worm of a man you are, my dear Squit. A pathetic wretch who deserves to be slowly digested by my stomach acids… My bidding will again be the tune to which you dance. The Egg led me to the Orb once. It will do so again…" As Sebastian's head slowly sank beneath the surface of the water, an unspoken thought glimmered in his mind – *Next time, we must be gathered. All of us together. Together we can destroy them all!*

CHAPTER THIRTY-TWO

The world was on fire…again! Slobber sat bolt upright in his bed, and with panic in his eyes, looked sharply around his room. He was home. He knew that. He had known that every morning for the past week but, as with those other mornings, it had taken him some small measure of time to realise it.

On this particular morning however, things felt a little different. He didn't know exactly why, only that the nightmarish dreams that had haunted his sleep that night – as they had for the past week – were somehow different. Something new had appeared, something created... No, not created... Slobber struggled to explain it to himself. Something new had been *introduced*. Yes, that was it.

He had never been terribly good at remembering his dreams, and for the last few days, his mind had really only permitted him to recall details for the briefest of moments.

"Need a reminder?" said Tree cheerfully, sitting on the window ledge, taking a moment from bathing in the brilliance of the morning light.

"Quiet!" returned Slobber sharply, desperately attempting to

clarify the new image that his unconscious mind had presented him with – "Bugger! It's gone."
"Now do you need a reminder?" pressed Tree, his question born of experience. His large companion had been in something of a deluded state for the past week, since passing out on the beach, where he and the others had inexplicably found themselves.
Believing it to be nothing more than garden-variety exhaustion, the decision had been taken for the newly reconstructed Matchwood to take him home, accompanied by Pot and Tree. Frutely had elected to remain – anxious to report to her Paymasters in the Government, but more anxious to return to Mantura, to answer the several thousand questions that had begun to rotate through her scientific mind.

The weekend away had taken its toll on the large blue man. He had ably managed to cope with being terrified on the journey to Gweep. He had managed to cope with being half drowned. Believing his friends dead – only to quickly discover that they weren't – was also something he had managed to take in his stride. Meeting a large 'extinct' monster, as well as a Clan of 'extinct' moles, had been something of a surprise, but had all sunk in quite well, without causing any major psychological trauma. No, the blame for his recent condition it must be said, lay squarely on the frame of Matchwood. Seeing bits of his floating companion burning away on a large fire, had been troublesome to say the least, but this was nothing compared to the damage inflicted by Matchwood intentionally stabbing Slobber in the thigh.
The wound itself had been relatively small, and the pain it caused had been reduced by the amount of adrenaline flowing through Slobber's veins at the time. The problem had truly been caused by an infection, permitted to gain entry into Slobber's system by way of the small puncture left by the large Matchwood splinter.

"Hey, you're awake!" said Potfondle cheerfully, as he walked into Slobber's bedroom, his arms weighed down by a rather heavy breakfast tray.
"OK. Let's get started…" he said, placing the tray on the bedside table. "Just over a week ago, you and I met in a pub. After several drinks you agreed to come to Gweep, and help me discover the cause of a spate of recent groundshakes…"
"He knows that!" interrupted Tree.
"Don't need a reminder, then?" asked Pot, his voice tinged with a hint of disappointment. He had rather enjoyed recanting the tale over the past few mornings – he was, he felt, getting pretty good at it too. In fact, hearing himself tell and retell the story, had given rise to aspirations of writing it all down in some kind of book.

With Pot and Tree in close observation, Slobber bit on a slice of toast, and swung his legs out over the side of his large, waterproof sleeping vessel.
Planting his feet firmly on the wooden floor, he rose to his full height, instinctively clutching the fresh bandages of his now healed thigh.
He excused himself and quickly sidled down the gallery corridor to his bathroom.
"Good morning sir!" barked Sergeant Enamuelle, as his employer strolled into view, offering a salute that could slice through Zintal. "Right..!" he said, permitting himself to stand easy. "A little over one week ago, you departed base camp en route for Gweep. Upon arrival you rendezvoused with the rest of your squad, and employed the services of one Match Wood for safe passage upstream..."
"It's OK, Sarge", interrupted Slobber. "Synchronised firing of the grey rifles today", he said, gently tapping his temple.
"Understood, sir."

Slobber, his mind quietly tormented by the evasive images of his dream, quickly concluded his bathroom business and made his way back to the bedroom. Stopping briefly at the

bathroom door and half turning his head, he quietly said:
"Fancy a little trip later, Sarge?"
"Going back, sir?"
Slobber left the question unanswered for what seemed to Sarge as an eternity. Indeed, he was about to repeat himself when Slobber, with a sudden feeling of acquired clarity replied softly, "It's time."

CHAPTER THIRTY-THREE

Festulas Squit sat uneasily in the office of his superior, staring up at the mountainous peak of the large desk, behind which sat an imposing carved, wooden chair. Festulas's unease heightened, as behind him he heard the sound of the large double doors push open, and then swing shut again.
His gaze remained fixed ahead as Flalian Trapp, Director of Development for the PEA glided past him, seating himself on his throne, and fixing a long, hard stare on the shuddering man before him.
"Mr Trapp, sir…" he offered, his words cut down by a silent, long finger, that reached out and sharply halted his voice with a single, slow point in the direction of the ceiling. Flalian Trapp then forced his subordinate to sit in uncomfortable silence, while he slowly leafed through the pages of a darkly covered file – occasionally raising a long finger to his mouth, where it was greeted by the lick of a serpent tongue that flicked out of its soulless home.
"Well, Squit," came the words from behind the desk, Trapp intentionally sitting far back in his chair so as to prevent Festulas from looking upon the deliverer from his low seat, "I must confess to feeling a degree of disappointment with your

efforts in Gweep." The conclusion of this somewhat negative statement, was followed by a pause of sufficient length to allow Festulas to believe it was now his turn to speak. As the pause lengthened, Squit found that his nerves had reached the point where his vocabulary was now their prisoner, opening his mouth on several occasions, only to find nothing but silence escaping. He was almost relieved when a single word managed to free itself from its incarceration, and fly out into the void – "Well…"he began, hoping that the success of this single word would prompt others to follow its route, before the finger of Trapp once more cut him off.
"Please don't interrupt me when I am speaking", he said quietly. In actual fact, Flalian had finished at that point, or at least, he had intentionally given Festulas that impression. Being something of a cruel man, one of his favourite pastimes was to intimidate the 'lower ranks'.
The 'fooled you' pause as he called it, was one of his more obvious tools in successfully achieving this aim – simple, yet highly effective. His office was another. The whole room had been carefully constructed according to his design, to make even the largest of men feel small and insignificant.
"As I was about to say," he continued, as he slowly leant forward and into view, "before I was so rudely interrupted..." he paused once more, this time allowing a firm, unwavering stare to penetrate the very heart of the increasingly shrinking Squit. "Perhaps I was not clear about my expectations of you in this matter", the stare continued, preventing the 'fooled you' pause from being a useful pitfall on this occasion. "I appointed this task to you personally. All you had to do was cut your way through a little Zintal and locate the Orb of Skeltenna. What happened?"

The report that Flalian had taken such pains to slowly leaf through was, in his view, incomplete. He firmly believed there was much more to this saga than had been submitted by Squit. True, the task Flalian had personally set him was not an easy one. Firstly, there was the fact that cutting through

Zintal was believed to be virtually impossible. Secondly, and this was a point that Squit himself had raised at one point during their meeting – in a brief moment of uncommon courage – was that there was absolutely no proof whatsoever that the Orb of Skeltenna was anything more than a particularly unbelievable myth.

The terror of his meeting with Trapp over, Festulas Squit sat outside, his head once more buried in his hands. More and more he was feeling like an ill-used pawn in some giant chess game. His meeting with Flalian Trapp had not gone well – not that he had expected anything else, mind you.
Of course his report was incomplete! He had only given half-truths about the Clan of moles, and made no reference at all about how he came to secure their services. He had not mentioned the gang of uncontrollable villagers, played down the severity of the groundshakes, and said nothing of a large, blue man and a couple of Pillicks. His report obviously referred to the moles, but their exit from the scene – as well as his own return to Head Office – had been blamed on a massive rock fall. The moles, it was claimed, had been killed in a disaster of their own creation, and that he had been lucky to come out alive... Frankly, given that his briefing made positively no reference to Sebastian either, it must be said that he had displayed a real talent for creative writing.

As he sat, desperately trying not to lose his mind in all this double-life stuff he had found himself living, a single, frightening thought streaked through his mind. Quite simply, Flalian Trapp was far too clever to be so easily mislead by the rubbish he had submitted. Squit turned his head and looked up at the window of Trapp's hellish office and his face dropped.
The single, frightening thought had become a seed, from which was quickly sprouting a terrifying plant. This 'plant' began to form a consciousness of its own, which spoke to Squit in words he did not wish to hear: *'Trapp isn't fooled by*

any of this – he is too clever. Do you honestly believe he would be where he is today if someone like you could pull the wool over his eyes?'

Squit began to reason with himself, hoping to put some kind of mental order to it all: *He gave the task personally... He gave me the task personally. He never gives tasks personally. He tells someone, they tell someone else and so on... My reports were to be submitted to him only – no others were to be contacted or advised. All monies and materials were supplied from external sources, not the central PEA deposit...* Festulas sat, his eyes still fixed on the window high above. The frown on his face deepening: *How did you know about the Orb? Only my Master knows about the Orb!* Until that time, he had given it curiously little thought. His PEA Master had summoned him to his office a couple of years ago. Until then, Squit wasn't even sure where his office was, let alone been asked to go there. There he had met with Trapp and been told what he was to do, and how he was to start out. Stealing Dr. Gaiberond's plans for the Comparometer had been Trapp's idea, as too had been the suggestion of a possible location for a lost Clan of moles! *How much does he actually know?* Squit asked of himself, staring down at the ground. *Does he know as much as my Master? Or...* looking back up at the office window: *Do you know more?* If Festulas had begun to feel overwhelmed in the halls of Mantura, this was a feeling of complete and utter suffocation. A few minutes ago, he had begun to feel like a pawn. Now he was starting to think that he wasn't even a dirty mark on the board. Standing, he looked sharply all about him, and then up again at the window. *Are you one of Trapp's spies?* he thought of anyone whose gaze even vaguely looked in his direction, as he began to shuffle down the footpath. One thing Squit had decided for certain: he must get back to his Master – wherever he was. A strange sense of safety began to fill his heart, as he made his way through the busy streets, desperately trying to avoid eye contact with anyone, for fear that his every move was now under the scrutiny of Flalian Trapp. He knew that in the company of his Master he would be safe and free – well, relatively free – from the torment of the PEA hierarchy. True, his Master didn't tell him everything, but that was alright because he made no pretension that he ever would. And true, his Master was incredibly rude, and left Squit with the terrible feeling that he could be terminated at any moment... Actually Festulas found it a little tricky to find anything terribly acceptable about that one, since on the one and only occasion he actually saw his Master, he was eaten by him! With that in mind, Festulas found it difficult to give himself any assurances that death by the hand of his Master would be anything like quick and painless. Right now, it all boiled down to one simple thing in his mind – power. His Master, he was convinced, had more!

CHAPTER THIRTY-FOUR

Sebastian stood in the centre of the great hall of the Northern Palace and beckoned for silence. Turning slowly to look upon the faces of the assembled congregation of some 50 surviving Nassians, he smiled. "The time is close at hand, my people!" he said, holding his arms out at his sides, ushering in their attention to his solid words. "For too long have we been forced to hide away in the deep places of the world – skulking in caves and swimming silently in the dark lakes and wide oceans. Some of you may consider this freedom, but how many of you run in fear at the sounds of their ships and their tunnelling devices?" His congregation looked at each other, some nodding in agreement, perhaps recalling such occasions. "How soundly have you slept these past 1000 years, knowing the Landwalkers' infestation across our once glorious realm grows by the day?" Sebastian looked into the eyes of his congregation assembled there, together for the first time in centuries. He saw the fear, and he heard the unanswered questions, that ran through the minds of those whose conviction to the task at hand was not strengthened by his illogical rage.

"We are only 50!" shouted one, "while their numbers multiply

like ants on an invader!" Sebastian's eyes flashed with fury at this – his anger fortified by the murmurs of agreement that echoed around the great hall.
"THEY ARE THE INVADER! THEY DESTROYED OUR RACE WITH THEIR DISEASES AND THEIR INTOLERANCE FOR OUR SUPERIORITY!" He moved closer to the one whose comment had angered him so much. "You, Stennaron", he said – his voice soft and empathetic. "You fear their numbers and their machines!?"
"I do. What concerns me Sebastian, is that you don't!"
Sebastian laughed and turned his back on Stennaron. The others looked at one-another quizzically. Stennaron's point was a valid one. There were far more Landwalkers than there were Nassians, and the Nassians who remained were old and nearing their time. It was true that many, if not all, did look back on greater days with a sense of loss and anger, more so in recent years, since Sebastian had begun to make his presence felt once more, with promises of glory and power. Until then, the Nassians who remained had resigned themselves to an existence of hiding and skulking. They had in the past made efforts to co-exist with their smaller and often furrier cousins on the land, but this had usually resulted in witnessing lots of screaming and running away. Stennaron however, still harboured a desire for peace and understanding between the races – after all he, in common with many of the survivors, only had a few hundred years left to live. What was the point in wasting that small amount of time starting a war they could not possibly win?
"The days of glory of which you continually speak Sebastian, are long gone", he said, seemingly the only voice among them who was prepared to question their self-appointed King. "Our time is passed. Accept it. Their time, as annoying and distasteful to many of us as it may be, is just beginning."
"THE DAYS OF GLORY ARE ABOUT TO BE RE-LIVED!" came Sebastian's quick, and unsurprisingly angry response. Turning away once more, he reached into his mouth and carefully removed a small object, taking great pains not to

allow its gentle glow to be seen by anyone. He carefully gripped the stone between the claws of his thumb and forefinger before turning, sharply raising his hand high above his head. At first no one noticed that he was holding anything at all. Its soft energy lost in this huge space.
"PELLAEONATH!" Sebastian commanded, and in response, the small stone's light began to shine as brightly as the sun.
"The Orb!" came the immediate, reverential utterances of the assembled crowd. "He's found the Orb!"
"YES!" came Sebastian's gleeful reply to the increasing excitement that began to echo around the hall. "YES, MY PEOPLE. THE ORB IS ONCE AGAIN IN OUR POWER...!" he shouted, his twisted ego filling to capacity with the adoration that began to emanate from his subjects.
"KELTREMANCIAN!" he commanded, and the walls about them came alive with glowing colours of the shimmering veins within.

The room became alive with the manic, jumping about of power-crazed giants. Through the years, Sebastian's continual promises of glory, along with his hissed anger at the Landwalkers' responsibility for their virtual demise, had created the foundation. With the Orb now apparently in his possession, that foundation now had a proud, strong building upon it – a construction of angry bricks and spiteful mortar. Stennaron watched as his race bathed themselves in the vision of power and blood, his heart sickened by the sight of what his people had allowed themselves to become. He watched with virtual fury as Sebastian absorbed their lust for power, that fuelled their growing, misguided love for him. He soon found what he witnessed to cause his stomach to churn. So sick did he feel, that he soon found himself with no alternative but to quietly slip away, unobserved. "Not in my lifetime!" he spat angrily to himself, as he slid his way down the smooth corridor and out into the cold Northern Sea.

CHAPTER THIRTY-FIVE

Despite claims that his memory of the events of a week ago was complete, Slobber clearly had to fill in one or two blanks. As he and Potfondle strolled down the road towards Slobber's Ferry & Taxi Services (International Rank), it became clear to Pot, that not all the pieces of Slobber's mental jigsaw were in the box. At one point, for the second time that morning, Slobber had asked the whereabouts Frutely.
"She is *still* at the dig site, and we are *still* going to meet her there!" answered Tree abruptly; whispering to Pot, as he swung back and forth in his bucket – "He's not ready for this!" Slobber, overhearing this, had to admit that perhaps he was still a little hazy, but, for reasons still unclear to him, the journey back to Gweep had to be made now.

At Slobber's suggestion, the eight – including five Toothwranglers who were bedded down in the rucksack, uncomfortably situated between a pair of socks and a change of underwear – walked the three miles down to the jetty. He felt it prudent to give his mind as much time as possible, to adjust to the fact that he was once again venturing across the water. Actually, the main reason for his decision, was that he was concerned not to run into his taxi-driving cousin again – as polite a man as he was, he did find many of his extended family to be rather tedious people.

Matchwood sat patiently, a large 'Private Hire' banner displayed on his stern. "Hello Fountain Head", he said warmly, as Slobber and the others clambered aboard – Slobber's replacement Vacuhat, choosing at that moment to send a single jet of mouth water arching into the blue sky above.
"I still can't get over it..." responded Slobber, patting and stroking Match's side – paying close attention to the area where the splinter, that had so brutally attached itself to him, had come from. "You were smashed. Bits of you were burnt. Gods, a piece of you was stuck in my leg, for crying out loud! I just can't get over it!"
It was a mystery, of that there could be no denial: *When is a smashed up boat, not a smashed up boat?* was the curious brain-teaser that they were all faced with. For this question, at the present time at least, there was no answer. To the other mind-tickler – *When is a group of people standing in a cave, not a group of people standing in a cave?* – there was a solution, but the answer – *When that group of people is sitting on a beach* – was not a particularly satisfactory one, correct though it may be.

With all aboard, Match set his Filer Paddles in motion and they glided gently out of Vomit Bay and into the Big Blue. The trip was, as you might expect, not to be a silent or thoughtful one. Far too many unanswered questions remained – the WHAT, WHERE, WHY, WHEN, WHO and HOW of it:

- ➢ WHAT the hell had happened?
- ➢ WHERE had everyone gone? They knew where *they* had gone. They knew that the villagers had gone back to the village. Even the man who had been first to take up a stick

and allow his paranoia to get the better of him, had been returned to the beach.
They had seen him further down from where they found themselves sitting, scratching his head and looking mightily confused. They had no clue however, as to the whereabouts of the moles or Sebastian, although they did recall where the pale streak that was Festulas Squit had ended up.

- WHO had sent everyone away?
- WHY had they done it? and what's more...
- HOW?

The WHEN was a question still being worked on but, for the time being at least, WHEN will we get an answer to the other five questions was good enough.
Matchwood, as you might expect, was the one to whom many questions were directed. After all, he was telepathic, possessed biological independence, and was the oldest. Match was, he had to concede, utterly without even the merest hint of a clue about any of it. In all his 278 years – tree and boat – he had not so much as heard of such an occurrence ever happening before.
The sight of Sebastian had been something of a shock to him... As a salty-old-Sea-dog he admitted his belief in such creatures, but in the back of his mind he had accepted that the actual existence of such a being was highly unlikely. He was, of course, utterly wrong!
It was hoped that the eminent Dr. Gaiberond might be able to shed a little light into the dark corners of their curiosity – she was, after all, a scientist and regardless of her scientific discipline, scientists were usually quite intelligent people. Potfondle had seen Frutely three days previous. She had been filled with excitement over the prospect of joining a group of archaeologists, who had been given government permission to survey the ruins of Mantura – much to the irritation of the PEA.

As their journey progressed, aided by an extremely calm sea, Matchwood was introduced to Enamuelle and the others. At first he thought Slobber had brought mice aboard, but after one singularly impressive salute from the squad, he was convinced that these tiny men where solid and worthy of free passage. Enamuelle's description of Matchwood as 'a clearly experienced warrior of the water', hadn't hurt either.

The trip had reached that point where, regardless of how much there is to talk about, the conversation just runs dry. All sat in dreamy silence, no doubt still puzzling over the obvious, but quietly – to themselves. Slobber trailed his hand in the water, as Match continued to cut through its glassy surface, and once more attempted to draw nearer, the distant and unclear image of the individual who had presented himself in his dreams. The harder he thought on it, the more he realised that it was not just the previous night this person had appeared. For the past several nights his unclear visage had been there – shadowy, elusive, but ever present. As he continued to dwell on it, the sounds of the gentle sea, punctuated occasionally by yet another saliva spurt hitting the water, a friendly sleep drew him in – welcoming him to its bliss. Before long all concerns over past, present and future drifted away like so much flotsam, as the calm surface of the water matched the blue man's mental state... Until the dream began, that is!

Crashing rocks, lunging monsters, death, mayhem and destruction all presented themselves, as his tranquillity was smashed into a thousand pieces. He shuddered and convulsed as his mind attempted to remove him from this terrifying place. Then…silence. Stillness. Slobber watched this mental disaster as the images before him slowed and then stopped. As the horror with which he was faced began to melt away, his view pulled back.

He was watching himself standing in a place he did not recognise – a moorland of sorts, with rocks of grey, and heathers of brown and dark green. Above and all about him the dark clouds swirled and mixed, blocking out the clear blue that he hoped was still present behind their gloom. He sat cross-legged, patiently awaiting the arrival of his visitor. His conscious mind had no recollection of this place, but his dreaming mind knew it well – it had been here on more than one occasion. *Hello. This is new. What are you doing here?* his dreambody thought, as he observed that his companions had suddenly appeared at his side. The new arrivals said nothing, just sat cross-legged – with the Toothwranglers taking up positions on available knees and shoulders, for fear of sinking without trace, into the sea of moss that surrounded them. All sat, their faces patient and hopeful. The question of why they were there was largely irrelevant – it did not matter.

"There you are", thought Slobber's dreambody, as the tall figure slowly drifted towards them.
"Hello, my friends", came the reply from the elderly figure that now stood before them – his long, grey cloak flowing smoothly down to the ground.
"What..?" began Potfondle.
The figure held up his hand. *"No need to speak your words, my dear Pot. No need to think of what to say before you say it. In this place..."* he said, arching
his hand slowly above his head, directing their attention to their surroundings, *"in this place all thoughts are heard. All life is."*
"All life is...what?" thought Tree, joining the echoing telepathy of the conversation.
"All things Butsmell, will be understood... In time."
"Butsmell!?" thought the others in unison. Inappropriate as it felt in this place, and in this company, the necessity for a quick fit of the giggles could not be denied. *"Is that your name, Tree? Butsmell? It's not is it? It can't be! Butsmell!?"*

The man smiled as the hilarity continued, smirking at the wonderful irony that so much depended on a small group who still found things like that funny.
Actually, he found the whole thing vaguely amusing too but, being the grey figure of mystery, he did not permit himself to join in.
Slobber noticed his retreat, as did the others. Fearing their levity had insulted him somehow, Slobber 'shouted' after him:
"Is that it then!?"
"For now, my friends. Yes. Be aware of what has been said, and give no fear to that which is past..."
"Past what!?" said Pot, forgetting that this was a telepathic conversation.
"That which appears the same can often be different…" concluded the figure, as his image grew distant, before finally disappearing altogether.
"All life is!? The same is often different!? He's not shuffling with a full deck, that bloke!" suggested Tree, a little irritated that the others had been afforded such a good laugh at his expense.
The grey clouds above began to change, breaking up and dispersing. "Sorry, guys," said Slobber, "time for me to wake up now. If I can I'll try to remember some of this... No promises, though."

The eyelids of all aboard slowly opened, and all quickly looked for some sign in the others that what had just happened was real. A dream admittedly, but a shared experience.
"All life is…" said Slobber, looking straight into the startled eyes of Potfondle.
"That which appears the same can often be different…" added Enamuelle, drawing their attention to his small, uniformed presence.
Pot, in turn with the others, looked from face to face – eye to eye. A frown slowly appeared on his brow, then a cheeky smile appeared on his face.

"Butsmell!?" he said, looking down at Tree.
"Asses!" replied Tree, still more than a little peeved that his secret was now out.
Slobber smiled to himself, happy for one, that the thing he had struggled to recall was now clear – even if his message wasn't. He now remembered that last night the grey man's message had been simple, and at the time, obvious: *"Leave today, my friend. Take the others and go",* is all that he had said. It was those words, secure in his subconscious, that had motivated him to leave his sickbed that morning.

Slobber's relief from the realisation that he was not going mad found Itself suddenly interrupted, as he noticed that the water moving past his trailing hand was now faster than before...
"Match, are we in some kind of hurry all of a sudden?"
"We're being followed!" said Match. Causing all to swiftly scan the rear distance for signs of a vessel of some kind.
"Not *on* the water, under it", said Match, noticing their confusion at a clear horizon.
Slobber lurched forward, inadvertently spraying his companions with yet another spit-jet. "The same thing as last time!?" he enquired urgently, obviously concerned about their experience of a week ago.
"Not sure", replied Match quietly, "But I'd appreciate it if you wouldn't move about... It throws off my aqua-dynamics."
Slobber did nothing, his response delayed by an attempt to understand what Match meant by 'aqua-dynamics'.
Realising Slobber's lack of understanding in this particular matter, Matchwood considered explaining politely that his continued movement rocked the boat, and prevented efficient transit through the water. Deciding however, that this would take too long, he simply barked "Sit down, drool boy. You're buggering up my balance!!"

For over an hour Matchwood's tubes worked at full tilt – pushing the vessel ever faster through the water. At length he slowed, returning to his sedate pace once more. "Blimey!" he puffed, clearly exhausted by his efforts.
"That was a close one."
"What was it!?" came the panicked enquiry from all but the Toothwranglers – hardy soldier types, they were reluctant to display even the smallest amount of fear.
"Don't know," replied Match quietly, "but when a big, unidentified thing is following you, the law of the sea states: 'Get your backside out of there!' Trust me, you don't want to be around when something of that size is attempting to creep up on you!"
"Sebastian?" offered Slobber.
"Perhaps", replied Matchwood. "Looked a lot like him... Somehow different though..." Match prevented himself from announcing any more observations, choosing instead to offer simply, with a thoughtful tone: "That which appears the same can often be different."
These words caused surprised reaction in his companions. None of the others had seen him in the shared dream. No boats, no furniture, not even a nice campfire. Moreover, how could he have been there? That would have meant he was asleep. He couldn't have been asleep, he had to have been awake in order to notice he was being followed.
"My port side…" he offered, in simple reply to their repetitious questioning, "My left side…" he clarified to his land-dwelling friends.
"We all know which side is port!" spat Tree. "What are you talking about!?"
Matchwood patiently explained that his port side, save for his Filer Tube, had been asleep at the same time as the others. This was apparently quite usual and nothing to be scared of... Having cellular, biological independence, Matchwood had the ability to allow different parts of himself to sleep, while others remained awake.
"I didn't see you!" said Pot. "Where were you?"

"You could have materialised as a bench or something", added Tree.
"I was behind you, Butsmell", replied Match. "A rather fetching, small picket fence, as it happens...I've always wondered what it would be like to be a fence. Quite dull actually."

As the final four hours of their journey passed, the WHO, WHAT,
WHERE, WHEN, HOW and WHY returned:

- WHO was the man?
- HOW did he get into the dream?
- WHY had they all had the same dream at the same time?
- And WHAT in the world did 'give no fear to that which is past' mean?

The WHERE and WHEN of things, it was decided, would have to wait...mainly because they didn't have questions to attach to either, although the publicly offered reason was that there simply wasn't enough time.
With absolutely no tangible evidence to offer in support of any theory suggested, the whole group was frankly relieved as they sailed into, and up, the Great Twit – towards the archaeologists camp and the waiting figure of the eminent Dr. Frutely Gaiberond.

CHAPTER THIRTY-SIX

Sebastian sailed through the deep ocean like a giant torpedo. His speed matched only by his purpose, as he approached the shore, and into the hidden cave entrance. Through and up the cylindrical pipe he swam, his speed quickly slowing, as his head breached the surface and rose silently into the chamber of another long forgotten place. With little more than his eyes on show to the empty room, he glanced around, ensuring that his privacy was secure, before moving further out of the water and into the typically domed design of the cavernous vault.
“Keltremancian!” he whispered, and in compliance with his request the walls illuminated, adding their distinctive lines of warm colour to the magnificence of this vast space. “I knew you’d be here”, he hissed, his sinister utterances echoing around the smooth walls and vaulted ceiling. “Why do you insist on hiding from me? Do you not see as I do, that our future destinies walk the same path?”
Standing in the centre of the hall, Sebastian watched through frowning eyes, as the veins of colour in the walls gently writhed and pulsed: *“I am not an object for destruction”*, came the soft sounds of an unexpected reply. *“You would use me*

for carnage and mayhem. My purpose Sebastian, is far removed from your petty ambitions for power."
Sebastian quickly composed himself, thrown somewhat by the gentle words that floated without echo through the stale air. "I *am* power!" he hissed. "You are merely a tool. A thing to be used in support of that power." He slowly turned around and around, glaring at the walls, as though wishing to see some visible presence of his opponent in this discussion.
"You lust for power as though it is a thing you can keep and control. Do you not see that power is an animal that will not be caged by any single entity – not even you, my dear Sebastian?"
Calming down, and reminding himself of with what, and who, he now conversed, Sebastian chose to attempt reason – hoping to make the owner of the gentle words understand his desires, and appreciate its own importance in the future of the world...at least the future as he saw it. "I do not seek glory purely for myself. It is for the Nassian race that I pursue you. You must see the impact these Landwalkers choose to have on the world. Do you truly believe that any good can come of permitting their domination?"
"What we are today, does not always truly reflect what we were yesterday. Nor is it an accurate reflection on who or what we may be tomorrow... Life is, and will always be, Sebastian. All but those of you who fight to remain, knew this to be true. Your time is gone, Sebastian. Bring the others to me, make me as one again. Let me travel as I was meant to. Come with me, Sebastian."
Sebastian said nothing for a moment, choosing instead to stare down at the floor. Only after a period of thought did he finally, with a sad shake of his head, announce – "My time is now, Orb. You've travelled once already this year, and transporting so many before could not have been easy. You are here, and you will remain here, until I find you, and *I* choose for you to move again." With that Sebastian turned in

the direction of the large doors, allowing his long tail to swing, hitting the wall – a gesture of defiance against that which he sought.
He moved down the long, wide corridor – setting light to the ancient torches that still hung from its walls, as he went. Down and out into a smaller chamber he moved, running his hand gently over the surface of its rougher lining, until he found what he was looking for. At this point he stopped, one hand gently patting the stony surface, the other clutching the tiny, glowing pebble still in his possession. "There you are. Finding you is becoming too easy", he mused to himself, his face wearing a smile of smug contempt. He extended a large claw, and marked the spot where digging was to begin, before retreating into a nearby connecting room. This area he chose not to illuminate with flame, preferring instead to permit darkness to live there.
He stood in silence, his breathing low and heavy, and his eyes glowing red, as the strain of concentration found itself displayed across his features. *"Squit,"* he mentally broadcast, *"Squit. The time is now, Squit. Gather my moles and bring them to their Master. Move swiftly, Squit. Move silently, and ensure you are unobserved."*

Festulas Squit sat upright on the foot of his bed, his expression vacant and lifeless, as his mind filled with the voice that he had so desperately needed to hear. As the words filled his mind, his grotesque mouth moved as he vocalised an occasional phrase: "Moles. Yes Master... Where? Oh. Yes Master, I see. I will, Master. Eastern Lands... I understand. Roundabout... Left at lights... Yes Master, I will."
The message received and understood, the limited acknowledgement that a life was there at all, returned to Squit's grey, leathery face. He placed his hat gently on the top of his head, and reached for his cane, before setting off on his newly acquired mission in life.

Ensuring he was not followed, he quickly secured passage to the Eastern Lands – a region that lay some 800 miles from his present location. Upon arrival, he had no trouble in locating the Clan of moles – they had been returned to the hibernation cave where Squit had first found them. Once there, and since they once more had no close contact with their beloved Egg of Gertrude, they had simply chosen to go back to sleep.
Since Squit did not have the Egg in his possession, he quickly had to think of another way to awaken the slumbering workers. Understanding that time was of the essence, he simply threw stones at their heads, until all were once more in the land of the living.

Lying through his teeth, or what passed as teeth in his horrid skull, he told the moles that he knew where to find their highly regarded Egg, and that they should obey him without question until they reached it. On arrival at their destination, he promised faithfully that he would turn the Egg over to them – allowing them the un-dreamed luxury of self-determination. Perhaps it was the fact that they had only just woken up, or maybe that they were all now suffering from mild concussion, but not one mole – not even Graith – found it curious that they were being given orders by a man who had, only one week ago, been swallowed whole by a giant, lizardy thing. They blindly accepted his word, and moved with haste into the large, wooden shipping crates he had provided.
As though possessed by inspirational demons, Squit quickly had the crates loaded onto carts and whisked to the nearest docks where, without losing momentum, they were hoisted onto a waiting vessel – its destination, the Northern Lands of Skocia.

CHAPTER THIRTY-SEVEN

It was a highly excited Frutely who greeted her friends – jumping and waving frantically, like a joyful child.
As Matchwood pulled up to the temporary jetty, quickly constructed near the recently discovered opening to the Palace of Mantura, she could barely contain herself – "You will not believe it! I don't believe it! None of us believe it!" she blurted, her words rushing from her mouth at a speed that could only just be clearly understood. "It's amazing, you must come and see…" the sheer level of her enthusiasm made it difficult for her to control her virtual impatience, at the length of time it was taking for her friends to shore up and alight.
Recognising Slobber, her greeting to him was almost an afterthought – "Hi Slobber, glad to see you up and about. Everything OK? Good", she hurried, as he planted a foot firmly on dry land. He barely had time to acknowledge her expression of greeting, and vague concern for his well-being, before she rushed them hastily up the bank and through the small opening in the rock.
Her sheer exhilaration at what had been discovered, displayed itself all too clearly, as her speed of speech continued – her little legs trying to keep pace as her body propelled itself

through the gap and down the tunnel – both of which looked recently carved out of the ever solid Zintal rock.
As she sped, ushering her companions to keep pace, she attempted to explain: “See this?” she said, “This we know, is new. There is no way it would not have been discovered in the past...” By the light of the torches, they could see the faintly coloured veins of colour beneath the smooth tunnel walls.

Down the tunnel went, out and into the larger cavern, where Slobber and the others had been held captive by the moles, and the odious Festulas Squit. It was here they recalled, that the aforementioned creature had met his end – swallowed whole by the still mysterious Sebastian. Down into the earth they continued, through the larger tunnel that led, eventually, to the much larger chamber where their previous adventure had ended so abruptly.
With floor-standing torches equally dispersed around the room’s full circumference, the gang could at last see just how vast this area really was.
Ahead of them, the entrance to the mole toilet – only a faint whiff of the evil that lay within escaping through the large, heavy curtain the archaeologists had erected. To the side of that, the recently excavated tunnel, which led to the room where the glowing ball had been disturbed. All about them lay tools and wooden boxes – some new arrivals, brought by the archaeological team; others left by the mole gang.
Dr. Gaiberond stood silently at last, permitting her friends to soak up the sights and smells around them – allowing their memories to recall the events of last week. It all seemed so long ago!
“We had to cut our way back into here”, remarked Frutely, referring to the mysteriously blocked entrance. Drawing everyone’s attention to a giant, fully blocked arch, now visible in the light, she commented, “Not the first time, some force chose to deny immediate access to this place…the smaller

entry though, was only filled by a few inches of newly created rock."
Potfondle, though not blind to the magnificence of his surroundings, or deaf to the puzzling observations made by Frutely, suddenly found a curious query enter his head. Turning to Frutely, he whispered "On the surface... You were waiting for us."
"I know", she replied with a smile.
"*We* didn't even know we were going to be here today... How did you?"
She looked into Pot's eyes and then into the eyes of Slobber, his attention drawn by Pot's question, "This is going to sound pretty weird, but I dreamed you would arrive today. I even had a rough idea of what time."
Pot and Slobber exchanged serious glances before their eyes returned to Frutely. "It sounds bizarre I know", she offered quietly, hoping to persuade her friends that she was not mad, nor did she possess some kind of second sight. "In my dream, a man..."
Slobber cut her off – "Old guy? Tall, grey hair, grey cloak?" he quizzed.
Frutely offered a frown so deep that the creases on her forehead looked like narrow canyons. "Don't worry about it..." said Slobber, his attention taken by the sound of a spit-jet hitting something large and metallic, "we've met him too. Didn't tell us anything quite so obvious though", he concluded, turning to see what he had hit.

Quickly joined by the others, Slobber moved towards the object of his distraction. A large, round curiosity, seemingly of ancient origin, it looked like a large, elaborately designed claw, with six long poles as handles, protruding out from its head – the tips of its six claws almost joined at a central point at the bottom.
"We think that's how they used to move it from place to place", said Frutely quietly, almost thinking aloud.

“Move what?” said Gobswane, poking his head from Slobber’s rucksack and scaring the life out of Frutely who, quite naturally, thought he was a mouse or some-such. Slobber quickly made the introductions and allowed Frutely to answer the question.
“The Orb”, she said, a smile lighting her face.
“The glowing thing?” asked Slobber, looking for clarification.
“The glowing thing”, repeated Frutely, turning slowly, smiling and winking. Beckoning them to follow, with a sideways nod of her head, she began to move casually towards the Orb room entrance. “No need for torches in here”, she said, gazing in wonder at the walls – still glowing softly with the light of the now still streams of colour.

All about her, scientific Pillicks busied themselves, studying this, analysing that, scratching heads, chewing pencils and generally going about their scientific business.
Frutely directed her friends’ attention to the carvings on the walls. Other carvings, like those they had discovered last week, had been uncovered elsewhere in the Palace. Diagrams and stories of past events. They were different however. Those carvings looked scratched, as though chiselled into the rock by inexperienced hands... Any writings they had found had always been in ancient tongues – forgotten languages. Here though, the carvings were fine and detailed, and the writings were in the language of the present.
“Wow!” offered both Slobber and Potfondle, amazed by the work, but not recognising the true significance.
Frutely looked into the faces of her friends, and quickly appreciated why their amazement was at half the level of her own. “Look at the carvings more closely”, she suggested softly, a large smile dominating her face, a smile that soon turned into a grin, a grin that issued laughter of pure delight in a small body that began to jump with joy, as Pot, Slobber and Tree suddenly found themselves filled with astonishment and, quite irritatingly, several thousand more unanswered

questions: the WHAT WHERE, WHEN, WHY, HOW and WHO of things suddenly taking itself to an entirely new level of complexity!

The two men and the little tree studied the carvings, as had been suggested. Eyes slowly began to widen uncontrollably, and jaws found themselves dropping lower and lower.
"This is us!!" uttered Slobber, turning to Frutely, a trembling finger pointing in the general direction of the wall behind him.
"Yes!" replied Frutely, giggling excitedly.

On the walls all about them were carved images of a story... A tale of two men, one woman, a small tree, and a boat. The diagrams displayed in some detail, their journey, Sebastian, Squit, the moles... everything – even things the group had known nothing about! Squit kneeling before the dark cave of his Master; details of where they had all been sent by the Orb; images of Sebastian coughing up Festulas Squit, and lighting a fire for him.
"I knew he couldn't be trusted!" offered Tree, acting on behalf of the non-present Matchwood.
Staring at the walls, they looked upon impossible images. Events that had, only now, elsewhere, begun to unfold: The gathering of the Nassians in Skocia could be seen...one of their number slipping away. The repulsive Squit...once more disturbing the pitiful, gullible moles. Everything! Everything that had happened, right up to that precise point in time... there was even a carving of the three of them staring at a wall!

Potfondle's knees gave way and he collapsed in a heap on the floor. The sheer weight of what he saw overpowered his mind, and left him feeling sick.
"Don't worry," said Frutely rushing to his aid, "the same thing happened to me." Slobber effortlessly picked up the small, hairy man – "I think we could all use a little air", he offered, surprised at how calm he was feeling about the whole thing.

On the surface, Slobber quickly found a sheltered spot and set Pot down. Witnessing the emergence of the group with an incapacitated Potfondle, Matchwood shouted up from the jetty – "Well!?" he said impatiently, somewhat put out that he had been forced to remain outside. "Would somebody like to let me know what the hell is going on!?"
Leaving Pot in the capable hands of Dr. Gaiberond, Slobber strolled down to the water's edge, and briefed Matchwood on the revelations of the cave below.
Upon receipt of the news, that everything they had done had somehow been set out on the subterranean walls, Matchwood sat in silence for a while before eventually finding the right words to express his dismay... "Bloody hell!"

With darkness quickly falling, the camp ate, and settled down for the night. It seemed only right for Matchwood to be carefully dragged up, high onto the shore, to join the others, as they segregated themselves from the rest of the community to share their thoughts and theories over what in the world was actually going on. Quickly it was decided that their shared dreams, involving the man in grey, should be kept strictly between them. Mentioning it to the other men and women, that daily came and went from this ancient place, would not be sensible.
"Whatever is going on here," Frutely announced, "has more to do with us than with scientific knowledge." She received no argument from the others, even Tree had lost his usual cynicism, and concurred that somehow their unintentional involvement with this deepening saga, was now irrevocably linked to a possible future – the nature of which was totally unclear.

Though far too much had happened to promote sleep in the original adventurers, sleep they did. First Pot, now more or less recovered from his mental overload, fell. Then, one by one, the others quickly followed.

CHAPTER THIRTY-EIGHT

The wind howled as the group sat in the heather of brown and dark green. Overhead, the grey clouds swirled and mingled as the strong winds of high altitude stirred and bothered them.
"So," said Tree impatiently, "where is he!?" Realising, as they all did, where they were, Tree was anxious to get this dream out of the way since his last encounter with the grey stranger had left him the potential butt of many a joke.
Slobber and Potfondle looked behind them, this time taking the time to notice the existence of a small picket fence, adorned, as it was on this occasion, with five tiny figures – Sergeant Enamuelle and the others.

Once more the grey figure approached from far in the distance. At first vague and shadowy, becoming clearer as he moved closer.
"Hello, my friends", came the calm tones of the old man, his cloak barely moving in the wind that whistled through the gathering.
"OK", said Slobber, deciding, that since it appeared his association with the stranger was the longest, he should be

the spokesman for the group. “We get it...”
“Do you?” interrupted the stranger.
“Actually... No! We honestly don’t have much of a clue. Not even Frutely here, and she’s really smart.”
“Please,” requested Frutely softly, hoping that patience and understanding might prove more successful in obtaining answers, “clearly you want something of us...I mean us in particular. What is it?”
The man stood in silence for what seemed like an eternity. For a moment it looked as though Frutely’s plea for clarity was to be unanswered, when at last he spoke...or rather thought:
“Sebastian’s lust for power grows by the hour, driving a once peaceful creature to increasing madness. In a matter of mere days he will uncover the Orb, and quickly set about the task of using its’ power to bring catastrophe upon this world.”
“What exactly do you expect us to do about it!” said Tree, the impatience that comes with fear, clear in his words.
“We’ve seen the wall”, said Pot, adding his own voice to the choir of underlying fear, that in truth now filled all present. Even the Toothwranglers, if they were honest, had to admit to some small measure of concern with where the stranger’s words were taking them. “We know Sebastian isn’t alone. How much use would we be against one, let alone an army!?”
The figure smiled softly: *“Power and greatness are not inseparable. Nor can it be claimed that great size and overwhelming numbers can assure victory.”*
“Great!” muttered Tree, “He’s gone back to being all enigmatic!”
“It is enigma that brought you here in the first place, my dear...Tree. It is the continued mystery of what you saw, and continue to see, which brings you back. What there can be no doubt over, my intrepid friends, is that your path is clear.”
“North!” said the fence, realising exactly what the stranger wanted of them, “You want the ten of us to go North – to Skocia.”
“You must. The future of everything depends upon it.”

“Oh great!” came in Tree’s usual sprinkle of sarcasm. “Just so long as there’s no pressure!”

The grey stranger once more offered his smile of gentle understanding and slowly turned, making his way back to the distance from whence he came: *“You will go”*, he said as he once more drifted into the blurry mists of his origins. *“You must succeed.”*

CHAPTER THIRTY-NINE

Chokkle swung his pick and pulled out yet another chunk of granite – "Why are we doing this?" he asked of his colleagues, as he stopped for a moment to wipe the sweat from his bald, pink head, "This stuff is easy to shift. That tall, thin bloke doesn't need our skills to dig a hole, any idiot with a pair of arms could do it!"

"I don't know why we just don't Pobble Strike it!" said Stoop, as he picked up yet another piece of debris, clearing the path of their growing tunnel. "It would be a damn sight simpler!"

The moles were in generally poor spirits. The promise of being reunited with their honoured Egg of Gertrude had not yet come to pass, and many were of the opinion that Festulas Squit was not a man to be trusted. Nor was he a man to give anyone a gentle wake-up call, as the still present bruises on their heads stood to prove. Graith however, for some unfathomable reason, seemed to maintain a small measure of respect for the 'living skeleton' – as the others had now termed their one-time Master, and holder of the Egg. Despite this, his brethren, being moles, found it not within their nature to oust him as Clan leader, and continued to follow his orders, as relayed by Squit.

As the work continued, making quick pace in this relatively soft rock, Graith stood at Festulas Squit's side, waiting patiently for the words of their Lord and Master.

"In three days, my brethren will arrive. In three days, your men will have reached their destination. In three days, you will retrieve the Orb of Skeltenna and bring it unto me", Sebastian's words came, as though escaping from the grave itself, as they echoed around the outer chamber. "Once I have it in my possession Graith, I will return the Egg to you."

Graith bowed his head, and quickly backed out of the blinding light of his Master's audience hall – returning to the relative darkness of the newly constructed granite corridor.

Festulas Squit stood alone, silently – his bony hands clutching the tip of his ever-present cane, as he waited patiently for his instructions. From the darkness, his Master spoke again:

"Have you reported to your superiors at the PEA, as to the current location of our excavations?"

"As you instructed Master, I despatched word yesterday morning."

"Good. Go now to the surface and wait. I will call upon you in due course."

His Master's words heard, Squit immediately did as he was instructed, and made his way out, up through the small, curiously smooth tunnel that twisted and wound its way to the surface.

Outside, Festulas picked out a suitable rock and perched himself upon it. There he sat, surrounded by plants of brown and dark green, staring up at the gently passing flight of grey clouds. In their hypnotic, rolling movement, he hoped to find some peace, or at the very least, some assistance in finding the answer to his unuttered question: Why should his Master specifically want the PEA to know what they were up to? To him it made no sense but then, when he thought about it, very few of his actions of the last few years had served any obvious purpose that he was aware of...not at the time of doing them, at least.

Again he tried to put things in order, hoping that more of the jigsaw would become visible to him: *Flalian Trapp knows about the Orb. Does he know what it does? For that matter do I know what it does?* Squit had to confess on this question he did not have a clue. The simple truth was that he had only recently found out about the Orb – more recent still, discover-ing it went by the name Skeltenna.

Back in the depths Sebastian sat in darkness, musing to himself – an inscrutable grin dominating his huge face. The message he had instructed Festulas to send was designed with one aim in mind, to bring Flalian Trapp to Skocia. It simply read:

Have re-located the Orb, and it is within my reach.
It sits in land owned by a powerful Lord.
He has discovered us and is angry that we are conducting work without his permission.
He demands meeting with you in person – here.
He demands financial compensation from the PEA and full disclosure of our activities.
Will speak only with you.

Flalian Trapp, thought Sebastian, *Director of Development for the PEA...Welcome to the final days of your life!*

CHAPTER FORTY

"I cannot believe we are actually doing this!" exclaimed Tree, as Matchwood glided out of the Great Twit, and into the wider expanse of the ocean once more. His words were not born of cowardice, more a sense of the utter futility of a small group (comprising himself, a small tree with extremely limited movement, a large, blue, walking fountain, two small Pillicks, and five 'toothpicks'...not forgetting Matchwood who, despite centuries of life experience, including actual combat, was little more than a mode of transportation, and other than possibly getting stuck in the throat of an angry Nassian, he failed to see what possible assistance he could be) travelling half-way around the world to stop a gang of thoroughly irritated giants from taking over the planet. "Does no one else think the grey, dream guy is a tad off his rocker on this!?" he asked of his, as he saw it, clearly deluded companions. His question went unanswered, even though not one among them could honestly say they thought this journey would produce anything other than utter disaster.

The passage of time once more permitted itself to drift quietly by, undisturbed by rough seas or even conversation. Other than Tree's earlier observations on the stupidity of their expedition, no one had uttered a word. Even the question of WHO had been pushed from their minds. They still had no idea who the grey stranger, or what his connection to all this was, but the strong possibility of impending death and/or mutilation had somehow driven away petty concerns over the 'why's' and 'wherefores'. So preoccupied with nothing were they, that not even Matchwood noticed the gentle ripples in the water behind them. Only when their movement inexplicably slowed and halted, did anyone stir from the state of oblivion they had slumped into. All aboard quickly busied themselves, scanning this way and that. Plunging their heads into the water in an attempt to glimpse the cause of their immobility. "Is this the same thing as before, Match!?" said Slobber, a truly incredible lack of panic in his voice – a curious side effect, he considered, of coming to terms with impending doom.

"Sebastian?" suggested Frutely.

"Quite likely", agreed Matchwood.

"Please don't panic..." came a gruff but strangely gentle voice from behind.

All eyes rotated in their sockets, before reaching a point where the head needs to turn, if more is to be seen. Expecting the vision of Sebastian to be present, all looked skywards. With no giant creature dominating the view, their eyes moved slowly down, and down still further, until they hit the horns atop a large, familiar head.

"Please hold on tight, my emergence may cause a wave or two...I understand that one of you can't swim", said the head as it slowly moved away from the boat, gently rising before them.

All available eyes watched in horror, as the Nassian reared up and out of the water, towering above them, obscuring the sun. "Grey guy said nothing about getting eaten before we even get

there, did he!?" announced Tree, his voice positively dripping with an air of, 'I told you so.'
"I have no intention of eating you", said the monster who, just like Sebastian, was possessed of excellent hearing. "Tell you what," he said, quickly concluding that perhaps rising to his full magnificence might be viewed as a tad intimidating, "I'll come back down." As the wake of his re-submergence caused waves to buffet the boat, the creature gently reached underneath, and steadied Matchwood's violent movements – causing him to giggle.
"Are you OK?" asked the creature, unsure if these noises were a sign that he had caused the vessel some pain.
"Ticklish", replied Match, a little embarrassed.
"Who are you?" asked Slobber, unconvinced that a little courtesy could be taken as proof that this Nassian was to be trusted. After all, Sebastian had been quite pleasant, and he had turned out to be a power-crazed lunatic.
Stennaron introduced himself with a polite, and very gentle bow of his head – "I am sorry to sneak up on you like that…" he said. "Actually, I have been trying to make contact with you for a while now…"
"You followed us yesterday?" enquired Matchwood cautiously.
"Aye. That was me. I backed off, though. Thought I was scaring you." This observation though true, went unanswered, since no one who had been aboard wanted to freely admit their fear.
"And last week?" said Match, his caution still present.
"No. That was a wee cousin of mine... Both times, actually. He was going to drag you under, but I convinced him not to. Hope you weren't hurt."
The general lack of reaction to this statement, made Stennaron realise that he would have to do more than display general consideration for other seafarers, in order to secure the trust of this particular group. Quickly, he explained what had brought him to this particular point in time and space. He advised those before him of Sebastian's plans for war – "Less

of a war more of a war-k over!" he said. He explained that over a period of decades, Sebastian had turned normally passive Nassians into bloodthirsty vessels of hatred. "This way is not my way", he said. "Life moves on. One race goes, another arrives. We should never have stayed in the first place." None of his audience knew what he actually meant by his last remark, but by that time it was pretty clear that Stennaron had something of the poet in him.

His tale told, Stennaron sat back, while the tiny people below debated his credibility. As the debate grew increasingly heated, he piped up once more – a degree of frustration beginning to tell in his voice. "Look here! Not all Nassians are the same", he said. "I may *look* like Sebastian but I am not him, I promise you!" His argument seemed to give little comfort, and the debate continued as if he had said nothing. "Listen here, you! Not everyone who sneaks up from behind is a bad guy. The only reason I was behind you is because you were in front! It's just a question of time. Past is behind, future's in front... You know?"
"What is he going on about!?" said Tree, as he and the others listened to his ever curious ramblings.
It was Potfondle who finally saw the light. An almost visible moment of true enlightenment suddenly flowed across his face – not that this was immediately noted by the others, who had become strangely fascinated by Stennaron's monologue on the differences between front and behind.
"That which appears the same can often be different", he said loudly, causing all those about him, including Stennaron, to give him their close attention.
"Give no fear to that which is past."
"Gods!" exclaimed Tree, "Now *he's* at it!"
"Past…" he said, looking up at the face of the giant.
"Behind...Back...Past."
The group looked at one another in silence, as the meaning of what had been said slowly sank in.
"Of course!" announced Frutely. "Obvious really!"

"That which appears the same can often be different…" said Slobber, his head nodding slowly, in agreement with Pot and Frutely's interpretation of the grey stranger's words. "You said it yourself, Match... Yesterday... Remember?"
"Oh well," said Tree, the utter negativity of his forthcoming sentence clear from the cynical delivery of his first two words, "if a guy in a dream says he's OK, he must be!"
"Shut it, Butsmell!" came the reply from more than one passenger.

CHAPTER FORTY-ONE

The odd collective sat high on the beach, staring passively into the orange flames – each one attempting to reconcile the very real possibility, that he or she would be extremely dead in the next couple of days. Even Stennaron, a giant in comparison to the others, sat in silence – lost in the energetic movement of the vigorously dancing flames.

“Can anyone fire a bow?” enquired Matchwood softly.

“Why?” asked Frutely, turning her head slowly to face the intentionally beached boat.

“I was just thinking that when we reach the shores of Skocia, you could turn me into a whole load of arrows – big ones.”

Looking up at Stennaron, and observing his mass, Slobber offered a half-hearted smile: “I don’t think a few arrows will make that much difference, my friend.”

It wasn’t the damage of physical wounds that Matchwood had in mind, but the potential for causing years of mental torment. The others listened patiently as Match laid out his plan… The arrows would easily be large enough to carry sufficient consciousness to permit speech. If they were then fired hard enough, and with great accuracy, at the Nassian hoards –

penetrating their inner ear – he could have endless fun driving them absolutely insane with incessant chit-chat. “The battle may be lost,” he suggested, “but the war might eventually be won!”

The tongue-in-cheek idea was fully discussed. Frankly, everyone that night was relieved to have something to take their minds away from funereal music and headstones. Even some degree of humour had been discovered in Matchwood’s desire to make the supreme sacrifice, as suggestions began to spring up as to how the Match-arrows might accomplish their long-term objective: Constantly singing out of tune; repeating everything they say; constantly asking ‘Why?’, like a young child; undermining personal confidence by telling them they smell, or by constantly saying ‘The others don’t really like you, you know’; when mental arithmetic is apparently taking place, randomly offer numbers until they lose count; prevent them from falling asleep by continually whistling…out of tune and really shrilly…

The possibilities were endless, and many of the suggestions did actually start to make sense. Stennaron even delivered a graphic demonstration of how an exceptional shot could hit the target, by pushing a fence post into his ear. The onlookers cringed, as he effortlessly inserted the large piece of wood. They cringed even more when he withdrew it, along with a rather large ball of wax that he had skewered in there.

“OK”, announced Frutely, with a dramatic clap of her hands, “Is anyone here skilled in archery?” Regrettably the question was met with shaking heads.

“Strap an arrow to our backs and we could deploy them manually”, suggested Enamuelle, but this idea was ruled out when Match explained that each arrow would be roughly 30-times their length, and more than 40-times their weight.

The group chatted on for some time before, one-by-one, the arms of sleep began to wrap themselves around their weary bodies.

With the new morning but a few minutes away, the now group of eleven lay, staring up at the swirling grey clouds above, their bodies once more cushioned by the heathers of dark green and brown. "You know, I am getting pretty sick of this place!" said Potfondle, pre-empting a similar, and expected comment from his ever-present wooden pal.

"Blimey! What happened to you!?" said Matchwood, once again a fence, observing the reduced version of Stennaron that now sat beside Slobber.

The creature drew up to his now much smaller size and looked himself up and down. "That's amazing!" he said, "I've never been able to shrink before!"

"It's a dream", said Frutely, offering just a hint of sarcasm with her tone, and in her smile.

"Aye lass," he replied, his smile denoting his obvious pleasure at his new height, "I know. But when you're a walking mountain, little things like shrinking are worthy of comment. I mean, you try finding decent clothes off the rack. Its bloody near impossible!" he joked.

"Been here before?" asked Slobber, noting Stennaron's lack of intrigue.

"Of course I have", replied Stennaron, scanning the scenery. "These are the Higher Lands of Skocia. My summer home is just to the South of here, as a matter of fact."

"Um, we're not actually in Skocia yet," explained Slobber, "this is all just a dream."

"A dream!?"

"Yes," said Frutely, "a shared dream."

Between them, the group explained that any minute now, a tall, grey man would shimmer into view, and offer a whole load of rather vague advice. Stennaron was truly amazed by it all. Not only was this his first shared dream, but to the best of his recollection, the only dream he'd ever had that didn't involve chasing fish, or hiding from men in colourful skirts… "They're nice enough chaps, you understand," he said, "but when you see how they treat those poor creatures with the tartan

tummies, long noses, and hollow legs... Well, let's just say I'd rather not find out where they'd try and get a tune out of me!"
"Welcome Stennaron", said the grey stranger as he drifted towards them once more. *"You look well."*
"Have we met?" asked Stennaron, looking at the man with a frown of vague recollection.
"You were very young", replied the grey man, as he looked across the faces, branches and neat fence-posts of the others, leaving the creature silently struggling to recall a previous encounter. When he eventually spoke – or rather thought – again, it was in brief, punctuated sentences: *"You will arrive at your final destination tomorrow, my friends. Move swiftly to where you are now… That which was once whole, is close at hand… Use the stone… Bring together. Reunite that which was divided…the task must be done. When the time comes, you will know."* These instructions were more obscure than anything said before, and the travellers looked at one-another, their faces displaying clearly their total lack of understanding at what had just been said.
Slobber turned to face the grey man: "What...?" he said to the empty space that existed there. "Bugger me, he's gone again!"
Before anyone could offer any further words of surprise and confusion, their surroundings too, vanished, as back on the beach, with the rising sun gently warming their bodies, all awoke sharply as if ejected from a nightmare.
"What, in the name of every arse on the planet, was that all about!?" cried Tree. "Can anyone here honestly say that any of that made any kind of sense whatsoever!?"
"Why did you come!?" snapped Potfondle, at last weary of his small friend's attitude.
"What!?"
"You could have stayed behind. I wouldn't have minded. Frankly, given your continued comments, I doubt anyone here would have had any real objections. So, I ask again. Why did you come!?"

Tree was somewhat taken aback by this scolding from his oldest friend, and he sat, silenced by the snapping tongue of his favourite Pillick.

"WELL!?" shouted Pot, his anger forcing his impatience to burst out.

How could Tree say it? All his life he had managed to tolerate the insanity of the world around him, by living with the belief that absurdity was a normal part of bipedal life, and as such, not something that anyone should view with even the merest hint of honesty or seriousness.

"You're pathetic!" spat Potfondle, taking Tree's silence as yet another display of ignorance and childishness.

The others quickly moved to block Potfondle, as he attempted to dramatically storm off. "We're all scared…" they all said, as they tried to temper his temper, all confused. This is just Tree's way of dealing with the pressure!" came their viable explanation, as Pot continued to spit his venom in the direction of the little plant. In the midst of this storm, Tree's quiet words gently floated up. Like a solitary leaf caught in a lifting breeze, his simple, honest words grabbed the attention of all who were there: "I don't want you to die."

Pot turned slowly and looked silently down on the shuddering branches of the Bonsai.

"I don't want you to die", he repeated, struggling to hold back the flood of emotion that began to overwhelm him, as he finally confronted the demons of his own particular truth. "You're my best friend and I don't want you to die. OK?"

Pot looked down at the little tree, as his heart filled with shame at the way he had spoken. "I'm sorry!" he said, dropping to his knees, the uncorking of Tree's emotional bottle forcing Pot to tackle a truth or two himself. "I know you're scared…we're all scared," he said, with tears beginning to well up in his eyes, "but if we are to die, then let us feel strong through the knowledge that we will die together... Friends to the very end."

That was it for the observers of this clichéd drama. Tears it seems, just like yawning, can be contagious…once one person starts, those around will quickly follow.

Revelations quickly began to surface, regarding the concern and remorse Tree had displayed when, during the previous week, he had believed Pot drowned. Then in the midst of this massive surge of emotion, with everyone allowing the floodgates to open, Pot's adoration for Frutely 'hit the headlines!'

It was Potfondle's own admission to her, during one of several embraces that took place that morning, which caused a sudden pause in activity. At arms length, with tears flowing down his face, three little words just popped out. Three little words that, if said in earnest, tend to cause a reaction.

They were three little words that Pot found himself hearing as, powerless to prevent them, they shot from his mouth, ejected by the raw emotion of the situation: "I love you."

With quivering chins the others looked on, their eyes locking in a fixed exchange. All were suddenly hushed, as silent questions simultaneously ran through their minds: *What will she say?*; *What will Pot do if it's bad news?*

Frutely, herself rather stunned into silence, could do nothing for a moment but stare into Pot's eyes. Eventually, her analytical mind produced a question: "Is this because I kissed you?" she asked, her mind forced to make the assumption that there was a simple, rational explanation for this curious, and rather irrational admission. Potfondle thought for a second. The damage had been done, there was no taking it back, and even if he could, he wasn't sure he wanted to. That said, however, he did, for the briefest of moments only, toy with the idea of putting the whole thing down to the stress of the moment...the very real possibility of impending doom and so on, but, rather sensibly, rejected it. He did love her and, truth be known, he had done so ever since he caught sight of her glorious image drifting into camp that day. She was bright, intelligent, courageous and she had really nice legs – always a bonus in his eyes.

"Perhaps," he said at length, "this is a discussion best left until..." Well, that was just it! Left until when? Until they were about to be devoured by a charging Nassian? Until they were lying in the mud, their limbs strewn about in the bloody aftermath of a disastrous battle? Pot gently snorted a single laugh. A recognition of the absurdity of it all. At that moment he suddenly realised, with a certain sense of how obvious it all was, that Tree's cynical approach to life was not a lifestyle designed to hide anything, more a product of the realisation that life is...well, pretty stupid most of the time. Tree's approach was one of simple expectance of that fact – a 'see it for what it is, and don't let it stop you from being whoever you want to be', kind of deal.

"Forget the 'I love you' bit", he said, smiling the smile of a man who has just discovered the secret of life. "Assuming we're not all dead…killed in some gruesome way in the next few hours, could I take you out to dinner sometime?"

"Sure", said Frutely, surprising herself with the speed of her response. "Why not?"

CHAPTER FORTY-TWO

Sebastian stood in the darkness, the look of sheer concentration evident across his sweating brow…his eyes tightly shut – visible evidence of his use of sheer will once more: *"Gather, my brothers and sisters. The time is now. The place is here. Gather unto me."* His thoughts floated up and out, crossing the land to the place of his people's gathering – the Northern retreat, Stenneron's summer home, as he called it. The words pushed their way through the earth, and into the hall of this once great meeting place. There his words found body, as they began to echo around the walls and through the corridors. Slowly, the eyes of the assembled monsters began to open, as their minds gave recognition to the commanding whisper that grew in their ears.

In answer to the call, they steadily filed out of the hall and down through the tunnel that led to the lake – one of only two remaining channels of exit in these wondrous caverns. Unconcerned about the presence of witnesses, they breached the grey surface of the water and marched across the land – their uniform strides causing the ground to shudder, as it vibrated to the beat of their advance.

"Do you feel that!?" whispered Slobber, his mind instinctively telling him that the gentle shuddering he felt beneath his feet was something to show concern for... Something for fear.
"It has begun", replied Stennaron mournfully.
From behind they heard a creaking, then a cracking, as fibres of wood stretched and contorted, twisting their way free of the greater body. Turning, they saw a plank of wood lying on the ground, separated from Matchwood's side by sheer will.
Smiling, Slobber approached and carefully picked it up. "I agree," he said with a smile, "it wouldn't be fair to leave you behind. Not now."
Turning, he rejoined the line of unlikely heroes, as together they looked forward into the grey horizon, and the ultimate end to their journey.
"Let's kick some scaly arse!" cried out Sergeant Enamuelle, as he poked the top half of his body from under the flap of Slobber's sack, "No offence, Stenny."
"None taken, tiny warrior."

As they reached the top of yet another hill, the eleven stopped to survey the land ahead, and the sea behind.
Slumping down on a nearby rock, Slobber scanned the grey heavens. "Does the sun ever shine in this curious place?"
"Oh yes…" Stennaron assured him proudly. "Skocia in the sunlight is unlike any other place in the world."
Potfondle stood – his interesting friend tucked, bucket and all, under one arm, his other hand tightly gripping Frutely's waist – scanning the rough sea below.
"Ships!" he announced excitedly, as his eyes rested on the sight of 10...no, 12 ships approaching from the West. The others quickly rushed to his side, and together they witnessed the Armada crash its way through increasingly stormy seas toward them. "An army?" queried Slobber.
"A massacre!" replied Stennaron. "They're PEA."
Perhaps he was right. It certainly was an impressive sight. A hopeful sight, All watched with interest as the ships continued their unstoppable approach.

"The PEA has an army?" asked Tree, "Cool! Looks like we might survive this after all!" To him, and indeed the others, this grand vision permitted the belief that actually being alive to see another dawn, was a distinct possibility.

"Think they'll win, then?" asked Frutely, looking up at Stennaron, her confidence in the group's continued survival raised by the creature's talk of massacre.

"They don't have a prayer!" said Stennaron. "To be frank," he added, "this is the one and only part of Sebastian's insane plan that I have less than a decent level of sorrow over." The others watched as the giant lay himself flat, concerned that his image on the hill, if caught through a telescope, might lead the approaching force away from the main battle site.

He bore malice to no one really, but the PEA was something he had little time for.

"You want all those people to die!?" said Slobber, scarcely able to believe his ears, the disappointment thick in the tone of his words of disbelief.

"All those ships smashed?" added Matchwood, keen that the sacrifice of the brave vessels, metal though they might be, should not go unnoticed.

"What are they doing here, anyway?" enquired Frutely, her keen analytical mind asking the obvious question. "How did they know?"

The destruction of the PEA was a gesture. The opening gambit in Sebastian's war against those who he viewed as polluters of the world.

It was, in fact, by using the Nassian's dislike of the PEA, that Sebastian had first sown the seeds of hatred for the Landwalkers. His thinking was, it must be said, quite logical, if somewhat simplistic: Better ports meant more trade, more trade meant bigger ships, bigger ships meant more people, more people meant greater exploration of the land. Exploration of new lands, leads to the discovery of yet more things to trade, and more things to trade, with more lands to trade in, meant more and bigger ports. Sebastian's argument,

though circular was, just like the theory behind it, simple: Ships take people to where they have never been before... Get rid of port establishment and development and the ships will have no place to go. "Destroy the PEA and you destroy the ships, preventing people from going where they don't belong", said Stennaron, giving verbal presence to the basic tenet of the whole argument.
"But that's just progress!" observed Frutely, once the spurious reasoning had sunk in. "You can't blame development, and the need for exploration, for all the troubles of your race. People will always want to see what's around the next corner. If they can't do it in big ships, they will do it in small boats."
"Ever been hit by a propeller!?" returned Stennaron, rolling over slightly so that the numerous scars on his back could be fully appreciated. "It bloody hurts!"

All things considered however, Stennaron did not want the death of all those people on his conscience. Standing up, he let out a tremendous roar, whilst frantically waving his arms about in an effort to distract the vessels from their course. It took some doing, but eventually the team rejoiced as the ships slowly turned in his direction, believing their original heading to be untrue.
"We'd better make ourselves scarce", suggested Stennaron, falling to his belly, so as to keep their direction of travel a mystery to the approaching ships.
"While they're farting about with landings and such, we'll be long gone."
Tree huffed loudly, drawing attention to himself: "Doesn't anyone else think that an army could prove useful to us!?"
"They are expected", said Stennaron. "We are not... Besides they'll only slow us down."
Noticing the amount of mud beneath and ahead of him, Stennaron suggested that everyone climb on his back:
"Anyone been sledging recently? Come on, the sooner we get there, the sooner we'll be able to..." he stopped talking... that was just the point. What were they supposed to do? For

some reason, none of them – not even Dr. Gaiberond – had made any attempt to formulate any kind of plan! Only now, in the eleventh hour, was it clear that they still had absolutely no idea whatsoever, what the grey stranger had been going on about. "He said we would know", muttered Slobber, as he scrambled aboard – using the now obvious scars on the creature's back as foot and hand-holds. "I don't know. Do you know?" he enquired of Frutely, as he quickly hoisted her up. "Pot? Any clues?"

Pot grabbed the outstretched hand – "Not a one", he replied, with a surprising lack of concern.

"Anyone!?" asked Stennaron, as their slide down the hill irrevocably and irreversibly began.

"Yes!" shouted Gobswane, clinging to the edge of Slobber's sack with the other Toothwranglers – anxious to enjoy the full exhilaration of this extraordinary ride. "I know!"

CHAPTER FORTY-THREE

Festulas Squit sat on his rock and watched in horror, as the ships he had been observing, slowly turned away from their course. He still had no idea why his Master should wish the PEA's presence, indeed he had no real idea about anything his Master demanded of him. He sat contemplating his options. Should he rush and tell his Master, and risk the aim of his wrath being directed firmly on his shoulders? Should he again turn his allegiance away from his Master and back to Flalian Trapp, undoubtedly aboard one of the vessels that now moved toward the wrong shore?

Whilst deliberating his limited options, Festulas found his attention suddenly removed from the rough seas ahead, and directed towards the increasing volume of the rhythmic drumming, coming from the land behind. Sliding from his perch, he quickly scrambled behind it for cover against the possible view that his elongated presence might provide to the mass of giants, he now observed, as they cut their way through the bleak landscape below.
If the sight of ships turning from their intended course had filled him with horror, the terrifying vision before him served

only to overload his sense of fear, causing his eyes to widen beyond their design, as his tortured mind debated whether continued existence was really worth all the effort.

Far below and beneath, Sebastian drew himself out of his dark retreat, to take personal charge of the valuable work the moles were about to undertake. From the darkness of his cave, he guided the large, metal claw by which the Orb of Skeltenna could be safely moved by Nassian hand.

The Clan of diggers all stood, rooted to the spot, in the blinding light of their Master's audience chamber. A strange, unuttered, sense of foreboding had begun to descend upon the group, growing slowly from nothing, into a true, yet undefined sense of dread. In the Palace of Mantura, they had liked, even revered the creature, but now..? None of them could quite put their finger on it, but there was something different about this Sebastian. Something not quite right. There was an obvious look in his eyes that none of them had seen previously…a dark sort of something that lurked silently, flashing into view very fleetingly, seemingly making its presence felt, as if of its own mind.

Through squinting eyes, they watched as he guided the heavy object towards them. "You need not fear me, my friends", he said – returning to the tone of voice that had so easily fooled Slobber and his companions into thinking he was anything other than a beast of destruction. "I may look fearsome but I assure you, I am still the same Sebastian who regaled you with stories, and defended you from the angry hoards. My intentions towards you, and indeed all living things, are nothing but peaceful."

"Bb…but…th…th…that Squit fellow..." stuttered Graith, referring to the previous devouring – needing to find some expression for his virtually subconscious paranoia.

Sebastian chuckled charmingly: "Oh you don't want to set any store by that", he said, with a gently dismissive wave of his giant hand. "If I had not acted in his defence, those others might have killed him… I'm afraid dear Mr Squit can so easily

be misunderstood by other surface dwellers. Besides, you have seen for yourself, he is fine. Aside from a little fluid in the lungs, Mr Squit survived my gullet with no permanent damage." Sebastian smiled a smile that indicated very definitely that this conversation had now concluded. Calmly gesturing in the direction of the claw, drawing the moles' attention to it, he politely instructed them on its use, irretrievably changing the subject. "A little push here, a little pull there and it unlocks... You see?"
The moles nodded energetically, their silent concerns over the character of this Sebastian not entirely resolved.
"A little twist that way, another this way and it opens... You understand?"
Again, his instruction was met with vigorous, silent nodding.
"Place it gently over the Orb, do the reverse and it closes up again... Yes?"
"Um…" said Chokkle, without really thinking, "what if it should choose to make us all disappear again, sir?"
Sebastian moved his head down, close to the originator of this enquiry.
"Have no fear, my friend", he said, his voice now slightly tinged with the mindful, silent presence that had hitherto, been dwelling behind his eyes. "It did that to prevent itself from falling into the hands of those others...the drooling fellow and his band of robbers", he paused slightly, and moved even closer to the tiny mole. "We are its friends. It has no need to hide from us", he concluded with a grin of true insincerity.
Using the claw, Sebastian requested they bring the Orb out of the smaller tunnel they had constructed, and deliver it unto him.

"Righty-ho, here we go!" said Graith, his voice echoing the strain of his muscles as, working as one, he and the other moles, carefully slid and guided the large, glowing ball out of the tunnel mouth and into the presence of Sebastian. Upon sight of his long-sought treasure, Sebastian clapped his hands with delight – creating such a noise as to almost deafen the poor diggers – and giggled with sheer pleasure and joy. He even managed a little jump in the air, nearly smashing his head on the curved ceiling high above.

Carefully reaching down, ensuring that absolutely no part of his hand touched the surface of the Orb, he picked up the claw-like receptacle. Staring into its bright glow, his eyes widened, in keeping with his tooth-displaying grin, and his brow slowly dropped, creating a sinister awning for his wildly staring eyes. "Now," he whispered, his voice utterly devoid of the charm-filled inflections he had previously employed, "you and I will shake the planet to its very core. Bringing order from chaos!"
"Well, sir. There you are... There you have it… One glowing ball thing", said Graith, pushed forward by his men, and required to ask for their promised payment.
Sebastian, transfixed by his own thoughts of what was about to come, didn't even glance down at the nervously shuffling mole. "Ah," he whispered, his tone more sinister than ever it had been, "you wish the Egg I suppose?"
Graith actually *felt* the words, as though they were some evil force penetrating his body and soul – filling him with an unspoken, instinctive feeling that this conversation was unlikely to end on a positive note. "Th…th…th…that is wh…wh…wh…what was agreed...sir", he trembled, his words meek and feeble, his head already withdrawing into his shoulders, as his eyes held themselves tightly shut, in expectation of some vicious blow that he knew was on its way.

Sebastian at last moved his now craze-filled eyes down to the ground, observing the cowering, pink creature below. "I'm afraid that won't be possible…" he said, and without even the merest hint of a warning, he swiftly brought down his huge, flattened hand – crunching and breaking the bodies of those who had served him so tirelessly. With his hand flat on the cavern floor, he twisted – grinding and squelching the forms beneath into an unrecognisable pulp of blood and gore.

Without ceremony. Without conscience or apparent thought, every single mole in the cave that day was murdered in a most brutal, terrible and pretty disgusting fashion.
Raising his palm, and observing the mess that now clung to it, Sebastian wiped his hand carelessly across the ceiling and sides of the large chamber, trailing evidence of his terrible crime over its surface. “That,” he said, looking down at the mole soup that now pooled below, and wearing a sickening smile of satisfaction, “is why people shouldn’t bunch!”
Returning his attention to the glowing power in his grasp, Sebastian adjusted his hold, carefully guiding the claw into position, and attaching it carefully to the jewel-encrusted brooch that he had attached to the centre of his chest. Then he stood, arms outstretched and head raised – the Orb’s glow seeming to originate from the creature’s very heart – allowing every fibre of his being to bathe in the insanity of his deluded ego.

CHAPTER FORTY-FOUR

From behind his rock, Festulas Squit's lifeless eyes reflected the happenings below. The marching army of Nassians neared their goal, stopping suddenly as the visage of Stennaron racing towards them at an alarming speed, caught their attention. Sebastian too, watched this amazing sight, as he rose up from the newly opened scar in the land, created by a simple wave of his hand, through the power of his new heart.

Curiously, Stennaron's absence had been barely noticed by his brethren. The sudden realisation that he had not been with them on the journey, was prevented from raising questions as they now cheered at the sight of his dramatic advance. As he neared his brothers and sisters, Stennaron quickly shouted instructions for his passengers to jump, fearing that their presence might be noticed as he approached – the other Nassians unlikely to greet *their* arrival with warmth. More likely, they would choose to bring swift conclusion to their 'insignificant' lives.

His passengers did as they were instructed with little hesitation, the sight of so many giants, offering great incentive to take their chances with gravity. Off they flew, some to the right, others to the left. The Toothwranglers spilling out of their snug home, and flying into the air in all directions as they, and the others, hit the soft earth with squelching thuds. Striking the ground before rolling down – following their vehicle's lead – as they waited patiently for the laws of physics to slow their uncomfortable tumbling.

Slobber's was the first journey to conclude, his trajectory suddenly and painfully halted, as his legs straddled Matchwood's plank, which had buried itself like a spear into the ground.
"You OK?" asked Match, as Slobber struck.
Slobber sat, the upper part of his body resting against the vertical plank, his facial features utterly distorted – displaying the shock and utter discomfort of the emasculating winding he had just received. With tears flowing down his cheeks, he winced his response: "Fine!" he squeaked, with the last gasp of breath still available to his lungs.
Pot and Frutely eventually ceased their acrobatics and quickly recovered themselves, scrambling on their bellies through the mud and plant life – keeping low, so as not to be observed, as they made their way towards their incapacitated friend. On arrival, Frutely quickly eased Slobber onto his back and removed his Vacuhat – remarkably still attached to his head. Potfondle wrestled with the plank, withdrawing the wooden sword from its muddy scabbard. "I've got to find Tree!" he said, as Frutely administered some caring attention to the groin-clutching Slobber.
"The guys…" strained Slobber – alluding to his patrol of Toothwranglers, "they flew off over there somewhere", his collision still denying him full lungs of oxygen, as he struggled to lift an arm and point in the general direction.

The small, furry Pillick quickly located Tree. He found him lying on the ground, his branches, as if it were winter, all but one…removed by the force of his rough landing. His flight had thrown him clear of his bucket, and his crashing impact with

the ground had snapped one of his major limbs – the sorry limb only connected to the trunk by a thin thread of wood.
Pot leant in close to his friend: "Tree!" he muttered, the panic that his friend may be critical, already setting in. "Tree!!" he repeated, desperate for some response from the broken plant.
"Pot?" muttered Tree, barely able to force the words. "Pot? I can hear you buddy, but I can't see you."
Potfondle buried his head in his hands and began to cry softly. Though no tree surgeon, it was clear to Pot that his childhood companion was nearing the end. Tree took a deep breath, struggling to gasp life into his small wooden structure.
"It's OK," said Pot, choking back the tears, "you'll get better." He began scraping out a hole in the mud with his hands. "I'll replant you. This soil is good... You'll get better." He carefully placed his dirt-covered palms under the Bonsai and raised him close, cradling him and gently stroking his hand over the now bare branches. "Say something!" he commanded. "Tell me this is all my fault. Blame me... Anything!" Pot knelt, his head raised to the grey sky above, his sobs of grief calling his companions to join him at his side. Frutely grabbed Matchwood, and aided Slobber as they crawled quickly to be with their friend. The Tooth-wranglers too, heard Pot's pain and regrouped – their overall position near to where their wooden comrade had apparently met his fate.
"Oh, Pot…" said Frutely, placing a consoling arm around his shoulders and offering a long kiss to his head.
"He was right", he said, looking across the group, before resting his eyes back on Tree's broken body. "Life is stupid, and death is the only answer to its stupidity." His observation was met with silence. Maybe they disagreed...they probably did, but this was no time for a debate.
"No…" came a single, breathless word from the object of their sorrow, "I was wrong, Pot. The challenge of life should not be met with cynicism. It should be..." his battle with life as he had so often put it, was drawing to a close. He had so desperately wanted to finish on a positive note, but it was not to be.
"Oh great!" said Pot, forcing an attempted laugh to break

through the enormous lump in his throat, “Now you decide to get philosophical.” His comment produced no response from his friend. His last remark had been made. The final word he had so often won in life, was to be denied him in death, it seemed.

CHAPTER FORTY-FIVE

Stennaron slowly slid to a halt, his nose finally resting on Sebastian's clawed feet. He lay for a moment, attempting to regain his bearings, before looking up with one eye and acknowledgeing the presence of his self-appointed leader.
"Sebastian", came his casual greeting, "OK there, pal?"
"Stennaron", offered Sebastian, "Interesting method of travel! Why did you not remain with the others?"
Stennaron slowly rose to his feet and brushed himself down, using the time to come up with a plausible explanation. "This is my home, Sebastian. I fancied a walk." From the look in Sebastian's eyes, his attempt was failing. "Did you know there are a load of ships out there?" he said, changing the subject and pointing over his shoulder with his clawed thumb.
Sebastian smiled patronisingly. "Of course. They are PEA. They've generously agreed to come here so that we might feast on their bones."
His words produced cheers of appreciation from the assembled Nassian army that moved to surround him.
"Oh..." said Stennaron, leaving an enigmatic pause, before offering a half-defiant look into Sebastian's eyes, "but they're not coming here. At least not straight away... They've turned

about, you see? I was just watching them."

A look of anger flashed across Sebastian's face, unobserved by the others who now all stood behind him. Not wishing this news to appear troublesome to him, Sebastian raised a hand and beckoned Kolm to him.

"Take a detachment of ten..." he quietly commanded, his gaze remaining fixed on Stennaron's defiantly smug expression. "See what they're up to."

As his trusted, and newly appointed lieutenant did as instructed, Sebastian added, "Stennaron, you go with them."

This was inconvenient. This was not in the plan. Stennaron felt his place should be here...with Sebastian. No, wandering off over the hills was not at all convenient. He had no choice, he couldn't risk separation; he couldn't wait for the others to make their way down, he had to act now! In a single lunge he went for Sebastian. The sudden, abrupt movement took his foe by surprise, but his reflexes were such that he managed a slight step back, causing Stennaron's advancing arm to miss his body, glancing off his shoulder and across his chest. Quickly realising the direction his blow was taking, Stennaron flattened his fist, reaching out with his fingers and flexing his claws. Sebastian shouted with pain as the sharp points of his adversary's weaponry scraped into his flesh – cutting shallow furrows as they headed for his glowing heart. Stennaron saw what he might do as Sebastian twisted, desperately trying to form a retaliatory strike. With a powerful counter blow from the power-rich Sebastian, Stennaron buckled, as the talons of his cousin buried themselves deep into his unguarded stomach. He felt himself on the verge of collapse, as the daggers of Sebastian's claws dug their way ever deeper into the interior of his body. Stennaron buckled, but fought courageously to maintain control over his still battling arm – guiding it down, across Sebastian's chest, before finally connecting with the radiant brooch – knocking it from its deeply embedded fixtures and sending it hurtling through the air. Kolm, turning quickly to witness this sudden and unbelievable spectacle, let out a gasp of horror as the separate blows found their mark. With his, and the others' attention firmly fixed on this unprecedented fight, the swiftly sailing travels of the precious Orb escaped notice, as it continued its speedy flight, eventually landing with an unceremonious thud, half-burying itself in the soft mud.

To Sebastian's aid the others now moved, their initial response slowed by the speed and ferocity of Stennaron's attack. As hands grabbed to pull his already crippled body away, Sebastian, his hand now deeply embedded in his assailant's flesh, commanded their retreat. "He's mine!" he spat, his eyes flashing with insane rage. Sharply withdrawing his daggers, Sebastian watched with great satisfaction as Stennaron stumbled and swayed, struggling to maintain his balance and remain on his feet, as he clutched the fearsome hole that now gaped in his middle. Through the pain and the sweat, he observed Sebastian move in, clearly intent on delivering a decisive assault on his rival. With all the strength he could muster, the badly injured Stennaron – now bent double – rose up, twisting his body, guiding his powerful fist to its unsuspecting target. A shattering crack echoed through the still air, as his final attack made firm contact with Sebastian's head, knocking him sideways with its shock and power. Reeling from the punch, Sebastian in his turn, stumbled and swayed as *he* tried to maintain *his* balance. He crashed to his knees, taking a moment to recover himself, before turning his head to deliver a look of pure hatred upon his enemy – now lying in contorted pain on the ground. Sebastian threw aside all offers of assistance in getting to his feet, and pulled himself up – moving slowly to stand over the critically injured Stennaron. Sebastian's intrusive thrust had done significant damage to his internal organs, but it was Stennaron's final lunge – the twisting of his body, the dramatic power of his blow, that had caused him to be lying there now. Dying slowly.

Slobber and the others now close at hand and unobserved, watched helplessly as their new found friend writhed in

torment, clutching both hands to his wound.
"I know what to do!" said Gobswane, turning to his commander.
"So you said", answered Enamuelle pessimistically. "How?"
To that question, Gobswane had no plausible answer. All he could do was look into the eyes of his commanding officer, and assure him that somehow, he knew what needed to be done. He couldn't explain it, all he could do was ask for a leap of faith.
Sergeant Enamuelle looked deeply into the pleading eyes of his man. After a long exhale of air, he nodded slowly:
"Alright," he said, "I believe you. I don't know why I should, but I do." Deferring leadership, and trusting in his man, the Sarge and the others followed Gobswane's instruction and arranged themselves at one end of Matchwood's plank.
"What do you think you're doing!?" asked Matchwood, as the tiny men secured themselves to his part-body.
"Matchwood. Quick, there's no time", said Gobswane excitedly. "Tell Slobber to swing you like a bat."
"Eh!?"
"Tell him to grab your other end and swing hard...Tell him to imagine he is hitting an invisible ball at the monster's head", he instructed, pointing repeatedly at Sebastian.
Matchwood didn't claim to understand, but he too had heard Gobswane's earlier claim, and chose, as did Enamuelle, to trust in him. Quickly he relayed the instruction to Slobber, who raised up the instrument. "Are you sure about this?" he enquired, holding the Wrangler-laden end to his face.
"Don't worry!" assured Gobswane, "We can do this." Though his comrades had their private doubts, the honour of the group was at stake, and they duly offered their own words of certainty in their ability. "Aim high," continued Gobswane, "and swing. Swing with every ounce of strength you can find."
Slobber took up his stance, turned his upper body slowly back, tensed his muscles and then snapped round, whipping the makeshift bat round at an incredible rate.

Their eyes closed as the pressure of the g-forces smudged their faces, the brave Toothwranglers awaited Gobswane's single command. As the plank swung, Gobswane's unexplained instinct alerted him that it was time.
"Release!" he shouted, and those still with their feet firmly on the ground, watched in amazement as the tiny squad detached, and sailed through the air, arching high into the grey sky above, heading with incredible accuracy for the head of Sebastian – the only audible sign of their flight being the fading acknowledgement, from more than one, of the extreme terror their endeavour had produced: "Shiiiiiiiii!!!"

Sebastian barely noticed as the little flies approached, standing, as he was, with rage, over the still writhing Stennaron. He looked down and spat at him. "You fool!" he sneered, raising a hand to add drama to his next move.
"You could have been a Prince of this land instead of a frightened resident, too scared to show your face in sunlight."
He offered Stennaron a final glance of utter contempt before uttering: "Nathrach!"
Nothing! Nothing happened. Sebastian uttered it again, this time reaching to his chest, holding a carefully cupped hand over his 'heart'. "Nathrach!"
Looking up, Stennaron managed to find the energy to force out a chuckle. "What's the matter, Seb…lost something?"
Sebastian, trying to hide his puzzlement from the others, suddenly found his mind consumed with fear as the realisation dawned. The dreadful thought steadily moved to the front of his mind at precisely the same time as the Toothwranglers landed – quickly finding decent grips to prevent themselves from sliding straight off and down to their deaths.

As a trembling Sebastian quickly looked under his hand at the empty area beneath, Stennaron offered his last breath in a final and utterly defiant laugh, as his eyes caught sight of a waving Gobswane standing on Sebastian's head.

The team re-grouped and awaited the next step of the plan. Quickly Gobswane gave them instruction: "We have to go inside his mouth."
"Sure", said Enamuelle..."Why?"
"There's a stone in there. A glowing stone."
Enamuelle and the others looked at one another, a little confused but more than happy to follow orders and get stuck in. With skill and speed, the team quickly worked out the best route into Sebastian's mouth; tying their ropes to the horns on the top of his head, they abseiled down – taking great care not to swing within his field of vision. Once on the bottom lip, each man picked a gap in the teeth and signalled to the others with a single, silent wave. Then, acting as one, they entered.

CHAPTER FORTY-SIX

Sebastian quickly ordered his army to fan out, desperate to have the Orb returned to his possession. With eyes elsewhere, he reached up towards his slowly opening mouth.
"Bugger!" said Gobswane, as the jaw slowly opened, "We need more time...McCavity find a hole."
McCavity quickly did as he was instructed. He needed little guidance as to his next course of action, as he drew out his long toothpick and thrust it deep into the gaping evidence of decay. As Sebastian reacted, roaring in agony, McCavity – dodging the tip of the giant tongue that now snaked and writhed, seeking out the cause of its owner's discomfort – mused to himself: "Now we discover why good oral hygiene is such a must!"

Securely fastened by their harnesses, the troop swung this way and that, as Sebastian's gaping mouth afforded them the perfect opportunity to cast their eyes into every crevice.
"There it is!" shouted Pastey, pointing to a large boulder lodged towards the back of the mouth.
Gobswane ordered McCavity to cease his torment, and the team moved quickly, taking full advantage of Sebastian's

recovery time.
Working as one, the team managed to heave the giant, glowing rock out and onto Sebastian's now still tongue.
"Quick!" said Gobswane. "Tie me to it."
"You'll never carry this out of here, man!" shouted Enamuelle. "It's five times your size."
Gobswane took only a split second to calculate a strategy. Calling to Plaqueard, he instructed him to make his way up to the back of the throat and start making a nuisance of himself.
"A sneeze!?" queried Enamuelle. "We'll never survive a sneeze!" He had a point; the speed at which a beast of this size sends objects out in a sneeze, could barely be calculated. There was only one thing for it, they would *all* have to fasten themselves securely to Gobswane's binding ropes – there would be no time to tie everyone to the rock. The generator of the sneeze would have little time to waste. Once the sneeze began to build, he would have to race back and get himself sorted.

As Plaqueard reached his destination, Sebastian had already begun to reach up once more – he would have to act fast! As the mouth began to open, he began punching and kicking the back of the throat, whilst trying to maintain his balance on the now surfing tongue. More than once, Sebastian pressed the back of his organ to the area giving offence, but Plaqueard managed to skilfully avoid it. On and on he continued, scratching and raking his nails over the soft tissue, until eventually his objective had been reached and the sneeze began to build. With little time to spare, he raced towards the rock, that through hard work and sheer determination, the others had managed to maintain near the tip of the now protruding tongue. In the nick of time, he rejoined the others and grabbed the binding ropes, wrapping them around his arms and wrists. Then together, the five, incredible men waited for the inevitable.
Suddenly McCavity realised a tiny flaw in their plan: "Wait a sec...where are we going with this thing!?"

Gobswane, still convinced that all this had a guided purpose, was just about to suggest they trust in fate, when it happened... Like a bullet, the glowing, Toothwrangler-encrusted rock shot from Sebastian's mouth. The g-forces they had encountered at the end of Slobber's swing, were as nothing compared to those offered by the level of velocity they now experienced. The air moved so fast that it was impossible to take a breath, and all aboard the hurtling stone hoped their journey would soon be at an end.

As they arched out through the air, Gobswane managed to open an eye. His position was such that he could just about make out the image of the others, watching open-mouthed as they witnessed this unimaginable sight. Managing to move an arm he pointed ahead of them, though not truly understanding what it was he guided them towards.

Slobber somehow noticed the signal and the group ran, all the while maintaining a fixed view of their companions' trajectory.

"Oh bum!" announced Pastey, his eyeline offering a terrifyingly clear view of Sebastian's eyes, as they saw and recognised the article that was now flying from him.

Slobber and the others noticed Sebastian's reaction too, and exerted greater effort in their movement. As the stone fell, their only hope was that its size would make it difficult for the giants to locate in all this mud and heather. Their great height would also make it impossible for them to hear the cries of the Toothwranglers, offering guidance to their location.

As they saw where the stone landed, they rapidly understood how much rested upon their ability to get there first.

Sebastian also, had observed the landing site. He saw too, the nearby glow of the Orb of Skeltenna. He shook his head with disbelief and anger, as he also took notice of Slobber, Pot and Frutely as they neared the area. He understood. He knew what they were going to do, even if they did not. He had no time to spare as he lunged forward, shouting orders to his brethren, hoping to guide them to the Orb's location first. As he ran, a further complication caught his eye as, from over the hill, thousands of PEA men began to pour down towards them.

"No!" he hissed through gritted teeth, quickening his pace.

"Quickly", said Gobswane, as his team-mates pulled his face out of the mud. "Slobber, take the stone and find the hole in the ball there."
Though he did not understand, Slobber snatched up the pebble, as Frutely and Potfondle scoured the visible surface of the Orb, searching for a gash in its smooth surface – panic beginning to appear as no such breach could be seen.
With all now converging on their position, the group moved with the speed of terror, quickly freeing the Orb from its jewelled brooch and clawed container, and heaving it out of the mud.
"You are mine!" came the frighteningly familiar voice of Sebastian as he neared, stretching out an open hand – intent on crushing these small irritations into oblivion before retrieving his property.
"Here! Here!" shouted Frutely, grabbing Slobber's arm and pulling him around. "There! That's it."
Slobber looked up at Sebastian's hand as it closed in, heading down to crush them all, then at the pebble, and finally at the open wound that appeared to be its home. With a massive spit of defiance at Sebastian, Slobber raised the stone and brought it down hard, ramming it into the space available!

All stopped – frozen in time… The PEA masses on the hillside ceased their advance. The approaching Nassian army now appeared as incredible statues, and Sebastian himself, just hung in mid-air, neither moving forward, nor crashing to the ground – his incredible effort to dive for the Orb, thwarted. Even the grey clouds ceased their swirling. Only a group of eight people it seemed, were permitted freedom of movement, as they slowly opened their eyes and looked about in wonder and disbelief.
The Orb – the sphere at the centre of all this commotion and tragedy – pulsated with radiant light, as it slowly lifted off the ground and hovered just a few feet above their heads.

In the distance, a tall, grey figure slowly moved towards them, its shadowy image growing clearer as it approached.
"Is this a dream?" asked Slobber.
"Not a dream my friends", he said with a smile. His eyes searched the group before resting on the small frame of Gobswane. *"Well done tiny warrior"*, he said. *"I am so very pleased you were able to recall the details of our conversation."*
Gobswane looked puzzled. To the best of his knowledge, he had never had a direct conversation with the stranger.
"Some few years ago, you were close to death…" said the grey stranger – attempting to clear Gobswane's mind of his obvious confusion, *"During the brief time you spent between 'today' and 'tomorrow', we met."*
"He must mean your trip through Sir's stomach, Gobby!" suggested Enamuelle quietly.
"You knew then…about all this, I mean!?" begged Gobswane.
The grey stranger did not reply. Instead he suddenly looked up at the Orb and smiled. Raising his arms high in the air, he closed his eyes as the sphere throbbed and hummed. Slobber, Frutely, Potfondle, Matchwood and all the Toothwranglers watched in silence as one by one, the Nassians began to glow with the same light as the Orb. In turn, each creature vanished until at last, not one remained – even the body of their brave, fallen comrade Stennaron, vanished.
"So," sniffed Potfondle, his mind at last able to return to his loss, "do we all suddenly find ourselves on a beach – everyone alive and whole?"
The grey man looked down, offering only a conciliatory smile.
"I wish that could be so Pot, but my powers here are almost at an end. My reunification and the collection of those who remained, has been accomplished. For that you have my eternal gratitude."
"But what about Tree? He didn't deserve to die!" insisted Pot, desperately hoping the power that had once returned

Matchwood to his original state, would return the life of his dear friend.
"Nothing truly dies. Do not mourn those who leave you this day. Life is, and will always be…nothing that lives suddenly exists. That which lives, has always done so. What you are today, has no bearing on what you were yesterday. Nor does it reflect who, or what you might be tomorrow."
"And the Nassians?" intruded Frutely.
"They had their time. Most left. These remained. The damage I suffered prevented me from returning them."
Matchwood, displaying, once again, his greater wisdom, offered a thought in the form of a question to the grey figure – finally putting two-and-two together, drawing a conclusion as to the true identity, and nature, of this being: "You knew all of this was going to happen, didn't you? Why did you not simply tell us what to do at the outset…wouldn't it have been simpler…and far less messy?"
The grey man – the living embodiment of the Orb, thought quietly for only a short time before replying: *"Rules may, from time-to-time, be bent…just a little – the carvings on the wall at Mantura, for example. But there is a vast chasm between bending the rules and breaking them altogether…even I am not permitted to do that!"*
With this admission, came further questions from the group. Questions fed by such intense curiosity that answers were nothing short of demanded.
Suddenly, and without any organisation, all in the group began to hurl their inquiries at the enigmatic presence…all talking at once, all struggling to give their questions greater emphasis and prominence.
As the cacophonic volume rose, the grey man simply held up a hand. With a quiet smile on his face, he suddenly, without any form of warning or fanfare, vanished.

Above them, the Orb began to pulse again as it slowly moved across the land, finally resting above the PEA hoards. In a single, blinding flash, the hillside was clear – the boats moored in the sea below also vanished, and the group of intrepid explorers were left alone, as the wind once more began to gently blow, and the clouds high above began to swirl and clear, offering dreamy blue skies in their place.

Pot stood silently, looking in the direction of his fallen friend, a single tear rolling down his fuzzy cheek. “Now that’s what I call taking the pea”, he said, forcing a smile and wishing, in some small way, to mark the event in a manner his sticky friend would have appreciated.

With the others managing a supportive laugh, Pot turned to Frutely, asking: “Do you think he’s right? Do you think…do you believe that nothing dies?”

Frutely took his hand in hers: “After the past week,” she said, “I can honestly say that I haven’t a clue what I believe anymore…” Gripping his hand tightly and looking earnestly into Pot’s eyes, she added: “I’ll say this though...with all the things we’ve witnessed; all the power the Orb seemed to possess, if it says nothing dies, I would advise you not to leave Tree here. I imagine it gets pretty cold in winter!”

Overhearing this conversation, Slobber chuckled quietly to himself as he picked up the Match plank. “Now, Match,” he said, “you can knit this bit back into your greater body, cant you?”

“Erm...”

The End…for now, at least.